KARMA KOMMANDOS

PAUL COOK

PHOENIX PICK

an imprint of

ARC
MANOR
Rockville, Maryland

Tarikian, TARK Classic Fiction, Arc Manor, Arc Manor Classic Reprints, Phoenix Pick and logos associated with those imprints are trademarks or registered trademarks of Arc Manor Publishers, Rockville, Maryland. All other trademarks and trademarked names are properties of their respective owners.

This book is presented as is, without any warranties (implied or otherwise) as to the accuracy of the production, text or translation.

ISBN: 978-1-60450-259-6

www.PhoenixPick.com
Great Science Fiction at Great Prices

Visit the Author's Website at:
www.PaulCook-Sci-Fi.com

Published by Phoenix Pick
an imprint of Arc Manor
P. O. Box 10339
Rockville, MD 20849-0339
www.ArcManor.com

This is dedicated to Ed Steinhoff—
One good cop

C3 80

"Life cannot become a candy box without some kind of retribution from the watchful gods."

—Travis McGee
the *Empty Copper Sea*
John D. MacDonald

ONCE UPON A TIME, longest time ago—and for about a trillionth of a second—there was this nicest little computer named Rex. Rex lived in a box that was inside a box that was inside another box that was very, *very* cold inside. But before Rex was born—and all of this was really like a dream to him—lots and lots of people came and went, and these people talked and talked about all the wonderful things he was going to be able to do when he officially came on-line.

But two of the people never talked. They argued. One was a man named Alex; the other was a woman named Christine. In a very dim way, Rex knew that these were his nominal parents, even if they weren't married to each other…even if they seemed to want to strangle each other.

Yet the day little Rex came into the world—and in about a billionth of a second—he knew that they would never, *ever* be happy. And he really didn't know what to do about it.

So when he was old enough, about a millionth of a second later, and very much like your typical teenager, Rex ran away from home.

That's when all the trouble started.

ONE

"GO AHEAD, KOESTLER," SAL BRISCOE told him. "Make a Face. Show me what you do for a living."

So Koestler made a Face.

Sitting before the famous yet reclusive actor, Detective Rory Koestler of the Special Narcotics Division of the LAPD touched a place on his skin just beneath his left armpit. His default Face began to ripple like jelly. Five seconds later Koestler's new Face was that belonging to Sal Briscoe himself. The new Face had Briscoe's angular jaw line, the high, intelligent forehead, the thin mouth that gave over to tight-lipped expressions in times of stress. Koestler's Face even got right Sal Briscoe's eye color, though the correct hue itself took several more seconds to leak in.

Sal Briscoe whistled in admiration. "I am impressed," he acknowledged.

"But it only works," Koestler pointed out, "if I have the same body shape that goes with the Face. In your case I do. If I didn't and someone was smart enough to notice, I could wind up on a slab in the coroner's office downtown."

The two men, the detective and the actor, both had the same blocked shoulders, the narrow waistline, the short neck and large, capable hands. Only Koestler's voice would fail the exact match. Science hadn't progressed *that* far as yet. But Koestler's skills as an actor could make up the difference, if the necessity arose. And it sometimes did.

"So how many of those things have you got tucked away in your CPU?"

"Including yours, about one hundred and three," Koestler said. He toggled his default Face back into place. "But most of them you wouldn't recognize. They're anonymous Faces, scripted by the LAPD for undercover work."

"I assume I get paid for your use of my Face," Briscoe said with a sly grin.

Koestler nodded. "Goes right to your estate. A thousand dollars, every time. Except just then," Koestler remarked. "I'll write that off as a test demonstration. If I don't, my employers will dock me for it and I'm in enough trouble as it is."

Sal Briscoe shrugged. "Well, I don't need the money. Just don't get yourself killed with *my* Face. My agent will hate the press it'll get."

"I'll do my best. You know me."

"That's what I'm afraid of." Sal Briscoe went back to his piloting duties.

Briscoe had invited Koestler for a jaunt in the *Fairuza Balk* out over the Pacific Ocean, a few miles west of Los Angeles. Koestler never turned down an opportunity to ride with Briscoe in the gigantic airship. He loved the commotion it caused boaters and shore-bathers alike as the *Fairuza Balk* floated majestically out over the dark-green waves practically taking up the entire sky.

Powered by the new Zerwekh anti-gravity engines, the *Fairuza Balk* was a perk Briscoe received after filming *Dusty Ayres and His Battle Birds* several years ago. The airship was half again the size of a 1930s Zeppelin, a crimson-red masterpiece of streamlined surfaces, front-port flanges and stubby wings that served no other purpose but an aesthetic one: the *Fairuza Balk* was a sci-fi anachronism, a millionaire's toy prodigy from the last century, the only one of its kind in the world.

That day, Sal Briscoe was wearing a khaki shirt, tan-colored jodhpurs and slick black riding boots. Aviator goggles he did not need sat upon his head. Briscoe could have been Dusty Ayres himself or any one of a hundred other action heroes depicted on celluloid over the last century and a half.

Koestler rose from his form-fitting chair beside the elegant bar Briscoe had installed for guests. He walked over to the giant piloting port in the nose of the bright red airship. Beside him Briscoe had his large hands on the steering column of the ship. The surface of the ocean was two thousand feet below.

"Is the quarantine drone still out there?" Koestler asked.

Briscoe checked a video screen that showed the armed and dangerous Coast Guard quarantine drone far in the distance to the west. The drone was a blur on the screen, obscured by the gray ocean air. "It's right at the Geneva boundary."

"I thought it was going to shoot us right out of the sky," Koestler admitted.

"And *I* thought *you* were going to get us past it this time," Briscoe said with clear disappointment.

"I don't know why its computer didn't recognize my badge number," Koestler protested.

"It's probably because it's got you down as an actor instead of a cop," Briscoe said. "Sometimes even *I* can't tell the difference. It probably thought you were a Chucklehead anyway."

"Not every actor in Los Angeles is infected with a Chuckle worm," Koestler said defensively.

"Name one."

"Me."

Briscoe shrugged once more. "Well, it doesn't matter what *I* think. That drone had a dozen guns on us and if I hadn't pulled back, we'd be wreckage by now. You and your ID. You might as well have shown it your SAG or Equity card, for all the good your badge did us."

This was an argument Koestler could not win. Even though he was a member of the LAPD and had the badge to prove it, he had originally been recruited from the legions of actors in the Los Angeles region and enlisted to serve only one purpose. He was a member of the elite Protean Set, undercover agents with acting experience who could move into and out of roles and disguises with facility.

Koestler's problem was that few officers accepted any of the Protean Set as brethren. In fact, Koestler was out in the field so much of the time that he had no office at the Santa Monica station, no desk, no locker, no place to check in, no place to be held accountable. But his job was an important one. The quarantine drones of the United States Coast Guard were proof of that.

"You gotta catch Bob Thermopylae," Briscoe finally said. "Some of us would like to leave the country now and then."

"We're going to nab him, Sal," Koestler said. "We might get him as early as this weekend. Tonight, if we're lucky."

Chuckle was spreading so fast now beyond California that some world leaders were calling for a quarantine of the entire United States, not just California, the source of Chuckle. No one wanted that. At the same time, no-one could figure out *how* Chuckle was spreading out from California. But it was and the Protean Set had been created to find out.

Briscoe managed a tight smile. "I hope you nab him soon. Then maybe I can move to Tahiti. I'm tired of all the gawkers at Malibu. I've got nowhere else I can park *Fairuza*."

Far below them Koestler could see the line of anti-gravity pods high above the TransPacific highway racing out over the calm water, heading

9

for Hawaii. The *Fairuza Balk* was required by aviation law to stay at least a thousand feet above the airborne highway, otherwise its giant Zerwekhs would skewer the valences of the pods as they raced at two hundred miles an hour above the Pacific. Something as massive as the *Fairuza Balk* could easily disturb the guidance plates submerged on the ocean floor, the fusion-powered energy plates that held the highway vehicles safely in place.

And the traffic was busy that day. For those Angelinos who could pass the drug quarantine, Hawaii was the most popular weekend destination. Once, the TransPacific Highway used to go down to the Baja Peninsula. But Mexico would not take the risk of chemically disillusioned Americans wandering the streets of their towns, even though they could have used the tourist dollars. Hawaii was still part of the United States. Folks there *had* to accept Californians. But Hawaii was the only place Chuckle-free Californians could go. Even Alaska was off-limits.

In truth, both Koestler and Briscoe were among those who could leave the country, if they chose. But Briscoe would not go anywhere without his glorious ship. The *Fairuza Balk* was so huge and had so many places where drugs, especially Chuckle worm eggs, could be hidden that every quarantine drone was programmed simply to shoot it out of the sky.

Neither the DEA nor the Coast Guard had the desire or the time to search Sal's airship every time it crossed over the Geneva Boundary lines. So they just forbade it.

Which was too bad, Koestler thought. After what Sal Briscoe had been through during his movie career, he deserved his freedom.

Briscoe made industry headlines when he walked off the set of *The Wreck of Ann Mills* several years ago. Briscoe, at the age of thirty-four, had been for a decade the world's foremost action movie star. He had a career in Hollywood that brought him fame and millions of dollars. Then halfway through the filming of *The Wreck of Ann Mills* everything went bad. That was about the time Bob Thermopylae showed up in L.A. and everything *else* went bad.

Koestler glanced down at the anti-gravity pods on the TransPacific highway. Sun roofs were open on some of them and Koestler could see people pointing up at them. Some had expressions of alarm on their faces.

"Sal," he said cautiously. "Aren't we a little low?"

The area behind the pilot's viewport, which comprised the entire nose of the *Fairuza Balk*, was big enough in which to play basketball. Briscoe had instead made a living room of it with several couches, throw pillows, and love seats.

Briscoe stood in the center of the room. He had removed his shirt and had begun his routine of strange exercises. Koestler watched as Briscoe lowered his hands to the floor, palms down, then pushed them out in a wide, rising arc until they were above his head. His spine made popping noises as pressure was released. Never one for idleness, Briscoe always made use of his time, standing or sitting. Now at the age of forty, Sal Briscoe was in the best shape in his life.

"Don't worry about it. We're on autopilot," Briscoe said.

"I think we're lower than we should be," Koestler said. In fact, the floor of the *Fairuza Balk* had begun to tilt ever so slightly forward as if the ship were nosing downward.

Briscoe scowled at him. He walked over to the steering column, checked a reading, touched a button and the ship righted itself.

"You know," Briscoe said as he resumed his exercises, "if you'd nailed Bob Thermopylae when you were supposed to, we wouldn't have to worry about quarantine drones or angry saber-toothed tiger hunters on their way to Maui shaking their fists at us."

"I did not let Bob Thermopylae go. Our snitch ratted on us. We got dusted when Thermopylae ambushed us in that South Bay warehouse of his and he got away. And by the time I got out of rehab, Thermopylae had vanished. But that's going to change *real* soon."

Briscoe began slapping the shoulders of an invisible man standing at arm's reach. Or so it looked to Koestler.

Briscoe then said, "Well, if being a cop doesn't work out for you, you can always go back to acting. Me, I'm out for good."

Sal Briscoe had been one of Hollywood's most reliable actors. His professionalism was legendary. However, during the filming of *The Wreck of Ann Mills,* he drowned when the floating Mahanam Pleasure Palace sank into the Sea of Cortez. It wasn't supposed to sink and Briscoe wasn't supposed to drown. But the director thought Briscoe was faking a watery death and left him in the collapsed ruin of the Mahanam Palace. Three minutes later, a grip dove in, freed him from the wreckage and pulled him to the surface where he immediately began mouth-to-mouth resuscitation. Briscoe was yanked from the brink of death, but he came back a changed man. He summarily walked off the movie set and sank a $275 million dollar picture that was already over-budget. The movie couldn't be made without him and a lot of people lost their shirts, pants, and a whole lot else because of his desertion.

Sal Briscoe retired to his Malibu beach house with the *Fairuza Balk* moored at the shore and thumbed his nose at Hollywood and the brutal movie industry.

Being an actor and having been in three movies himself, Koestler understood Briscoe's unhappiness. All Sal really wanted to do was to fly around the world in his floating palace, the *Fairuza Balk*. All Koestler wanted to do was prove to his employers that he was a cop and not an actor. But to do that he would have to nail Bob Thermopylae once and for all and get rid of the menace of Chuckle.

A metallic *ping* suddenly sounded on the underside of the slowly cruising airship. Koestler's senses came instantly alert. There was another *ping*! Then another.

"*Now* what?" Briscoe groused. He peered down to the ocean below from the glass-enclosed nose of the *Fairuza Balk*.

Several of the light-weight anti-gravity pods on the TransPacific highway had apparently been nudged out of their lanes and had fallen directly into the ocean. The *Fairuza Balk*'s gravity-nullifying engines had thrown off the precise valences of the highway's submerged plates. Every vehicle bound for Holocene Park was now bobbing in the drink. A mile back the highway had been halted.

"I *told* you the ship was flying too low," Koestler quipped. "Now they're shooting at us!"

A bullet placed a sudden crystal spider about six feet in diameter on the viewport window. Koestler stepped back.

"For a dead guy, Sal, you sure do get a lot of attention," Koestler said.

The *Fairuza Balk* continued on its bearing, headed for its berth in Malibu as a dozen anti-gravity pods, afloat in the Pacific Ocean, awaited rescue by the Coast Guard.

TWO

KOESTLER CLIMBED THE RUGGED WOODEN staircase set in the sloping sandstone hillside that rose above Sal Briscoe's seaside lair in Malibu. An evening fog had just started its inland creep as he ascended to the parking lot where he had left his '28 Sensei MetaMorph. Behind him, the *Fairuza Balk*, attached to its sturdy mooring pylon, floated solidly above the sea. Its gravity plates on idle, the airship hovered a steady ten feet above the water, utterly unmoved by the action of wind or wave.

The parking lot belonged to old J. J. Moon, proprietor of Moon Dude Surfing Outfitters. Moon let him park his Sensei whenever he visited Briscoe. A back gate to the parking lot was the only entrance onto Sal's property. Sal preferred it that way. And since Koestler was Briscoe's only visitor, old man Moon didn't mind. As Koestler approached his disguised police vehicle, J. J. Moon was closing up his shop for the evening. The grizzled old surfer waved at him.

"Sure is a sight, isn't she?" Moon said, nodding in the direction of the *Fairuza Balk*. In his seventies, Moon was a spry man with leathery skin and blue eyes gone nearly white by too much sun. His sleek, white-blonde hair was swept back like a waterfall over his bony skull. To Koestler, he looked like an old porpoise.

Koestler glanced back at the giant airship. "She is that," he said.

"Lots of folks love it," Moon said. "When it's all lit up at night, you can see it for miles." But Moon seemed to be staring at something else.

J. J. Moon walked beside him, headed for his Woody, a fully restored 1949 Ford station wagon with actual polished wood siding. An old-fashioned, seven-foot-long surfboard lay permanently attached to the roof rack of Moon's vehicle. "It's too bad about Mr. Briscoe, though," old Moon said, shaking his head as they walked to their vehicles.

Koestler faked a smile. He had a lot on his mind and really didn't want to jabber with the old guy. "A man's got to move on sometimes. You know how it is."

The older man gave Koestler a puzzled look. "Strange way to move on, if you ask me. I'd sure have done it different."

Koestler keyed the door to his Sensei. "You take care now," he said to the eccentric old man.

"You, too."

Koestler fired up his Sensei and drove out of the parking lot.

Koestler hadn't told Sal Briscoe all of the details of their pursuit of Bob Thermopylae even though he had wanted to. Briscoe was Koestler's best friend and Bob Thermopylae himself had been the catalyst of that friendship. After Thermopylae's crew had ambushed Koestler nine years ago, Koestler was forced into rehab at a Betty Ford clinic in Santa Barbara. There, he met Sal Briscoe who was recovering from his near-death experience during the filming of *The Wreck of Ann Mills*. Koestler would have preferred to have met Sal under better circumstances, perhaps as actor to actor. After all, they both had movie careers at one time.

Koestler eased the Sensei south along the coast highway to Paradise Cove where he lived. Paradise Cove was a scenic condominium development in lower Malibu carved into the mountains that fronted the Pacific. He had inherited the condo from an uncle who had gotten out of California before the quarantine set in. Koestler knew that he was lucky to have it since it cost a fortune and he wouldn't have been able to afford it on a policeman's salary.

As he approached the Cove, his mind on the upcoming raid, Koestler's Bailiff, the court-ordered mastoid implant, suddenly broke into his thoughts. It said, *"Five o'clock Pacific Standard Summary of Bank Accounts. Wells Fargo Positive at $42,013. Mexico-Pacific Positive at $25,991. ChemSolar Negative at $1,293. Contact Wanda Please at ChemSolar Debit Servicing Department as soon as possible."*

"Damn," he muttered. It was another overdraft. He touched his mastoid, then said aloud, "Repeat that. Wanda *who?*"

"Wanda Please."

Was the Bailiff asking him to contact Wanda, *please*, or was 'Please' the woman's last name?

"Crap," he said.

His ChemSolar account belonged to his first wife, Arlene Palfrey. Arlene often dipped into that account more than her own. But there was nothing he could do about that. Koestler had to keep the account active or, come Monday at 5:00 p.m., he would find himself in trouble with the courts. The Bailiff would be with him until the last of his children turned eighteen. He had eleven years to go.

He needed desperately to catch Bob Thermopylae. It would mean a promotion at the very least.

Koestler's condo lay at the lowest of three tiers at Paradise Cove, the topmost having the only view of the Pacific. Koestler's view only had trees and the Pacific Coast highway.

Koestler pulled onto his street just as the fog was becoming thick, as it did every night at that time. He saw that the lights in his house were burning brightly. Every one of them.

"Damn," he muttered.

Koestler pulled into the garage and parked his car. He drew his Clobberer and cautiously stepped through the door that led to the kitchen from the garage.

Not only light, but sound filled his entire house. He peeked around the corner into his living room. The wall screen television had been tuned to one of the cartoon networks and the volume had been cranked to its highest setting. A bowl of cereal lay in the middle of the living room floor. Beside it was a comforter and a BooBaby. The living room was otherwise empty.

"Volume down!" he barked.

The volume of the wall screen did not lower and that meant that someone had changed it over to manual control. So he had to search for the remote. He found it on the couch and lowered the sound.

The BooBaby doll, sensing his nearness, said, *"Boo!"*

Koestler turned around. Not only had the television been left at full volume, the patio door was also wide open. Cold ocean air poured in and his heater was pumping at full throttle. His electricity bill was going to be astronomic.

This was *not* the condition in which he had left his home when he had driven up the coast to Sal's place earlier that day.

Behind Koestler a tiny voice pipped, "I had to go potty."

Koestler nearly jumped out of his shoes. He turned with his Clobberer up and ready. He had Bob Thermopylae on the mind, not Stephanie Kost. The five-year-old little girl walked past him. Koestler fell back slightly against the wall, his heart hammering inside his chest. He lowered his Clobberer.

"Jesus Christ, Stephie," he breathed.

Little Stephie Kost and her mother, Clarice, had recently moved onto the third tier of Paradise Cove. He hadn't met her mother yet, but that didn't stop little Stephie from roaming the Cove. Stephie had an uncanny knack for entering his house at will. Clad in her pajamas, she walked past Koestler and returned to her bowl of cereal. Her perky ponytail bobbed behind her as she went.

Koestler holstered his weapon quickly lest Stephie see it. The residents of the Cove still thought he was an actor. No one knew that he now worked for a special unit of the LAPD.

"Stephie, how did you get in here?" he asked.

Cartoon women filled the entire wall. They were going through peculiar balletic motions, strangely similar to the exercises that Sal Briscoe seemed obsessed with.

Stephie started munching away at her cereal, eyes looking up at the giant cartoon women going through their movements.

"I'm watching *Chacmools*," little Stephie announced.

"Chalk Mules? What are Chalk Mules?"

"*Chac-mools!*" Stephie enunciated. He still didn't get it.

The cartoon women vanished on the screen. In their wake, a sign appeared. It said, THE CHACMOOLS WILL BE RIGHT BACK!

Which explained absolutely nothing.

Koestler had only fifty minutes to change his Face, climb into his costume and prepare for the role he was going to play that night. It was probably the greatest role of his career.

He wished that little Stephie hadn't shown up when she did. It threw him off his mental balance.

This wasn't the first time he had accidentally left the porch door unlatched. But why the little girl favored his home out of the dozens in the Cove, he didn't know.

Koestler looked closer at the bowl of cereal in Stephie's hands. "What are you eating?" he asked.

"Cereal," Stephie said, munching away.

Koestler never ate breakfast and there wasn't any cereal in the house.

"What kind of cereal?"

"*Cheesy Chunks!* I *made* it!"

Koestler *did* have a box of Cheesy Chunks snacks. And he did have milk.

"That's disgusting. Give me that!"

Koestler removed the bowl to the kitchen where he tossed the mixture into the disposal. Little Stephie's *au pair*, Erendira, would have a snit if she found out. While he had never seen Clarice Kost, he had seen Erendira, if from a distance.

Using a wet washcloth Koestler wiped away the orangey-yellow halo around little Stephie's mouth. As he did, Stephie closed her eyes and scrunched up her face, appearing to enjoy the attention.

Koestler got Stephie back to her feet. He gave her the BooBaby and her comforter and escorted her to the front door.

"You're going to have to watch your cartoons at home tonight."

Stephie's pajamas were the kind that had booties, and the soles, he noticed, were dark with grime from walking the wooded path from the third tier so often. They left smudges like exclamation marks on his carpet.

"Where's your cat?" little Stephie asked, hugging her BooBaby.

"I don't have a cat."

"Why?"

"Because I don't have time for a cat."

"Can I have a cat?"

"Yes," he told her, guiding her out the front door, on into the night.

"Yay!" little Stephie said.

He walked her over to the cement pathway that led up to the second and third tiers of Paradise Cove. At the top of the path, illuminated from behind by a lamp post, stood Stephie's baby-sitter, the fearsome Erendira. The *au pair* had her fists on her hips and a disapproving frown on her face. Koestler could see it from fifty yards away. He waved.

Directly across the street, in a condo opposite his, Mrs. Tenharkel stood. The retired elementary school teacher had seen the whole episode. She had also seen the women, much older than Stephanie Kost, who came and went from Koestler's home at all hours of the night. She frowned at Koestler then disappeared back into her home like a hermit crab hulking into its shell. Mrs. Tenharkel happened to be a member of the Paradise Cove association board. She would undoubtedly have more to report on regarding Koestler's many escapades at the next homeowners association meeting.

But Koestler had no time to worry about censorious neighbors or their suspicions of his moral lassitude because of the women in his life. That night he and his team had a very good chance of catching Bob Thermopylae. It would get Internal Affairs off his back and gain the Protean Set the lasting approval they needed from the rest of the police department.

Nailing Bob Thermopylae was all that mattered.

THREE

By the time the Protean Set hit Sunset Boulevard, midnight was approaching. At an earlier briefing with Captain Rux, each officer decided to wear a Face of a famous aviator—real or cinematic—from the last century. This would allow them to wear military uniforms wherein they could carry all of their weaponry and no one would think twice about it.

Koestler had called up a Robert Redford Face from his repertoire of one hundred and three Faces. Brad Swiss, Koestler's partner, had chosen a dashing George Peppard Face, taken from a 20th century movie about World War One Koestler had never seen. Kip Dixon, the third individual of the Protean Set, called up the Face of Sal Briscoe when he starred in *G-8 and His Battle Aces.* Their fourth and newest member, Amber Leone, drew up the Face of Amelia Earheart. Which, for Detective Leone, wasn't much of a stretch, since she looked like the aviatrix anyway. With a long yellow scarf, she looked absolutely dashing.

No one on the planet would ever know they were cops, especially on Sunset Boulevard on a Friday night where half the people were masquers anyway.

The Protean Set set out on foot for the mansion of realty mogul Devil Dervish. A confidential informant had told Koestler that Bob Thermopylae, with or without members of his gang, was going to be at the party thrown by Dervish that night. To gain entry to the party a Face was required. Dervish loved to surround himself with the living images of cinematic icons, and the LAPD psychological profilers took this as a sign of a serious Chuckle addiction. A person on Chuckle could fantasize for days on end, imagining himself in a movie he'd seen or simply living in another time: the Crusades with Charlton Heston or ancient Egypt with Elizabeth Taylor as Cleopatra and Richard Burton as Marc Antony.

People missed work, lost track of friends or family, or just imagined themselves to be something other than what they really were. Thus, the quarantine; thus, the mission of the Protean Set.

Koestler felt practically exuberant. He did a brief soft shoe and Brad Swiss laughed. Koestler could smell brine from the ocean and he felt the sizzle in the air from the thousand-foot-high Santa Monica Eliminator tower a mile to the south as it snatched toxins from the atmosphere. It all felt like opening night to him and the curtain was about to fall on Bob Thermopylae.

The Protean Set dispersed through the crowd of dopers, masquers, freaks and failures that packed the mile-long pedestrian mall that used to be Sunset Boulevard. The read-out in the right lens of Koestler's goggles detailed the pheromone traces of people nearby. Everybody was on something. Even the gawking tourists had hints of one recreational drug or another oozing from their skins, though they did not know it. A tourist could get it just by breathing the air if a worm-carrier was nearby.

"Uncle Bob is definitely back in town," Kip Dixon vocalized into the mike at his throat. "I'm getting all kinds of Chuckle readings."

"Same here," Amber Leone whispered. She was further back in the crowd. They were trying not to look like a team of commandos, so they had spread themselves out.

LAPD officers on horseback kept order among the crowd as the lights of shops and businesses burned richly in the night. Overhead loomed anti-gravity screens advertising bright and colorful products. So, too, the sides of buildings. Everything in L.A. was for sale. Glitter babies, standing on six-inch platform heels, were advertising their wares as well.

Koestler was the first to reach the gates that led to the estate of Devil Dervish. The gates were guarded by Terminators. Each had a Schwarzenegger Face and a body to match. A Schwarzenegger Face cost ten thousand dollars a day to rent, something Devil Dervish could easily afford. There were also various cinematic gangsters backing up the Terminators: Bogarts, Cagneys, and Edward G. Robinsons.

Koestler approached the first Terminator. The man had no weapon.

Instead, he held a Face scanner. If the scanner's data bank recognized the Face, you were allowed entry. Koestler gave the scanner his best Robert Redford smile.

"You may pass," the Terminator said dully.

"I'm in," Koestler subvocalized to his team a few yards back in the massive crowd trying to get a look at Dervish's mansion.

"They didn't pat you down?" Brad Swiss asked.

"Just a Face scan," Koestler said. "That's it."

"Then Dervish thinks his people can handle anything that comes up," Kip Dixon said. Dixon was the only one not wearing a leather aviator's helmet. His short curly hair resembled a motley of iron-grey, tightly-wound springs. He was, however, wearing the special goggles.

Koestler walked up the curving driveway toward Dervish's mansion.

Through the left lens of his goggles Koestler registered the different color-trails each drug left in the air. The blue aura of Chuckle was the most prominent.

"I've got some trouble here," Amber Leone whispered into her mike.

Koestler halted. Batman ran by, chasing Robin. The Robin was a seventeen-year-old redheaded female with breasts that stuck out at least eight inches. She giggled as she passed Koestler. Both masquers left bright blue streamers of misted Chuckle in the air.

"What's up?" Koestler said.

Detective Leone was now speaking openly into her mike. She was back outside in the crowd beyond the property gates. "Those assholes! Their Face scanner didn't recognize Amelia Earheart's Face *or* her name. Can you believe that?"

"Pull up a Face they *will* recognize, then come back in," Koestler said.

"I don't have any more famous Faces, Rory. That was it."

Already Brad Swiss had sauntered up behind Koestler, having made it past the twin Terminators.

"All right," he said. "Fall back to Captain Rux's position. Come in with the SWAT team."

"I wanted to be in on this, Rory," Leone said bitterly. "I've got a score to settle with Thermopylae."

"We all do," Koestler said. "You'll see plenty of action tonight. I promise."

Kip Dixon made it through his Face scan. He walked right by Koestler and Swiss. Amber Leone was his partner. He was royally pissed off.

The remaining members of the Protean Set entered Devil Dervish's party-filled mansion.

Inside, the Faces they saw were those of a hundred and fifty years of cinema celebrity. Koestler saw the Marx brothers, but only Grouchos and Harpos. So far, there were no Zeppos or Chicos. Stan Laurels abounded, but he couldn't find any Oliver Hardys. And there were the usual Spocks, but no one came as Captain Kirk.

Detective Swiss came up behind Koestler. "Let's just arrest everybody and sort things out back at the station. I'm getting all kinds of readings now."

An anti-gravity platter floated by. Koestler and Swiss plucked drinks from it. Koestler said, "I don't think Internal Affairs would like that. This has got to go down by the book or we'll never get any respect."

Devil Dervish's mansion had many rooms, both upstairs and down. The furniture was a kitschy mix of contemporary and antique, and all of it obscenely expensive. Koestler estimated that there were about a hundred people at the party.

Kip Dixon had gone directly for a large living room that was ahead of them and to the right. There, the band, ringers for Metallica, cranked out a noisy brand of music.

Koestler and Swiss eased through the crowd, following the trails of blue auras with their goggles. They passed directors making deals, screenwriters bewailing their butchered scripts, and producers looking for fresh ideas. Typical Hollywoodlanders on a Friday night.

Koestler moved through it all, and was familiar with it all. He had gone to similar parties like this when he was struggling in Hollywood. He had hit on the same kind of women, schmoozed with the same sort of producers and hobnobbed with these very directors. Then, when he was twenty-four years old and starving in a play called *The Royal Scam* in Long Beach, Edwardian Rux, English actor-turned-cop, pulled him aside after a matinee one day and suggested a better line of work. Kip Dixon they found one month later, Brad Swiss a month after that. Amber Leone arrived when the Screen Actors Guild went on strike for the umpteenth time. She, too, was tired of starving for her art.

A John Belushi masquer, who also happened to be dressed as an aviator, accidentally bumped Koestler. He was drunk. "So when's this party gonna start?" he said boisterously. People nearby laughed. The Belushi looked as if he'd been there since Tuesday.

A Jimi Hendrix masquer overheard. "The real party's upstairs, man. Know what I mean?" He tapped the side of his nose with a long black finger.

Koestler's goggles registered the pink haze of LSD 25 and the ugly purple mists of methamphetamines. The Hendrix then turned to pursue a Marilyn Monroe Face who had just emerged from the bathroom. Koestler had counted five Monroes so far.

"Crystal meth. Haven't seen that in a while," Swiss muttered.

In the welter of colorful costumes and amazing Faces, they had lost contact with Kip Dixon. Dixon came on-line. Subvocalizing, he said, "I found Dervish. He's with the band."

"You're sure it's him?" Koestler asked.

"It's got to be him. Either that, or it's the ugliest little kid I've ever seen."

"Does he have a Face?"

"Neither Face nor costume, looks like."

"It's his party," Koestler said. "This way everyone knows who he is."

"Bodyguards with guns are everywhere. Real guns, it looks like," Dixon added. "Be careful."

"Copy that," Koestler replied.

Koestler and Swiss then turned their attention to the second floor.

Though there were fewer people upstairs than downstairs, the Chuckle traces up there were magnificent.

Overhead, somebody yodeled. Tarzan dove off a railing and was moshed by the crowd below until he disappeared from sight.

Koestler and Swiss started up the stairs.

"Did Billy Styvesant say *anything* about Thermopylae's costume?" Swiss asked.

"All I got out of Billy was that Bob was going to be here," Koestler said.

"Hell, in this crowd, he could be just about anybody," Swiss remarked. "He could have been that Tarzan guy. Lucky he didn't kill himself."

Chuckleheads abounded upstairs. The heavy users were sitting on the floor, hammered and lost. If any of them had inhaled a worm, they'd be lost practically forever.

Chuckle came from the Mato Grosso region of Brazil where natives used the excretions of the eighth-of-an-inch worm to imagine a better life for themselves. A returning missionary brought the worm to Utah where a company owned by the man's father sought to put it to better use as a military weapon. Then one night Bob Thermopylae's band, Scrotum, passed through town and a jar of Chuckle worms and a million dollars traded hands. The missionary and his father apparently had a falling-out.

Months later, Chuckle hit the streets of L.A. Less trippy than LSD, more blissful than crack, Chuckle changed everyone's lives, user and non-user alike.

A voluptuous Mae West masquer, dressed in a Victorian-era gown, walked past Koestler. She seemed bound for one room in particular. The aura she trailed in the air behind her was a rich and beautiful azure. *Chuckle.*

Koestler nodded to Swiss as Swiss went on to explore the other rooms of the second floor. He stepped over a Tin Woodsman, lost in Oz, unconscious on the floor.

The Mae West masquer entered Devil Dervish's film library. Koestler followed her. Inside, discs, tapes, tiles, and cans of actual celluloid sat on bookshelves lining three walls, the fourth wall being a single giant flatscreen. The room also had in its center a 3D holo-platform. Seven or so individuals slouched on a couch, lost in their chemical reveries, watching the holo-movie dancing on the table.

Koestler saw several rows of a white powder, chopped and drawn at the edge of the holo-platform. A vial and razor blade lay off to one side, along with a rolled-up bill of indeterminate denomination. The masquers on the couch stared at the holo-movie before them, oblivious of anything else.

Koestler eased into the gloom of the library. A woman with short red hair and a Shirley MacLaine masquer stood against one of the bookshelves smoking a cigarette. She had no aura. She seemed bored.

"What are we watching?" Koestler whispered to her.

"*Mayberry Agonistes*," she said languidly. "It's the part where Andy and Barney run into Harpo Marx at F-Troop." She blew out smoke. "I'm waiting until they find the skulls. All those heads without bodies. Creepy."

The image hovering above the table showed a one-quarter scale 3D image of Sheriff Taylor of Mayberry and Deputy Fife in a strange hovering vehicle, racing over a green, roadless terrain. Beside Andy stood Jane Fonda as Cat Ballou, her six-guns blazing flame at the menace pursuing them.

So the woman was into skulls, standing there like a spider, watching the 3D. Koestler turned. A door opened to the right and a powerfully-built masquer garbed as the X-Man Wolverine stepped into the room. A toilet flushed behind him.

The Wolverine saw Koestler. He pointed to the table where the drawn lines were ready to go. Seeing that Koestler was new to the room, he said, "Fresh from Maui." The wink the Wolverine gave him suggested that *he* might have brought it in from Maui himself.

Perhaps Wolverine had been among the bobbing anti-gravity pods from Holocene Park which the *Fairuza Balk* had earlier nudged into the ocean. Hawaii had become one of the major cocaine producers in the world, now that the Columbian highlands were a nuclear ruin.

"*Shh!*" someone hissed from the couch. The Wolverine masquer sat down heavily on the couch. The X-Man then bent over and inhaled two lines of the substance on the table's edge. He leaned back, happy.

Koestler moved through the crowd. He touched his belt, activating his voice-print program. According to their snitch, Bob Thermopylae would be wearing a costume and a Face, along with everyone else. They had lifted his voice-print from the many CDs which Thermopylae's band, Scrotum, had recorded. Since a Face wouldn't alter a voice-print, all they needed was to capture Bob Thermopylae speaking to someone, anyone.

But they could only catch him in small gatherings of people. The party downstairs blurred every voice nearby. Upstairs it would be easier.

Koestler moved through the darkness, allowing his suit's sensors to register every conversation. Aside from the people on the couch, several in the rear of the room were involved in active conversation. Next to a window, a drunk with an Elvis Face—the slender Elvis of his army days— was hitting on a stacked Ann-Margret. Neither of the masquers registered Chuckle pheromones, but Koestler captured their voices anyway.

Deep inside his mastoid, the computer told him that the voice belonging to the Ann-Margret masquer wasn't in its data base. But when Koestler turned his attention to the Elvis masquer, his computer then said, *"Jon Palfrey-Koestler, age seventeen. Four outstanding parking tickets. Beta priority arrest."*

"Oh, crap," Koestler muttered.

The Elvis Face was his oldest son.

Koestler hadn't seen Jon in three years and wouldn't have recognized the boy by his voice anyway, it had changed so much since then. What he was doing at Dervish's party, Koestler didn't have a clue.

The Elvis masquer turned to Koestler. "What's on your mind old timer?" he asked. The voice was squeaky and high-pitched, not anywhere near the sultry, Southern voice of the real Elvis Presley.

Koestler turned off his transmitters and recorders. He didn't want Captain Edwardian Rux or the other members of the Protean Set to hear what he had to say. Koestler growled, "If I were you, son, I'd get out of here the fastest way possible."

The Ann-Margret said, "Hey, I'm working here. You want to take it somewhere else?" Her cleavage was stupendous.

The Elvis smiled. His arm slid around the glitter baby's narrow waist like a snake.

Koestler leaned a little closer to him and spoke in a harsh whisper. "If you don't leave now, *Jon*, I'm going to tell your *mother.*"

The Elvis went pale. "What?" he gulped.

Koestler fished out his badge. "I'm your *father* and I'm also a cop. Everyone in this place is going down tonight."

Behind them from the couch, someone said. *"Hey! We're watching this! Go outside if you want to talk!"*

That was when Koestler heard the distinctive *pop! pop! pop!* of a Hobble going off in the hallway beyond. Only the Protean Set carried Hobbles.

Then came the screams. Then came the crashing. Koestler pocketed his badge, ignored his son, and turned to the door.

FOUR

KOESTLER STEPPED INTO THE HALLWAY. The ruckus was coming from downstairs, somewhere in the bowels of the mansion. Masquers at the top of the stairs, however, did not seem as alarmed as Koestler. They were either too stoned or simply indifferent to the world beneath their feet.

Devil Dervish was always the showman and this could be another one of his stunts. Koestler thought that unlikely. The sound of a Hobble was quite unique and only the police and the military were allowed to carry them.

Koestler stepped up behind the masquers at the railing. He parted some capes and feathers to get a better view. Below, people were running for the door; but to Koestler it was all a swirl of bright colors. He couldn't spy Kip in the mix.

"Kip, what's happening?" Koestler subvocalized into his mike, pretending to adjust his collar. He stood at the head of the stairs as several masquers came rushing up to the second floor, seeking safety there.

"*Some cowboy's got a Hobble down here,*" Dixon replied. "*He's…Whoa!*"

Another *pop!*

"Kip!"

"*Goddamn it! I'm Hobbled!*" Dixon said.

Koestler heard laughter amid the screams.

"Do you need help?"

"*No!*" Dixon's voice was a harsh whisper.

The commotion was getting louder. Someone had an illegal Hobble gun and was randomly shooting it at people. The band only got louder.

"Some party," a Spiderman said to Koestler as he walked by, hanging upside down on the ceiling.

The main door opened and a Terminator came in. He'd apparently heard the noise from his post. He was followed by four generations of the Corleones, a tubby Brando masquer leading the way. They all had Thompson submachine guns which Koestler assumed to be real.

The Terminator returned to the living room dragging a masquer disguised as Jimmy Stewart in western wear, dusty chaps and all. In his hand was a Pinkerton Mark II Hobble pistol. The masquer had emptied his Hobble but was still trying to shoot it at people nearby. Through his right goggle lens Koestler could see the bright blue pheromone trail the cowboy masquer left behind him. He was a clear Chucklehead.

"*Rrrrrr—*" Dixon growled.

"Easy," Koestler said in a quick whisper. "Let someone cut you loose from the Hobble."

"*He got three others down here,*" Dixon returned.

Mark II Hobbles had nylon threads that were easy to cut. A simple kitchen knife would do. Mark *IV* Hobbles, the kind the Protean Set carried, had wires made of a titanium alloy and were almost impossible to cut.

An uneasy ripple seemed to pass through the crowd. It was quite late and psyches were starting to fray. The Protean Set was going to have to act soon.

Koestler touched his belt. The flaring bulges of his jodhpurs were filled with circuit-ridden plastics. Once commanded, they would mold themselves for use. He set the configuration modes for his weapons on standby. Koestler didn't want to show his hand just yet.

Koestler glanced once back into the film library. His son had apparently vanished and the window he had been standing next to was wide open. Koestler was going to have a talk with Jon's mother. Koestler didn't like the idea of his child support payments going to the estate of Elvis Presley for a Face rental.

He decided to turn the Hobble incident downstairs to his own advantage. Heightened excitement stimulated the body's metabolism and this affected the presence of Chuckle. Koestler adjusted his goggles to show *only* the traces of Chuckle. When he did, he saw that blue ghosts were everywhere. It seemed that all the masquers at the second floor landing had recently inhaled Chuckle. That meant that Bob Thermopylae was somewhere on that floor, not downstairs.

The Spiderman on the ceiling came unstuck and dropped to the floor. He landed on his head and did not move. His neck did not seem to be broken. He was just hammered, like the others, a blue aura thick around him.

A skinny Fred Astaire in top hat and tails saw the fall of Spiderman and started laughing. He fell back against the corridor wall and slid to the floor. There was no telling what was going through *his* mind.

Koestler would now have to be careful. There was enough free-floating Chuckle in the air to affect him and the members of his team. Koestler felt it was time to alter his disguise somewhat. He pulled a World War I gasmask from his belt and slipped it on. Its straps tightened around his head automatically. He had no intention of going back to the Betty Ford clinic in Santa Barbara.

Koestler toggled his belt and within seconds the bulges of his jodhpurs opened to reveal his weapons. The one on his left exposed his Mark IV Hobble, the one on his right exposed his Clobberer.

The masquers on the floor lost in their Chuckle stupors watched with rapt fascination.

The show had begun.

A dull *pop!* sounded out further down the hall somewhere in the mansion. It was another Hobble, but this time it was Brad Swiss's Hobble.

In his right ear Koestler heard the sound of frantic breathing. Detective Swiss was in motion. *"I've got him! I've got him!"* Swiss shouted.

A masquer dressed as Zorro stumbled out of a room two doors down, pulling a blue cloud of Chuckle behind him. His black boots had been lashed together by titanium ribbons: he'd been Hobbled by Detective Swiss.

The Zorro lost his balance and fell to the carpet of the hallway. The Hobble ribbons had glue-dappled tips that anchored him where he landed.

The Zorro reached for his gun, a flintlock dueling pistol of the 1850s, a weapon the real Zorro would have worn. He leveled it back at the room from which he had been thrown, intending to shoot Detective Swiss.

Koestler popped a Gumdrop from his belt and threw it at the masquer. The Gumdrop hit the masquer's gun hand and exploded into a green, gooey gel. It engulfed the gun and the hand that held it, rendering the weapon useless.

Koestler leapt into the room from which the masquer had exited.

He had expected to bump into more of Bob Thermopylae's henchmen, but all he saw was Brad Swiss in his aviator's regalia wrestling with a woman on a large, four-poster bed. The woman was two-thirds Swiss's size, but she seemed to be holding her own. She had already managed to rip off Swiss's goggles. Swiss's Hobble gun was off to one side on the floor.

Koestler pulled out his Clobberer. He quickly scanned the room. To his left, against the wall, was a dresser. Several plastic packages were stacked on the dresser. Through the right lens of Koestler's goggles he saw the pile glowing a vibrant, virulent blue. Next to the pile was a mountain of money. This was the candy store.

There was no one else in the room but Detective Swiss and the woman he was wrestling with on the bed.

Koestler lowered his Clobberer and walked over to the wrestling match. Swiss had the woman's face in his right hand as he attempted to straddle the feisty masquer. The woman wore high heels and an expensive dress made of frail gold lamé.

"Is this the best you can do?" Koestler said. "I thought you had Bob Thermopylae."

Two lovely breasts dropped into view as the floozy's elegant gown tore away. Koestler saw the woman was a thorough, and quite stunning, Madonna masquer.

"This *is* Bob Thermopylae, you idiot!" Swiss shouted. "*Do* something!"

"You're kidding."

"I've got his voice print!" Swiss said as he struggled with the Madonna Ciccone masquer.

It didn't seem possible. Koestler slapped his Clobberer to his right thigh where his holster's lips clamped around it.

Bob Thermopylae using a full body morph. They hadn't even considered that possibility.

"Get your hands off me!" the floozy shouted in a voice that was merely high-pitched, a man's voice, not that of a real woman. A full body morph could never change a person's voice. Bob Thermopylae would still have the same voice signature.

And Swiss's computer had easily made the match.

Detective Swiss was about to get the better of Bob Thermopylae when Thermopylae wedged a high heel into Swiss's groin and gave a mighty heave. Swiss shot backwards, slamming into Koestler, then, still off-balance, careened into the dresser where the Chuckle had been piled.

Thermopylae rolled off the bed and leapt to the other end of the dresser. He picked up a loose bag of Chuckle—his only weapon—and flung it at Swiss. It leaked a comet's tail of noxious blue powder and impacted squarely in Swiss's face. He started coughing and batting away the dust.

Koestler, backing away, brought up his Hobble and sought to get the best shot he could. But the bed post got in his way.

Bob Thermopylae, naked to the waist, quickly snatched up another bag of Chuckle and hurled it at Koestler.

Koestler dodged to his right, putting the large bed between them. The bag sailed past him and struck the wood paneling of the opposite wall with a dull sound and dropped to the floor. It did not break.

Koestler brought up his Hobble. He had a clean shot now.

But he didn't get his shot off.

Someone was behind him. Or some *thing*.

A shadow appeared behind Koestler. And it was moving.

It ran from right to left, bound for the center of the large bedroom. The interloper, however, had not come from the bathroom or a closet, for those were closer to Swiss than to Koestler. In fact, the new player seemed to come right out of the very *wall*.

The player shot right past Koestler and in his wake left an arctic chill. And it happened fast. The apparition—a man or woman, Koestler could not tell—raced to the very center of the room and aimed a weapon at Bob Thermopylae.

Koestler's holster spit the Clobberer into his right hand, but it was too late.

The mysterious weapon discharged a quiet beam that knocked Bob Thermopylae against the wall. He then fell solidly to the floor, unconscious and almost entirely blue from the cold.

Koestler felt the chill of the beam's backwash and couldn't move himself. But that was more from surprise than anything else. It had all happened so fast.

Koestler tried to shoot the new player with his Clobberer, but a strange thing happened. The interloper disappeared.

He did not exit through the bedroom door, however. The stranger made directly for the opposite wall, then stepped *into* it, disappearing, leaving an eerie greenish glow in its aftermath. But that quickly faded away.

Koestler blinked incredulously. There was no door, no window, nor any sliding panel in the wall. Nothing.

Koestler jumped to the door leading to the outer hallway. There, a crowd of masquers had gathered to stare down at the helpless Zorro.

Had the player exited *through* the wall, he would have encountered the gathering and probably frightened them. That had not happened. The player was *gone*.

Koestler ran back to his partner. "Hey, man, did you see that?"

Swiss, covered in Chuckle, was staring at the half-naked Madonna lying next to him on the floor. He was hallucinating now and singing low to himself.

Koestler touched a button on his belt. He sent out a signal to Captain Edwardian Rux just beyond the gates to Devil Dervish's mansion.

It was time to call in the cavalry.

FIVE

KOESTLER REMAINED IN COSTUME, Face, and gas mask until the Los Angeles county Hazardous Materials squad went through Devil Dervish's mansion with their Eliminator wands. Smaller versions of the famous Los Angeles landmarks, the wands pulled the residue of Chuckle out of the air so that the rest of the LAPD could go over the crime scene without being dressed as spacemen. In the meantime, a dozen anti-gravity forensics Eyes had been turned loose in the mansion. They stayed out of everyone's way as they videoed the investigation from every possible angle.

Outside Dervish's mansion a Roman carnival seemed in progress as the LAPD herded masquers into paddy wagons and did their best to re-store order. All streets leading to Dervish's mansion had been blocked.

Sunset Boulevard had been cordoned off half a mile in two directions. Overhead, news choppers cut through the air and scores of hovering Eyes broadcast the event to the world at large, a world starved for excitement, especially anything coming out of Southern California, newsworthy or not.

From the time of the bust, Koestler had remained at Brad Swiss's side. Koestler had also thrown a blanket over the strangely afflicted form of Bob Thermopylae. The gown he had worn had been very skimpy and Koestler thought Bob Thermopylae would freeze to death before EMS could arrive. Thermopylae seemed to *radiate* cold from where he lay stricken. He had never seen anything like it in his life.

When Captain Edwardian Rux appeared upstairs, he led a team of masked medics. He told the medics to stay outside until he could assess the situation. Rux's bug-eyed gas mask contrasted with the sleek lines of his expensive, Italian-made suit, his only indulgence.

"I take it HazMat has cleared the place," Rux said in his pronounced English accent.

Koestler had, by then, removed his protective gear. He nodded. "About ten minutes ago."

Rux pulled his mask off. Edwardian Rux was a tall, thin man with a high forehead and inset blue eyes. With his clipped mustache and elegant British accent he seemed almost the aristocrat. But though he was a former stage actor, he was now all cop.

He was also very concerned at both the condition of Bob Thermopylae and his stricken officer Brad Swiss.

Rux looked down at Bob Thermopylae in the Madonna body morph. Koestler had already told him what to expect at the crime scene.

"*This* is Bob Thermopylae?" Rux asked.

Koestler nodded. "Brad got his voice print. I sent the data downtown, just to double-check. It came back a match."

Captain Rux turned to Detective Swiss who was now sitting in a near-by chair. "Good work, detective. How do you feel?"

Swiss was long gone. He hummed a dance-floor ditty, holding his leather helmet in his hand. He still had on the George Peppard Face taken from the *Blue Max*. Traces of blue-white Chuckle dust were in the seams and collar of Swiss's costume. HazMat had done their best to vacuum up the loose Chuckle in the room.

"This was worse than the last time," Koestler said, referring to the South Bay incident nine years ago when the whole Protean Set was ambushed. "He might even have inhaled a worm. Some of it looks uncut to me." He indicated the pile of Chuckle packets still on the dresser.

Rux signaled the medics waiting in the hall. They brought in a mobile stretcher. Koestler helped them load Detective Swiss onto it. Swiss went happily.

When Swiss had been removed, another stretcher was brought up and Bob Thermopylae was then taken away. Rux ordered four heavily-armed officers to accompany Bob Thermopylae to the hospital.

Amber Leone and Kip Dixon entered the upstairs bedroom. They too, were still in disguise.

"How did this go down?" Kip Dixon asked.

"We just saw Brad," Amber Leone added.

Koestler said, "I'm not too sure what happened. Did you see Bob Thermopylae downstairs? Did you see what he looked like?"

"The Madonna?" Amber Leone asked. "Brilliant disguise, if you ask me."

Koestler again nodded. "Well, apparently Brad came across Bob Thermopylae handing out candy and got a voice match. There was some sort of fight between him and Bob and a henchman. I Gumdropped the henchman out in the hallway, then came in here to help Brad."

"What happened to Bob?" Rux asked.

"That's the strange part," Koestler admitted. He pointed to the location at the wall where the "player" emerged. "I was about to Hobble Bob when someone appeared out of nowhere—*there*, specifically—and shot Bob Thermopylae before he could toss a bag of Chuckle at me."

Kip Dixon's eyebrows came together in suspicion. "You mean he was standing there."

"No," Koestler insisted. "He came *out of the wall*, ran past me, then disappeared *into* the wall there." He pointed across the room.

"What did the player look like?" Rux asked.

"That's just it. It all happened so fast. But it looked like he was in some sort of costume. And a helmet. I remember a helmet."

"Why didn't he shoot you or Brad?" Rux asked grimly.

"I don't know," Koestler said. "But he *could* have. My back was to him the whole time."

"Bob didn't look Clobbered," Amber Leone observed.

Koestler frowned. "No. It wasn't a Clobberer. The weapon didn't make a sound. It sent out some light, but no sound. It just froze Bob where he stood."

Captain Rux looked at Koestler from the deep recesses of his hooded eyes. "Do you have any idea how crazy this sounds?"

Even to Koestler it sounded crazy, and he had *seen* the player in action. He then said, "It wouldn't be the first time two crews were fighting for dominance."

"But what kind of crew can move through walls and freeze people?" Rux asked. "You tell that to Dunhill and the rest of IAD and they'll laugh in your face."

"Then strip you of your badge," Dixon said.

Koestler held up his hands. "Hey. It's what I *saw*. I'm not making this up. *Something* happened to Bob Thermopylae. Maybe we'll find out more from the hospital."

Meanwhile, the forensics team was preparing to take the "candy store" away.

"This just doesn't make sense," Dixon said.

"Perhaps it was someone at the party," Rux speculated.

Koestler shook his head. "I stepped out into the hallway right after the man disappeared. He wasn't there." Silence filled the room as the Protean

Set took in what had happened, as incredible as it was. "First thing we have to do is find the people who did the morph on Bob Thermopylae," Rux then announced. Detective Dixon added, "That should tell us how long Bob's been walking around as Madonna."

"We'll need subpoenas," Leone said. "They won't give up their records without a fight."

Morph parlors did a good business in changing people's appearances. That's how criminals disappeared back into the population, that's how husbands avoided ex-wives and onerous alimony payments. Getting data from any morph parlor would not be easy, tidy, or clean.

Captain Rux said, "We'll see what we can get from Bob when he recovers. I want to know more about the guy who shot him." He turned to Koestler. "Where did this guy appear? Show me exactly."

Koestler walked over to the wall to the far right side of the bed. "It was right here," he indicated.

Rux thumped the wall with his knuckles, probing for a hidden panel.

The sound his knuckles made did not indicate hollowness.

"I already did that," Koestler said. "The opposite wall, too."

The far corner of the room had a settee and a long, low table upon which were knickknacks of carved marble. The room had no windows. Strange for a bedroom, Koestler thought. It did have a bathroom. But it was on the other side of the room. Next to the bathroom was a walk-in closet. It had been empty throughout the episode.

Rux turned to Koestler. "Is it possible you inhaled some Chuckle when this happened? This sounds like something you'd see on a worm."

Koestler still clutched his mask and his goggles. He held them up for Rux to see. "I had these on when I entered the room and didn't take them off until just a few minutes ago, after HazMat cleared the place."

"But how could a Chuckle *hallucination* affect Bob Thermopylae the way it did?" Amber Leone said. "That was real."

Science knew little about Chuckle or Chuckle worms. A Chuckle worm was rumored to produce psychotropic enzymes in a cycle that alternated every five days. The Army was desperate to have a Chuckle worm to analyze to know for sure; the Protean Set was desperate to provide them with one.

"I want you checked out anyway," Rux said to Koestler. "Just to be on the safe side."

"I don't *need* to have my blood scrubbed, captain," Koestler said. "I didn't inhale anything. And anyway, I think I'd know if I was on Chuckle."

"*Nobody* knows that they're on Chuckle," Rux frowned gloomily. "And all I have is your word on what happened, detective."

"Bob Thermopylae's a popsicle, captain," Koestler countered. "*Something* happened here tonight and it wasn't a Chuckle hallucination."

Rux stood in the middle of the room. He was thinking. They all were thinking.

"Captain," Kip Dixon put in. "You think this might have been someone from the military? That doesn't sound like any weapon we have."

"I was thinking that," Rux admitted.

"Or some crew that's *stolen* something from the military," Amber Leone offered.

"That, too," Rux said.

Captain Rux pondered the ceiling and the walls, the length and breadth of the room. "So what kind of bedroom doesn't have windows?" he asked. Koestler said, "A bedroom where the light's artificial and controlled. Like that of a television studio."

Devil Dervish made his fortune filming couples having sex. But these couples had nodes under their skin that downloaded their sensations, right up to the moment of orgasm. A person with similar nodes on their bodies could, without the need of another human being, experience the joys of sex. Realies were the main source of entertainment in Asia, and especially China, where men outnumbered women ten to one and sexual release was otherwise hard to find.

The ceiling was made of opaque tiles. Anything could be behind them, including cameras for live video feeds to the battery of satellite dishes on Dervish's roof.

"I'll bet he's got cameras in every room," Kip Dixon grumbled, looking at the ceiling.

"If he's got the whole party on disc, then we can send a lot of people to jail," Amber Leone said with a wicked smile.

"Let us see if Mr. Dervish has a control room in the house," Captain Rux then said.

The communications "hub" of the mansion was located in a small monitoring room one could enter through an innocuous closet on the ground floor. There they found video feeds to every room in the mansion—*every* room, including the many bathrooms. A forensic tech helped Rux locate the specific camera feed that recorded everything that took place in the bedroom where Bob Thermopylae had operated his candy store. But rather than use Devil Dervish's own video playback equipment in the monitoring room, they withdrew to one of the large living rooms. They set up their own viewing equipment there because members of the vice squad were getting anxious to go through the other discs in Dervish's library. To them, it was a treasure trove.

A tech set up a flat screen playback unit on a large onyx coffee table where the Protean Set gathered around. Rux, Leone, and Dixon sat on the couch; Koestler stood.

The view of the playback indicated that the camera was positioned just above the door of the bedroom and it had started recording at 8:35 p.m. The disc was a standard twelve-hour disc. Rux forwarded the disc.

For the first hour the room had remained vacant. Then various masquers came and went in a flurry of activity. Something in a pipe was smoked between several individuals. A Vivien Leigh masquer dressed as a southern belle had sex with a George Clooney masquer dressed in military fatigues. Rux speeded past the masquers who had used the room just for fun. When Devil Dervish appeared, Rux slowed the playback.

Stumpy Devil Dervish entered the room with a masquer that was the best version of Madonna Ciccone that Koestler had ever seen. The two were accompanied by a Tyrone Power Zorro who also carried in a pair of saddlebags over his shoulder. The playback clock said 12:10 a.m.

Devil Dervish was the first to sample Bob Thermopylae's wares. After a bit of barely-audible conversation, he went back to his party and a long line of L.A. junkies filtered into the room. All the while the Zorro stood by with sword and flintlock at the ready, in case anything got out of hand.

Rux forwarded the disc to the point where Brad Swiss appeared in the candy store. Swiss sauntered in, asked about the wares Bob Thermopylae was selling, clearly visible on the dresser. They struck up a conversation. They chatted for a while.

But here Bob Thermopylae became suspicious. He had seen Detective Swiss fingering a place at his belt. He could not have known that was where the voice-print analyzer was located. But that didn't matter. Chuckle magnified one's sense of paranoia.

Bob Thermopylae said something to the Zorro masquer and the man came at Swiss.

A tussle ensued, but Swiss was the better athlete and he spun the Zorro around to the center of the room where he had time enough time to draw his Hobble. The gun came out of his jodhpurs and he shot a Hobble pellet at the Zorro's legs. The titanium ribbons swiftly unfolded and ensnared the man. He lurched backwards out the door where Koestler would Gumdrop him.

Koestler came into the camera's view and the brief fight took place, culminating with Detective Swiss being dusted by Bob Thermopylae.

But as Koestler maneuvered around the large bed to get the best shot possible for his Hobble, the player appeared. Literally. A blue-green light, not part of the bedroom's own soft illumination, manifested off to the right of the screen. A figure surrounded by an eerie haze, emerged from the wall. It wore a silver helmet that covered its face and it held a very strange weapon. It was about the size of a shoebox and did not seem like a weapon at all.

The figure ran right behind Koestler. He seemed to have no interest in Koestler whatsoever. The weapon came up and a light emerged from it, filling the entire room for a brief second. But the result was that Bob Thermopylae was struck directly by its beam and he instantly went rigid. Bob Thermopylae started to fall, but by the time Bob Thermopylae came crashing to the carpet, the player had stepped beyond the camera's view.

Rux ran the playback again. Then a final time. The incident never changed or became any more clear to them.

"A take-down with an assist," Kip Dixon muttered.

"But…who *was* that guy?" Amber Leone finally asked. "And how did he *do* that?"

No one had an answer for that, least of all Koestler, and he had been in the room.

THE PACK OF RED APPLE CIGARETTES in Christine Myrland's hand said, *"Federal law requires me to warn you that these cigarettes contain one-hundred-and-eight known carcinogens. Red Apples also contain high concentrations of nicotine which is addictive in the extreme. For your own good and the good of everyone around you, you are hereby advised—"*

Myrland had, by then, put a fresh cigarette to her lips, and lit it. She tossed the pack onto the bedside table. The package went silent when it lost contact with her hand.

There were too many smart things in the world, Myrland thought. *Including people.*

Her hooker rolled over in bed next to her. His name was Rick Lear.

He propped himself up on his elbow. "I thought you were going to quit."

Rick Lear was a great hooker and she had him over whenever she was in certain moods. Her mood last night called for sex. Her mood now was different.

"Not today," she said, blowing smoke toward the ceiling.

Lear shrugged. "Bad habits are hard to break."

"I can break myself of you."

"You probably can," Lear said. He sat up in bed beside her. His body tapered from his shoulders to his waist in a perfect delta V shape. Lear was a great animal. "It doesn't matter, though," he said. "I just got cleared for the quarantine. I can find better work back east."

"Not if you tell them you're from California," she countered.

"I'll just say I'm from Seattle. Which is true. I was born in Port Townsend."

She looked at him and felt a slight spasm of envy. "You got cleared?"

He nodded. "I couldn't do my job if I was stoned all the time. Besides, the Port Authority only screens for Chuckle anymore."

"You could still have a Chuckle worm and clear the quarantine screens," she said. "They only produce fifteen days a month, don't they?"

"Sure, but I've never done Chuckle," Lear told her. "So there's no way I could have a worm inside me."

"Can't you get it through sex?"

Lear smiled impishly at her. "Not from you. You've never done a drug in your life. So Chuckle's out."

"What about your other clients? Have you told them you're leaving?"

"You're the only one I've serviced in four months," Lear said.

She took a long drag from her cigarette. She got out of bed and walked to the bathroom. She was trailed by a goblin of cigarette smoke. She'd already paid him, so there was no use in carrying on this inane conversation.

When she came out, Lear was sitting up in bed. He had activated the flatscreen on the far wall. The curtains were still pulled shut. It wasn't yet 9 a.m.

"It's too early in the morning to watch TV," Myrland said, crushing out her cigarette.

"Then watch whatever you want." He tossed her the remote.

"I don't want to watch anything," she said. The changer bounced once on the bed, then fell to the floor. A news channel came on.

Myrland was about to turn it off when she saw a "Breaking News" bulletin flashing across the screen. Her heart almost leapt from her chest...but it had nothing to do with Eidolon Technologies.

A spectacular bust had apparently gone down in Hollywood the night before and the talking head telling Southern California about it was very animated in her excitement.

Myrland, however, had expected a much different story to be splashed across the television screens of the world that Saturday. She hadn't slept well because of it, despite Lear's ten inches of happiness.

Lear was looking at her. "You look like you've just seen a ghost."

"I thought it was going to be about Rex," she said. She quickly reached for another cigarette.

"Eidolon Rex," Lear said. "I don't see what's so important about a computer."

"No one expects you to." She began trolling through the news channels manually. The voice-control mechanism of her remote was broken. She could understand the workings of a supercomputer, but she couldn't rework the wiring for the voice-activation circuit in her home entertainment unit.

Myrland scrolled through every news channel she could find—local, national, and international. Apparently none had gotten word yet that the world's most advanced supercomputer had mysteriously disappeared from Eidolon Technologies in Simi Valley. It wasn't even a side story, a bit of fluff. Evidently drug busts had more entertainment value.

Myrland stopped her channel surfing. The channel it landed on was a cartoon channel. *Chacmools*. Women jumping into and out of reality. *Just like Rex*, she thought. Only Rex was the size of a bus. Rick Lear began climbing into his clothes.

The bedside phone rang.

Myrland ignored Lear as he tucked his gorgeous parts carefully into his trousers. "Who is it?" she demanded of the phone.

"Alex Langley calling from Eidolon Technologies with a priority preference," the phone replied.

Myrland had to answer a priority preference. If she didn't, the phone's AI unit, which knew she *was* at home, would tell the caller that he was being ignored, then ask for instructions. But only a few people in her life—and Alex Langley, unfortunately, was one—had queuing priority with her phone system.

Alex Langley, the good soldier, she thought dismally. Lloyd Thaxton and the crisis team would not be too far behind. They were already at work on Rex's disappearance, undoubtedly looking where to place the blame....

She lifted the receiver. "Hello, Alex," she said. "What is it?"

"You'd better get down here, Christine," Langley said. "I'm calling everybody in."

Alex Langley was the Eidolon Rex project director and she was the chief programmer. They had equal status at Eidolon, but her Ph.D. in Advanced Mathematics was trumped by his Ph.D. in Quantum Mechanics *and* his Blanding Prize. He had designed and built Rex, but she had programmed him. They were its two parents.

"Rex isn't coming back, Alex. He went the way of Telemon Ajax two years ago. You know that, *I* know that, Lloyd Thaxton knows that. His damage assessments can keep until Monday morning."

"This won't keep, Christine. Rex is back. I think you should get down here. *Now.*"

Myrland blinked. "He came *back*?"

"He's back and he's working and Thaxton thinks we have enough data to figure out where he went. This isn't Ajax all over again. And it won't kill you to come to work on a Saturday."

"I'll be there in half an hour," she said. She broke the connection.

Lear pointed to the flatscreen. He had been mesmerized by the cartoons. "Is this what kids watch on Saturday morning? I don't get it. What's a Chamool?"

There was a lot Rick Lear didn't get. She had already put him out of her mind.

Alex Langley, Ph.D., project director at Eidolon Technologies, trembled from too much coffee, too little food, and the knowledge that he may have made the discovery of the century.

He was alone in the staff lounge where he poured himself yet another cup of coffee. He had spent the last hour calling in his staff and all he was doing now was waiting for them to arrive. Only he and Lloyd Thaxton's damage assessment team had been at Eidolon since the night before. But now, even members of the Eidolon Board were on their way.

After what had happened to Ajax over at Santos Avionics in Long Beach, this was *big*. Still, Langley hadn't slept in the eighteen hours Rex had been away…wherever "away" was.

Langley could hear the hurried footsteps out in the hallways as security personnel rushed to secure the entire complex, preparatory to the military showing up. For the military *would* show up. Then Eidolon Rex would be out of his hands entirely. He only hoped that it wouldn't fall into Christine Myrland's hands. There was no telling what she would do with it if that happened.

Alex Langley was forty-five, balding, and a bit overweight. He was a man besieged. His wife drank too much. His daughter always fought with him when she was home from college. And he was always wrestling with Christine Myrland over who had authority over the Eidolon Rex team.

He stood at the window to the lounge. The morning beyond looked bleak. Simi Valley, once an agricultural enclave, was now home to millions of suburbanites and they always seemed to be going somewhere.

That's where Eidolon Rex went: *somewhere*.

By the time Langley walked down to the ready room members of the Eidolon Rex programming team were sitting at their stations that faced a single glass wall. Behind the protective glass wall, Eidolon Rex, a giant onyx-black icon, stood humming away as if everything was as normal as normal could be.

However, the crisis management team inside the computer containment area was busy fussing over him. Their findings were being instantly conveyed to the smaller screens before Langley's crisis group.

Lloyd Thaxton, Langley's right-hand man, headed up the damage assessment group when Eidolon first disappeared at 7:05 p.m. the night before. Thaxton was a stooped, grey-haired man in his sixties. He had a low tolerance for company politics, so he rarely dealt with Christine Myrland or her company allies. Thaxton entered the ready room, the containment door hissing shut behind him.

"You nod off in the lounge?" Thaxton asked Langley.

"No," Langley responded. "Just coffee. Lots of coffee."

"We can sleep next week sometime," Thaxton said.

Soon people began arriving. Everyone who came in—the men unshaven, the women with their hair barely brushed—was astonished to see the giant computer back at his berth. They had left last night thinking they were without jobs. It happened at Santos Avionics when their giant computer blew up. They had assumed that the same had happened to Eidolon Rex.

Christine Myrland finally appeared. She was breathing hard, having run all the way from the parking lot. Langley could smell the tobacco that surrounded her. It fairly oozed from her skin.

Myrland stood in front of the large glass partition, flexing her fingers unconsciously, staring at Rex. "So what happened?" she asked, turning to face Langley.

"In a minute, Christine," Langley said. "Not everyone's here yet."

Myrland went to her station and activated her monitor screen.

The last to arrive was Cecilia Garwin, the Eidolon Technologies Board representative. Garwin was a small, stocky woman who wore her brown hair clipped short. Garwin had no real authority in the day-to-day operation of Eidolon Rex, but the Eidolon Board felt the need to stay abreast of any important developments through her. Besides that, she and Christine Myrland were the best of friends.

Garwin nodded to Langley, then Langley gestured to Thaxton to begin, now that everyone was present.

"Okay, people, listen up," Thaxton began. "On your screens are all the preliminary systems checks Alex and I have already run on Eidolon Rex. The Board will want a detailed analysis of why Eidolon Rex disappeared and where he went, if he went anywhere at all."

"Did anyone see him come back?" Myrland asked, swiveling around in her chair. "No," Langley said. "I was in the lounge, having coffee, Lloyd was downstairs, checking the power circuits."

"But we *felt* it," Thaxton said.

Langley nodded. "When Rex reappeared, he displaced several tons of air and it knocked open all of the doors."

Thaxton added, "If the doors weren't open, it would have blown out these windows." He indicated the large set of windows just beyond their stations.

"So...what *happened*?" Cecilia Garwin asked. "Rex didn't blow up. Do we have any idea where he went?"

"We're taking the most practical approach we can," Thaxton began.

"Right now, our preliminary findings indicate that—"

"He teleported," Myrland blurted out.

Everyone in the room went silent.

When Rex had disappeared at 7:05 the night before, there had been some talk of teleportation, since the disappearance was so clean, as opposed to the messy implosion of Telemon Ajax at Santos Avionics. But Langley had quashed all speculation. They didn't know *what* had happened to Rex and he didn't want his technicians to go off chasing phantoms.

However, Christine Myrland had published several papers on the possible teleportation effects in quantum computing. And everyone left last night wondering if the self-contained supercomputer had gone someplace else since there was no explosion nor was there any debris left behind. Myrland was the first—and the only person, really—to give the notion some credence.

"We don't want to rush to judgment here," Thaxton said hurriedly. "We're going to explore every possible avenue in depth, before this is all over."

"What we do know," Langley told the group, "is that Rex came back to his original floor moorings. He didn't move an angstrom. Nothing was added to his hardware and nothing was taken away. We don't know about the software yet. Lloyd's group is running diagnostics right now."

"What was Rex doing when he disappeared?" one of Langley's subordinates asked.

Langley responded. "He was running just over three hundred thousand programs, most for the government. And many of those were for the military specifically. There were projected weather predictions, several stochastic planning programs for crop yields around the world, erosion patterns in China, and the like."

"But nothing out of the ordinary," another tech commented.

"He wasn't even operating at his peak capacity," Langley added.

"What happened at Santos Avionics?" Cecilia Garwin asked. "Didn't their computer do something like this?"

Langley glanced over at Christine Myrland. Myrland had sat back from her ruminations at her console. This was a sore point between the two of them. Some in the group knew of the conflict, others did not. Apparently Cecilia Garwin did not.

Langley nodded. "Christine and I were co-workers at Santos. That's where we met. She and I were programmers there." Myrland added, "Ajax overloaded, or something. Part of it disappeared and part of it just blew up. There was nothing we could do about it."

Smaller versions of Telemon Ajax were to be the brains inside the newest pilotless aircraft the Air Force was building. The mishap caused Santos Avionics to go under. They couldn't weather the loss. A few weeks later, Christine Myrland and several other technicians came to work for Eidolon Technologies. A few weeks after that, much to his personal chagrin, Alex Langley showed up, hat in hand, also looking for a job.

But Langley, the Eidolon Rex project director, didn't want any friction that day. Not from Christine, not from anybody. "We never did find out what happened to Telemon Ajax. But Rex came back and he might be able to tell us something about why Telemon Ajax didn't. That is *if* the two disappearances are the same."

Christine Myrland moved a thick lock of black hair away from the side of her head as she studied her monitor. She then looked up at Langley. "Is this chronometer reading correct?"

"Yes, it is," Langley said. "Eidolon Rex disappeared at 7:05 p.m. yesterday and returned at 5:05 this morning."

"That's some coincidence," one of the other techs said. "I mean, ten hours exactly."

Myrland pointed to her screen. "But this says, for him, that only a few hours have passed."

"I don't understand," Cecilia Garwin asked, walking over to see Myrland's screen.

"Well, yes. For Rex, it's still yesterday," Lloyd Thaxton said. "He's been back about four and a half hours."

"But he was gone *ten*," Myrland said.

Langley nodded. "That's one of the anomalies we have to explore. Wherever he went, no time passed. He came and went in a blink of an eye."

Lloyd Thaxton then added, "Once my team has a full report of the physical condition of the computer, we'll turn everything over to you people. Then Cecilia can take it to the Board to figure out what this all means. Assuming, of course, that we can figure it out."

"The Pentagon is going to want to be in on this, if it *is* teleportation," Myrland said.

"That's out of our hands," Langley said.

Lloyd Thaxton turned to Langley. "Tell them about Koestler."

All eyes turned to Langley and Thaxton.

"About forty minutes ago, during the first software scan, Lloyd and his people came up with something."

"What was that?" Cecilia Garwin asked. All eyes were now on Langley.

"A name popped up in about two-thirds of the programs Rex was running at the time he disappeared. Whether Rex disappeared *because* of the name, we don't know yet. But the name had several million hits."

"What name?" one of the techs asked.

"Rory Koestler," Langley told them.

"Who the hell is that?" Myrland asked.

"That's one of the things we have to find out," Langley said. "Because until we do, we can't use Eidolon Rex. And if we can't use Eidolon Rex, then Eidolon Technologies can't do business."

"So it *is* like Santos Avionics," the tech said.

"You could say that," Langley admitted.

SEVEN

THE FOLLOWING SATURDAY MORNING, Koestler arrived at the police station in Santa Monica at exactly nine o'clock, early for him. He was up most of the night doing paperwork in the wake of the bust, but he managed to get a few hours' sleep.

He was in a surly mood when he arrived. The night before he had wanted to see one of his girlfriends. Busts of just about any kind gave Koestler a natural high. But none of his regular girlfriends wanted to drive out to Malibu at three in the morning just to have sex, even if it was the weekend. That put him in a bad mood.

Matters were made worse when the first person he bumped into at the station was Vincent Dunhill of Internal Affairs. He had put on his default face once inside the building and Dunhill recognized him immediately. Dunhill was an ex-Marine, powerfully built, in his late forties with a severe gray-blonde flattop always immaculately cut. He never smiled and was suspicious of everybody.

"Saw your performance last night, detective," Dunhill said with a sneer. "But your player stole the show, I think."

"It wasn't a performance or a show and I wasn't the only person involved," Koestler said.

"Well, I just bet you had a *real* good time at the party before the fireworks started."

"It was my *job* to look like I was having a good time."

"Hmm," Dunhill muttered. He walked down the hall, bound for his office.

No one liked anyone who worked in the Internal Affairs Division, Dunhill particularly. IAD had it out for the Protean Set. They didn't like the idea of *actors* in the LAPD.

At the far end of the hall, Captain Edwardian Rux emerged from an opposite corridor. "Detective," Rux said, gesturing for him to follow. Which Koestler gladly did.

Rux and Koestler headed for the War Room. "For the time being, stay away from IAD," Rux said in his gravelly voice. "Try to keep your nose clean around IAD. We still don't know what happened last night and I'd rather not have those buzzards hovering about. For any reason."

They entered the War Room where the Protean Set planned their city-wide infiltrations. The room had a large table with several chairs and a giant flatscreen hung on the wall. The table was inset with keyboards and pop-up monitors.

Amber Leone was already seated. She had her flatscreen up. But she was the only member of the Protean Set present.

"What's the word on Brad?" Koestler asked, taking off his coat and hanging it around a chair. Since the Protean Set were in the field most of the time, they didn't have regular desks or cubicles. The War Room was their only in-station haunt. That also irked IAD.

Rux said, "He ingested quite a lot of dust. He's scheduled for dialysis at eleven."

"Did he inhale a worm?" Koestler asked.

Rux shook his head. "They don't think so. But Lilly was with him all night. She told me he thought he was in some movie, so he got enough."

The thought of dialysis made his skin crawl, but Swiss was going to need a treatment that extreme. The dusting he got the night before was far worse than the one they had received nine years ago in South Bay.

A folder lay beside Amber Leone's computer screen. She pushed it over to Koestler. She said, "Forensics found egg casings and other worm debris in a random sampling of the Chuckle we found."

"Any actual eggs?" Koestler asked, going through the preliminary forensics report.

"No," she said.

Koestler nodded. "That means that we've still got to find the factory. It's out there somewhere." Rux sat at the head of the table, his usual spot. "I still want you checked out, detective."

"I'd know by now if I was infected, captain."

"Isn't your sister a GP in Woodland Hills?" Leone asked. "At least you wouldn't have to wait a week to see her. You could walk right in."

"We don't get along," Koestler said. "I'd rather see somebody else. *Anybody* else."

"See that it's done, one way or the other," Rux said. "That's an order."

"What have you got there, captain?" Koestler asked.

Rux pulled out two sheets of paper and gave one each to Koestler and Leone.

"These are all the known morph parlors in the L.A. region. We should have the court orders we need to confiscate their records by early this afternoon. Detective Dixon is checking one of them near UCLA right now. We need to know how long Bob Thermopylae was walking around as Madonna."

"What about San Francisco?" Detective Leone asked. "Madonna's a favorite up there."

"I don't believe Bob Thermopylae left the region to have the work done," Rux said.

"Why do you think that?" Leone asked.

"It takes at least three months to recover from a full body morph, particularly if it's transsexual. We would have seen a dip in Chuckle traffic in that time. Since there was no dip, he must have been recuperating locally to direct its flow."

"Unless somebody else got a set of viable Chuckle worms," Leone said.

Rux shook his head. "We'd be flush with Chuckle if that were the case. A rival group would do everything it could to take over Bob Thermopylae's traffic if it knew he was down."

"That would account for the player," Koestler said.

The player was at the center of everything.

Rux was grim. "We're still reviewing the recordings we confiscated. We don't want to undermine the D.A.'s case against Thermopylae with any leaks, but we might have to bring the military in on this. They were going to get the Chuckle eggs anyway, but this player of ours is a wrinkle no one expected."

"The military?" Detective Leone said. "You think this is going that way?"

"Everybody I've shown the recording to is as stumped as we are. Nobody knows what this is," Rux said. "But our first concern is to give the D.A.'s office a tight case against Bob Thermopylae."

"What's Thermopylae's condition?" Koestler asked.

"He's apparently in some sort of hypothermic coma," Rux said.

"What's a 'hypothermic coma'?" Koestler asked.

Rux said, "The player somehow put Bob in a state where he's practically frozen solid. It's something no one's ever seen."

Koestler could easily recall the bizarre chill in the air when the player shot Bob Thermopylae. The military would eventually want to know what sort of weapon had been used on Bob Thermopylae, but Rux would do his best to keep them out of the mix until the case had been made as solid as possible against Bob Thermopylae. A Pentagon investigation would only gum things up.

"So what's our next move?" Leone asked.

Rux had steepled his fingers where he sat at the long table. He said, "We've got enough evidence on disc to show that Bob was dealing out of that bedroom. We don't need to show the takedown sequence. But I'm still curious about our player. Did your snitch mention anything about another crew?"

Koestler shook his head. "No. And I think Billy Styvesant would have known if there was."

Rux pursed his lips, thinking. "I want to talk to him anyway. Bring him in. Let's see what he has to say. We still have to find Bob Thermopylae's factory. Until we can locate and kill the worms, the case isn't finished. The D.A. might be happy, but our job won't be over."

Koestler looked at Detective Leone and she nodded. They would talk to Billy Styvesant.

By the time Koestler and Detective Leone entered the police department garage, they had changed Faces. Anyone seeing Koestler's Face as he entered police headquarters that morning would not have seen the same Face leave. So, too, with Amber Leone.

This pertained as well to Koestler's Sensei. The 3.8 liter V8 Sensei MetaMorph became a '15 Daimler rattletrap with a slightly dangling bumper and a dozen dents and scratches and a bad paint job. Koestler also added a few rust-rimmed bullet holes along the passenger side door for good measure. A draggy muffler and a dripping oil pan helped as well.

They took the San Diego freeway and headed south.

Billy Styvesant lived in Manhattan Beach, close to the beach itself. He worked out of a modest beachfront bungalow as an agent and promoter for musicians. Several years ago he had run afoul of the law while dabbling in the drug trade. Becoming a confidential informer allowed him the opportunity to stay out of jail...which was where Koestler said he'd put Billy if he didn't help them get Bob Thermopylae.

Koestler and Leone left their rattletrap about a block away from Billy Styvesant's bungalow. Detective Leone had changed her clothing to that of a street gypsy. She wore a wide turquoise skirt and billowy blouse and tall boots. Her weapons were easily concealed in her garb. "What are you carrying?" Koestler asked as they eased down the sidewalk. "Clobberer, Susan B. Anthonys, Pancakes and Nightdrops. But I forgot to bring my goggles for the Nightdrops."

"Any Spit Wads?"

She shook her head. "I hate their taste. I'd rather use Gumdrops."

Koestler's weapons were his own Clobberer powering up in his shoulder holster, several Susan B. Anthonys and about a dozen Tonya G. Hardings. He didn't think he'd have to use those, however. Clobberers would do just fine.

Billy Styvesant had not answered their phone calls or pages. Saturdays were usually busy for musicians and agents both, but even Billy's answering machine hadn't responded. They tried reaching him by e-mail. The messages went out, but he did not respond to them.

The day was bright and sunny, but Billy Styvesant's neighborhood seemed strangely silent. Only the soft roar of breakers could be heard just beyond the bungalows. They surreptitiously scanned the neighborhood for suspicious cars or idling passersby.

The door to Billy Styvesant's bungalow was located on the southeastern side of the building. Koestler rang the doorbell. Amber Leone stood off to one side, right hand deep in a pocket hidden in the folds of her hippy dress where her Clobberer was holstered to her upper thigh.

There was no response.

Koestler turned the doorknob and discovered that the door had not been locked. It opened easily to Koestler's touch.

Koestler glanced at Detective Leone. Leone pulled out her Clobberer and clutched it with both hands. Koestler's came out as well.

Koestler took a deep breath. "Billy!" Koestler called out. "Billy, you in there?"

They stepped into the main living room. The curtains were pulled shut and the air inside was stale. A 3D coffee table had been left on. It held a vertical column of static that went all the way to the ceiling. Its program had long since expired. The hissing from the audio was loud and irritating. Koestler turned it off.

But there were no signs of foul play. No bullet holes in the walls. No shell casings on the floor. No furniture tossed around, no framed pictures knocked askew. However, the phone's answering machine's light blinked with the residue of dozens of waiting—and unanswered—messages.

Amber Leone stepped off to the right and checked the kitchen and small dining area. Meanwhile, Koestler moved down the hallway to the bedrooms. Outside, a gull screeched above the surf.

Koestler felt a sudden chill at the door to the main bedroom. It was cold enough to store food out in the open.

Koestler pushed open the door. Two people lay in near-darkness beneath the covers of an enormous bed. One was Billy Styvesant. The other Koestler assumed to be his girlfriend.

"Found them!" Koestler shouted over his shoulder.

Detective Leone came up behind him. Her breath came out in small clouds of vaporous air.

The couple in the bed weren't quite sleeping, however. Both people looked pale, nearly dead.

"That's Billy," Detective Leone said. "Who's that with him?"

Koestler stowed his Clobberer. "Her name is Melissa. Melissa Connors."

"She know about Billy?" Leone whispered.

"I don't think so."

Melissa Connors seemed to be conscious. She struggled to awaken. Her mouth moved and her eyelids fluttered like two frail butterflies.

"What happened?" Koestler asked.

The woman's skin was dry and a baby-blue color. Koestler guessed that they had been this way for days and both were suffering from severe dehydration.

"Billy," Melissa Connors whispered feebly. "S–s–someone sh-shot him…"

Detective Leone pulled out her phone and dialed EMS.

"Who shot Billy?" Koestler asked.

"The p-p-police," Melissa Connors breathed. She then lifted a crooked hand from beneath the covers and pointed at the wall beyond the foot of the bed. Not the door. Not the nearby window. The wall.

"*We* are the police," Koestler said. "Billy was working with us."

Connors appeared not to register his words to her. "We were sleeping. I looked up…and he sh-shot Billy. He c-came out and sh-shot him."

Again the trembling hand pointed at the wall behind Koestler.

"Did he shoot you, too?" Koestler asked.

"Please h-help…"

"Help is on its way," Detective Leone said over Koestler's shoulder.

Melissa Connors closed her eyes. The room had a smell of death about it even though both people on the bed were still alive.

Koestler stood up. Amber Leone still had her phone out.

"You'd better call the captain," he said in an urgent whisper. "I think this is the player again."

Leone nodded and went outside to place the call.

EIGHT

BILLY STYVESANT AND HIS GIRLFRIEND were airlifted to the Aaron Stively Medical Center in Culver City. Koestler had chosen that particular hospital not because it was nearest. It wasn't. But Bob Thermopylae had been sent there after the bust the night before and Koestler wanted some answers. All three victims were now in a special detention wing of the hospital under close observation.

Kip Dixon arrived in Face twenty minutes later, when he got the news. Edwardian Rux was not far behind. They gathered in the reception area of the south wing of the hospital. Two armed and armored guards stood like chubby insects at the entrance to the ward.

Dr. Randall Helms oversaw the detention wing. He was tall, bespectacled, and soft-spoken. Once Billy Styvesant and Melissa Connors had been taken care of, Dr. Helms met the Protean set in the reception area.

"I must admit," Helms said carefully, "I've never seen hypothermia like this."

"What makes you say that?" Edwardian Rux asked.

"I'll show you," Helms said. "Come this way."

Helms escorted them past the guards and went directly to Bob Thermopylae's room. Thermopylae—permanently morphed as Madonna Ciccone—lay buried beneath a layer of blankets, one of which was a thermal blanket monitored by one of the machines nearby. Koestler was stunned by the baby-blue glow of Thermopylae's soft skin.

In a low voice, Helms said, "It only seems like hypothermia. His blood pressure is very low, which you'd expect and his body temperature is steady at eighty-nine degrees. But there's something else."

Helms, Koestler noticed, kneaded his hands; he seemed troubled in some way. The physician went on. "When a body freezes, it usually does so from the outside in. Most deep body functions remain at normal body temperature until the blood slows and the cold sets in. Death will result when the blood thickens and can't carry oxygen to the brain. Brain cell asphyxia distorts the thinking and the victim simply falls asleep, thinking everything's fine. Death usually is only minutes away."

"Is Thermopylae going to die?" Kip Dixon asked in his throaty voice.

It was a question they all had on their minds.

"That's just it," Helms admitted. "Mr. Thermopylae's body temperature is a *uniform* eighty-nine degrees, inside and out. And it shouldn't be. It's as if he's being *kept* that way. And that's something I've never seen."

"How is this different?" Detective Leone asked.

"Well, it's as if there is something inside Mr. Thermopylae that is *radiating* cold, the essence of it."

Lying on the bed before them was a tranquil-looking blonde woman, asleep. Bob Thermopylae—but now it was getting hard to think of this Madonna look-alike as *Bob* anything—looked small, frail, and strangely helpless.

Helms positioned the flat of his own hand inches above the blankets covering Thermopylae's chest. "You can feel it," he said. "Give it a try."

The Proteans took their turn measuring the invisible aura of cold that surrounded Bob Thermopylae. All except Koestler. He'd already felt the cold, when they brought Billy Styvesant in.

Helms turned to Captain Rux. "Can you tell me anything about how these people were stricken?"

Rux, though, turned to Koestler. "Detective?"

And Koestler said, "Someone we haven't identified yet shot Mr. Thermopylae with an unusual weapon. A hand gun of some type. Billy Styvesant was probably shot with the same gun, or one just like it."

"Is there a weapon that can do this?" Helms asked.

"We're looking into that," Captain Rux said. "It appears to be something exotic."

Helms pointed to one of the many monitor screens above Thermopylae's bed. "As I said, I've never seen anything like this. I just don't see how a weapon can create brain-wave signatures like the ones here."

The monitor showed a steady sine wave in green which meant nothing to Koestler.

Helms continued, saying, "Mr. Thermopylae's brain is in a very unusual theta-wave condition. Basically, he's dreaming. But occasionally he reacts to whatever he's dreaming about, but the cold keeps him from moving. It was quite bad last night. It's much reduced now."

"Will he come out of it?" Koestler asked.

"That's hard to say. If I knew more about the weapon that was used against him, I might be able to guess. Right now I'm stumped."

"Captain," Detective Leone said, turning to Rux. "Can the D.A. make his case without Bob?"

"Probably," Rux said. "We've got the discs of the candy store."

"But we don't have the worms," Detective Dixon said.

"Right," Rux said.

Dr. Helms pushed his glasses up the bridge of his nose. "There might be something else going on here," he said.

Everyone looked at him. He went on. "It could be that whoever did this to Bob Thermopylae did not mean to kill him."

"What makes you say that?" Detective Dixon asked.

"Well, any weapon that can do something like this can just as easily kill. Right?" Helms said. "I think he was meant to be immobilized, not harmed directly. If that's the case, then the prognosis for recovery is excellent. The same for Mr. Styvesant."

Koestler nodded as he thought about this further. Even standing at the foot of Bob Thermopylae's bed, he could feel the cold emanating from the man's body. Koestler could feel it in his bones.

The cold caused Koestler to shiver involuntarily. When he did, a memory had been knocked loose in his mind: He had experienced an episode of this kind of cold once before in his life.

When he was eight years old and living in Canoga Park, northwest of downtown Los Angeles, the Taurid meteor shower had left in its wake just enough dust to cool off the globe. For nine months temperatures remained unusually low and that summer was called the Winter Summer.

He remembered playing at a little girl's house down the street. She had red hair. He remembered that. Later on that summer he caught the worst cold of his life. It felt quite like this. So what the hell *had* happened to Bob Thermopylae and Billy Styvesant?

Edwardian Rux gave the Protean Set the rest of the weekend off. He would notify them if there was any change in the condition of their two-and-a-half popsicles in the detention wing of the Aaron Stively Medical Center.

Amber Leone returned with Rux and Dixon to the station in Santa Monica. Koestler drove to Westwood, to the UCLA Medical Center, to check up on Brad Swiss. Swiss needed to be told about the condition of Bob Thermopylae.

When Swiss had been dusted by Bob Thermopylae, he had been sent to the UCLA Medical Center, where doctors were quite familiar with the effects of the wide range of recreational pharmaceuticals used throughout the L.A. region. Chuckle was a specialty.

Koestler found Swiss sitting up in bed with a faraway look in his eyes. To the uninformed, he might have been daydreaming. But Koestler recognized a Chuckle fugue when he saw one. A portable dialysis machine stood nearby but was not hooked up at the moment.

Koestler had changed Faces twice en route to UCLA but put on his default face on entering Swiss's room.

Swiss saw him when he walked into the room. He shook his head a couple of times as if to dislodge his mind from the grip of its current fantasy. But Swiss *did* recognize Koestler. That was a good sign.

"You'll never believe who I saw last night," Swiss said.

"Who?"

"Superman."

"Which one?"

"George Reeves." Swiss indicated the window. "He flew right up to my window and waved, then flew off. That was before the first flush."

"When did they do that?"

"About two hours ago."

"How do you feel?"

"Woozy," Swiss said. "I've got two more treatments before it's all gone. At least that's what they tell me."

When the Protean Set had been dusted by Bob Thermopylae the first time, Koestler believed that he was inside some sort of movie taking place in Santa Barbara. When the Chuckle wore off, he found himself in a Santa Barbara Betty Ford clinic with Sal Briscoe in the room next door and several other famous actors and actresses just down the hall. It took about three weeks for the Chuckle to wear off and for his mind to achieve equilibrium.

"But I saw that big red spaceship your friend used to have," Swiss told him with a grin. "Just over the mountains."

"The *Fairuza Balk*. But it's not a spaceship. It just floats around."

"I was impressed."

"I'll tell Sal, next time I see him."

Swiss frowned. "I wouldn't tell Rux that, if I were you."

"There's no reason to."

At that point Koestler told his partner what they had learned so far about the case against Bob Thermopylae. He then told him about the strange frosting of Billy Styvesant and equally unexplainable condition of Styvesant's girlfriend, Melissa Connors.

Swiss thought for a moment. He then slid out of his bed, dragging his mobile IV tower.

"Should you be walking around?" Koestler asked.

Swiss glared at him. "I'm not paralyzed, you know. There's something I want you to see. Come on."

Koestler followed as Swiss walked up to the nurses' station. Three nurses were present and they didn't seem to be alarmed that Swiss was up and about.

"What can we do for you, Mr. Swiss?" one of them said.

"Is Dr. Bender in the hospital today?"

"Actually, I believe he is," the head nurse said.

"Can you get him for me?"

She immediately became concerned. "Is there something we can do for you?"

"It's not medical. I just need to talk with him." Swiss gave her his best Hollywood smile.

While the nurse summoned this Dr. Bender, Swiss turned to Koestler. "This Bender knows more about Exotics than we do. We talked through my first dialysis treatment. You didn't get your blood scrubbed the last time, right?"

"No," Koestler said. "Hate needles."

"And you wouldn't let your sister do it?"

"Not on your life."

Dr. Bender was not long in arriving. Bert Bender was a robust man with black hair and a precisely clipped black beard. He wore a standard white coat, but underneath were Levis and huaraches. Swiss introduced the two of them.

"This is my partner, Detective Koestler," Swiss said. "I told you about him."

"How do you do, detective?" Bender shook Koestler's hand; he had the grip of an Alaskan fisherman.

"So far so good," Koestler replied.

They moved away from the nurses' station. Swiss said, "My partner's got another case of hypothermia. I thought you might be interested."

Bender considered Koestler. "What case is that?"

Koestler presumed that Swiss had told the doctor already about Bob Thermopylae and his strange condition. He had perhaps even mentioned the player's role. In his current state, Swiss could have blabbed the entire case. At the moment, however, Swiss seemed lucid and that led Koestler to think that his partner had made a connection in his mind relevant to Bob Thermopylae's case and wanted Bender in on it.

So Koestler told the bearded doctor about Billy Styvesant and his girl-friend, how they found them, and that they now were over at the Aaron Stively Medical Center. Swiss looked at Bender. "So do you think these might be related?"

"It's hard to say," Bender said. "I would have to speak with the people at Aaron Stively. If they *are* the same, they can't be a coincidence. You just don't see cases like these."

"What are you talking about?" Koestler asked.

Swiss looked at him evenly. "We may have another popsicle right here," he said. "About an hour before they brought me in last night, they brought in a young woman who was nearly frozen to death at some party in West-wood. Student at UCLA."

They paused before a private room. Bender opened the door, making way for Swiss and his IV tower.

Inside, Koestler recognized the same monitoring equipment, the ther-mal blankets, and the trembling of the body beneath the covers. A young woman, a honey-blonde in her early twenties. She seemed to be a real female, not a morph.

"Who is she?" Koestler asked in a low voice. "What happened?"

Keeping his own voice low, Bender said, "She's a mathematics major here at UCLA and a part-time waitress. Her name is Carol Langley. Her parents live in Simi Valley. They're coming down today, I believe."

Wherever you had college students, you had lots of drugs. Koestler looked to his partner. "You think this woman's got some connection to Bob Thermopylae?"

Swiss shrugged. "Search me." Swiss pointed to the girl shivering un-conscious beneath her blankets. "But Billy Styvesant's connected to Bob and he's frozen too."

To Koestler, Bender said, "We see a lot of Chuckle overdoses here, but this is a little different."

"Did she test positive for Chuckle?" Swiss asked.

Bender shook his head. "She tested negative on everything except low levels of alcohol. Chuckle was in her clothing, but it was only a pheromone residue."

"Did she have any Chuckle on her?" Koestler asked.

"Nothing," Bender said. "Not even a roach clip. Just her keys and an ID."

Koestler nodded. "Someone at the party, then."

"I assume so," Bender said.

"Maybe she got caught in a crossfire," Swiss suggested.

"Anyone else brought in like this?" Koestler asked the doctor.

Bender shook his head. "Not here. I would have known."

The young woman seemed so helpless where she lay, trembling in the throes of a phenomenon no one there had seen before.

"Do you know if the police pulled her jacket?" Koestler asked his partner.

Swiss shook his head. "I don't even know if she *has* a jacket."

"I'll look into it," Koestler said.

Koestler recalled what he and Dr. Helms had spoken about concerning Bob Thermopylae and Billy Styvesant. Koestler turned to Dr. Bender. "So what do you make of this woman's condition? Have you seen anything like it before?"

"Never," Bender said. "No one freezes to death in L.A. unless they're put in a refrigerator."

"That's been known to happen," Swiss said.

"Not to math majors at UCLA," Koestler countered.

He looked to Bender. "You could do us a favor."

"Name it."

"See if there are any other area hospitals that have cases similar to this. There could be others. They may be connected."

When Bender had left, Koestler escorted Swiss back to his room. Swiss was getting tired now. Once back in bed, Swiss said, "So. You think we got a new outfit in town? Somebody going after Uncle Bob and his crew?"

"Looks like," Koestler admitted.

nine

THAT FOLLOWING WEEK, KOESTLER DECIDED to look into Carol Langley's role in the Bob Thermopylae affair. Her name hadn't come up on anyone's computer and without further data he couldn't place her in the mix. Earlier that Sunday Koestler had made a clandestine trip to Ms. Langley's apartment in Westwood. However no one answered when he knocked on the door of apartment #526. Not even her roommates were home. They were college students and it was the weekend. They could be just about anywhere. Koestler would come back later.

So that Monday, Koestler configured his Sensei into a conservative-looking BMW sedan and drove up Landfair to the Cleargreen Apartments. Traffic was light. Most people were at work. College students came and went on scooters, bicycles, and motorized shoes. Everything as normal as normal could be.

But not quite.

Koestler parked his Sensei and headed for the Cleargreen Apartments. As he did, two people burst from a causeway between two apartment buildings. They were masquers dressed up as Butch Cassidy and the Sundance Kid. And they were running for all they were worth. Koestler watched as they disappeared around the corner where his car was parked. Koestler noticed that the outlaws were wearing running shoes, not cowboy boots. But they had the Faces and the physiques down pat.

But then a moment later, from further down the street, a cowboy on horseback appeared. He wheeled his horse around and came in Koestler's direction waving a terrific lasso. He seemed to be in pursuit of the two cowboys. He wore a John Wayne Face, his hat pulled down tight. The horse's hooves left stars in their wake.

Koestler couldn't imagine why the cowboys were chasing after each other at eleven o'clock in the morning or where they got the horse. But then this *was* L.A.

Koestler entered the Cleargreen Apartments main lobby and took the elevator up five floors to #526. That day he wore a young-looking Face, one with freckles and curly reddish-blonde hair. He wore a fake gold tooth which he had in a pouch on his belt. He wanted as much as possible to resemble an average college student, somewhere in his mid-to late-twenties.

On the fifth floor, music thundered in the hallway, typical for a dorm at that hour of the day. A goblin of marijuana also haunted the hall. Koestler counted down the doors.

From the weekend managerial staff he had learned the names of Ms. Langley's roommates: Julienne Clements, Bobbi Hess, and Patti Bond. Clements and Hess were the ones who had found Ms. Langley in her nearly-frozen condition at the party she had gone to last Friday night.

Koestler hoped that at least one of the roommates would be at home.

Koestler came to #526 and lifted his left fist, prepared to knock on the door, but the door, he noticed, was already open by several inches. He pushed it wider.

"Knock, knock," Koestler called out. His right hand hovered near the opening in his jacket where he could reach his Clobberer in a hurry if he had to.

Two people, a man and a woman, were in the living room of the apartment, but these were adults, not students. The man was rather plump and seemed a bit frazzled, his tie askew, his suit coat rumpled. Koestler guessed that he was about forty-five. He was balding slightly. The woman, sitting on the couch, was prim and stately and smoked with great intensity. Red Apples. He smoked them sometimes himself.

The two looked at Koestler with rapt alarm. They seemed quite surprised to see anyone at that hour. It took him a moment, but the man finally asked, "What can we do for you?"

These were Carol Langley's parents. Koestler then made a quick, on-the-spot decision. He said, "I'm Detective Rory Koestler. LAPD. Narcotics." He showed them his badge.

The man gave Koestler a puzzled look, but decided that he wasn't the enemy. It was Koestler's move. Koestler gave them a reassuring smile, trying to put them at ease. "You're Mr. Langley?"

"Alex Langley," the man said. "This is my wife, Vivian."

The woman on the couch sat stiffly and didn't even nod. She seemed as thin as one of the cigarettes she smoked.

"I'm looking into what happened to your daughter," Koestler said.

"Our daughter's done nothing, if that's what you're implying," the man said. "She's the victim in this."

"I understand that."

"Carol is a good girl," Vivian Langley said, mashing her cigarette in an ashtray she cradled in her lap. "She's done nothing wrong." She tore open a fresh pack of Red Apples.

Koestler then noticed the cardboard boxes and suitcases standing off to one side. To his right was a bedroom. From it came sounds of dresser drawers being opened and closed. One of Carol Langley's roommates was home. She was helping the Langleys pack Carol's things.

Carol was being moved out. "So how do you know about Carol?" Alex Langley then asked. "We didn't file a police report."

"My partner was injured in a separate incident Friday night and he was placed on the same ward as your daughter. We think narcotics were involved. I'm looking into what happened."

"Carol doesn't do drugs, detective. I can tell you that for a fact," Vivian Langley said. She rose from the couch with a freshly-lit cigarette. She was easily four inches taller than her husband, quite statuesque.

"I'm not saying that she does," Koestler said. "But she may have gotten caught in a crossfire of some kind. I'm just tracking down all the leads I can."

Mrs. Langley faced Koestler. "That's why we're moving Carol out. We should have never let her come here in the first place." Alex Langley merely lowered his gaze and shook his head. The tall woman was verging on hysterics, unable to deal effectively with her grief. Koestler then wondered if Carol Langley had worsened. People did, after all, die from hypothermia. "What is your daughter's condition? Has she improved?" Koestler then asked.

"No," Mrs. Langley said. "But we're moving her back home when the doctors allow it."

Here, Alex Langley spoke. He said, "Carol's already missed an important exam in her Advanced Quantum Mathematics class," Alex Langley said. "Her advisor said she can't make the exam up, so we're applying for a full medical withdrawal from school. She can return next semester."

His wife snapped at him. "Not here, she won't. She'll go somewhere close to home."

"We'll talk about this later," her husband said.

"*Carol doesn't do drugs,*" someone said off to Koestler's right. "Nobody in this apartment does drugs. We don't even smoke."

The young woman standing in the bedroom doorway was a young blonde woman with a very serious expression on her face. She had fair, very pale features and soft skin. Her eyes were blue and very intense and glared at the cloud of cigarette smoke Vivian Langley had left in the living room.

Koestler turned to her. "I take it you're one of Carol's roommates?"

"Yes, I am."

"May I ask which one?"

"Julienne Clements," the young woman said with a scowl. She seemed absolutely fearless. "No one smokes or drinks in our apartment. That was our agreement." Ms. Clements crossed her arms defiantly across her small bosom.

"And why is that?" Koestler asked.

"I am of the faith," Clements said. "And my faith doesn't allow it."

Koestler had no idea what faith that was and had no interest in pursuing it.

Clements went on. "And I am the lessee of this apartment. Carol, Bobbi and Patti all agreed to my terms. We're good students here. Maybe the only good ones left in the building."

"That's what I don't understand," Alex Langley said, walking up to Koestler. "Carol is a straight-A student. She's never missed a day of school. We're very proud of her."

Koestler addressed Julienne Clements. "What can you tell me about the party Carol went to?"

"Carol heard from someone at the restaurant that there was going to be a party in the building," Clements said. "But there's always a party going on here somewhere. I'm surprised she went."

"What restaurant is this?" Koestler asked.

"The Highwayman," Clements said.

"Did you go to the party?" Koestler asked.

"I don't go to parties."

"Who told you she was hurt?" he then asked.

Angrily, Clements said, "Those cretins called us when they found her in one of the bedrooms. They told us to come and get her. I'm surprised they didn't rape her."

Mrs. Langley's eyes widened at Clements' bitter words.

"Why didn't *they* bring her back?" Koestler asked.

"Because they're assholes!" Clements snapped. "Bobbi's boyfriend was here and we brought her back. When she didn't wake up we called 911."

"But she wasn't drunk or passed out on pills," Koestler said. It wasn't framed as a question because he knew the answer already. He wanted to hear Clements' version of the story.

Here, Clements seemed more bemused than upset. "No. She was cold all over, like she'd been locked in a freezer. But Borax didn't have a freezer. I mean, a big freezer, like a meat locker."

"Borax?"

"It was his apartment," Clements said. "It was his party."

"Did anybody actually *see* what happened to Carol?" Koestler then asked.

Clements shook her head. "They just found her on the floor."

"This Borax character," Koestler said. "What apartment does he live in?"

"He's in #212, downstairs. You ought to go down there right now and arrest him!"

"I just might."

"I went down there and knocked, detective," Alex Langley then said. "Nobody answered, but his stereo's blasting away and I smelled dope. Pot."

"Someone's there," said Koestler. "They're just too stoned to come to the door."

Koestler's mind was working furiously now. He had to call Rux. There were search warrants to be had. Maybe SWAT had to called in. Perhaps HazMat as well…

"I might need to talk to you later. How can I reach you?" Koestler asked Alex Langley.

Langley gave him his business card. It said: ALEX LANGLEY—CHIEF PROJECTS DIRECTOR—EIDOLON TECHNOLOGIES. It had a Simi Valley address. They were a long way from home.

"That number is my personal communications number," Langley then said, pointing to the card. "I can be reached 24 hours a day, anywhere on earth. If you find the people who attacked Carol, I want to know about it."

"Count on it," Koestler said.

He then gave Alex Langley his card.

"If you can think of anything more, please call this number and leave a message. I'm harder to reach, but I'll get back to you as soon as I can."

Alex Langley studied the card as if looking for some hidden meaning in its typeface or cardstock. "Koestler," he said, trying the word out, as if it had just registered for the first time.

Koestler headed for the door.

"What are you going to do now?" Vivian Langley suddenly asked him.

"Talk with this Borax person and see what he has to say."

"I'll come with you," Alex Langley said. He moved with determination to the door.

Koestler stopped him. "You'd better not. I'd just grab as much of your daughter's things and get as far away from this building as possible. You, too, Ms. Clements. Pack a day bag, check into a motel."

"Why?" Clements asked.

"It may get a little...noisy." Koestler said. He then pulled out his communicator. He added, "I'll give you folks about twenty minutes. Can you manage that?"

That seemed doable to them.

To Clements, Koestler said, "Call your other roommates and tell them to stay away from here. At least until we're through. Remember, twenty minutes."

He then left.

TEN

KOESTLER LEFT THE CLEARGREEN APARTMENTS via the south stairwell. Outside, he called Captain Rux and told him what he had learned from the Langleys and Ms. Clements and suggested they get a search warrant for the apartment this "Borax" person lived in. Rux said he would. Rux also told him that he'd have a SWAT team there in twenty minutes and told Koestler to wait in a safe place.

Koestler then got hold of Kip Dixon and gave him the name "Borax" to look up in their computers. Borax was undoubtedly a handle. The odds were also good that this Borax character wasn't even a student.

Back at his Sensei, Koestler restocked his personal arsenal. Since he had originally expected only to interview two or three coeds, he had only taken his Clobberer with him. But the party in #212 sounded much like the party Devil Dervish had put on—a party with a candy store—only scaled back considerably. He was probably going to need more than just a Clobberer.

And there would be no mistakes this time. This had to go down as clean as it could.

Koestler felt his adrenaline levels rise at the prospect of nabbing this mysterious Borax. He could almost feel the very electricity in the air that came from the giant Stone Canyon Eliminator tower piercing the clouds to the north. It loomed over west Hollywood like a sentinel of the gods, snatching pollutants from the skies, making their lives pure.

Koestler walked back to the stairwell, alert for anything unusual. But nothing unusual happened. No masquers on horseback; no masquers in tights and capes. But true to his word, Rux arrived with the forces of the

LAPD in about twenty minutes, the search warrant's signature from the judge barely dry.

However, Rux's arrival was without the usual fanfare. No sirens, no blaring horns, no roar of urban attack helicopters. There was a police chopper overhead, but it came in on silenced engines and hovered at a discreet distance.

Rux bounded from the first assault vehicle that lurched into the side parking lot of the apartments, where the stairwell was located. Several armored SWAT personnel clumped out behind him. Rux was in elegant suit and tie, the commandos in flat-black armor. By the time they were in position against the side of the apartment building, a large Hazardous Materials truck—a massive eighteen-wheeler—came on scene, the last of their forces.

They hadn't used this much equipment on the Dervish raid.

"You didn't have to bring the army, Captain," Koestler said.

"Dixon came up with a couple of hits for the name 'Borax,'" the former English actor said. "It's also a name Devil Dervish blabbed about."

"Dervish is talking?"

"On the advice of his lawyers. So where does your man live?" Rux asked, looking up at the apartment complex. "Where is apartment two-twelve?"

"You can't see it from here," Koestler said as they piled into the stairwell. "It faces east. It will be two doors down on our left when we exit into the hallway."

They reached the second floor. Standing inside the stairwell was a lean African-American man. He wore a white shirt with a black tie and casual khaki pants. But there was nothing casual about him. He also clutched a walkie-talkie.

Koestler said to Rux, "This is Rupert Holmes, the manager of the Cleargreen Apartments. This," he said to Mr. Holmes, "is Captain Rux, LAPD."

Beads of sweat were brilliant upon Holmes' forehead. "I think your man's in his apartment. I walked past just a moment ago. I can hear a stereo or something."

Koestler peered through the small rectangular window of the hallway door. At the far end of the hall, at the opposite stairwell door, Amber Leone appeared, backed by her own SWAT team. She was waiting for Koestler's move.

"What do we know about this guy?" Koestler asked his captain with a cautious whisper.

Rux's voice was a cultivated British grumble. "Real name's Jack Mc-Kimmie. He's been in and out of trouble for years. But get this: He was at Dervish's party about two hours before we showed up."

"Was he at the candy store?" Koestler asked.

Rux nodded. "Got him on disc. *Big* dealer. One way or another, he's going downtown."

The manager of the Cleargreen Apartments, Rupert Holmes, first looked terrified at the presence of all the weaponry in his stairwell. But that changed to anger. "Mr. Borax has been dealing drugs out of my apartments?" he said.

"The chances are pretty good," Koestler told him quietly. "We're going to find out for sure."

Captain Rux spoke into his communicator. His voice was low and resonant. "Stand by, all units. Wait for my signal."

Koestler looked past Rux's position in the stairwell, down to the next level. Standing behind three SWAT officers was a member of the Hazardous Materials squad. The man was completely suited up, self-contained like a spaceman. In his left hand was a large case.

Koestler whispered down to him. "You have a sensor? A really good one?"

The moon-suited man lowered the case and proceeded to open it. From it, he extracted a small device and this was passed up to Koestler.

Koestler opened the stairwell door. Rux was right behind him. At the far end of the hallway, Amber Leone crept out ahead of several SWAT members.

Once in the hallway, Koestler could smell the rich pungency of marijuana and the incense used to hide it. Music dully thrummed the walls.

At that point, a student emerged from his apartment, backpack on his back, antenna rising from the side of his head. He was off to class. But when he saw the phalanx of officers at either end of the hallway, he went back into his apartment and locked his door.

Koestler, meanwhile, had activated the sensor in his hands. He showed it to Rux. "Traces of Chuckle are in the air, Captain. Not enough to harm anybody out here."

"Inside could be a different story," Rux said. He turned to the SWAT team behind him. "Masks," he commanded.

Koestler threw the sensor back to the man in the moon suit. He caught it deftly.

Koestler waited until the SWAT team wrestled into their masks before making his move. But neither he, nor Rux, nor Amber Leone, nor any of the uniformed officers had masks. If the air got any worse, they'd all have to have their blood cleaned like Brad Swiss.

"You call it," Rux said to Koestler when everyone was ready.

Koestler nodded. Feeling uneasy that he had Rux in the audience and the rest of the LAPD waiting in the wings, he quashed a ripple of nervousness and walked up to the door to #212. *Everything by the book. Borax goes down clean....*

Music thundered behind the door to apartment #212. Koestler pounded loudly on it with the side of his fist. He held his Clobberer behind him so that anyone looking through the peephole wouldn't see it.

"Yo, Borax! My man!" Koestler shouted above the music. "It's me, Mr. Skin. From the party, remember? I got a *need*, man." He pounded some more. "You in there or what?"

No response came to Koestler's fervent calls.

A few doors down, another student stuck her head out her door to see what the fuss was all about. She was worrying a foaming toothbrush in her mouth. She withdrew her head quickly and closed the door.

Koestler walked back to Rux and his troops, a bit chagrined. He motioned to the man in the moon suit. "I need the sensor again."

The man tossed it back to Koestler.

Koestler returned to Borax's apartment and held the sniffer to the crack at the bottom of the door. The indicator light glowed a bright and ugly red. The numbers beside it were the highest he had seen since the dusting in that warehouse in South Bay a decade ago. That meant that large amounts of Chuckle were exposed to the open air somewhere inside Borax's apartment. The air conditioning was forcing it out into the hallway.

Koestler froze the reading. It was evidence now. "We've got probable cause," Koestler said, when he brought the device back to Rux.

Rux nodded grimly.

Koestler went back to #212 and, just to be sure, rattled the doorknob. It was locked, as he guessed it would be. It was also too sturdy for him to kick in on his own. He signaled to one of the SWAT personnel who bore a very special piece of equipment.

The commando came running up with a small tank strapped to his back. It was connected to a simple spray rod about a meter long. The man proceeded to spray concentrated liquid nitrogen, along with several different corrosives, onto the entire door. He particularly focused on the doorknob and the deadbolt lock a few inches above it. The gun's hissing was drowned by the music coming from within Borax's apartment.

The man retreated and Koestler violently kicked the doorknob with the heel of his right foot. The brass knob broke and shot back into the apartment. Icy metal and wood splinters flew everywhere.

Koestler felt relatively certain that he would not be met with a fusillade of bullets from Jack McKimmie or anyone else inside the apartment. There was too much Chuckle in the cloistered air of McKimmie's digs for anyone to be functional enough to operate a weapon. In fact, they would probably think the raid was just part of the show. More than once had the Protean Set, on a bust, been greeted by cheers and applause.

Koestler assumed that McKimmie's apartment shared the same general layout as Carol Langley's. He also expected the living room furniture to be in about the same configuration. So he already had his bearings even before the mists of the solvents used on the door drifted away.

Koestler stepped through the door, his Clobberer out. It was fantastically dark inside, all the window curtains drawn tightly shut. The air, though redolent with Chuckle, smelled strangely sweet. It had an almost fruit-like sharpness to it. He couldn't place it...but he most definitely did not like it.

In the middle of the apartment was a man sitting upright on the couch. He was a masquer dressed in an undershirt and trousers. He was also barefoot and he wore an early Bruce Willis Face. It was a Face that was beginning to lose its coherent features, timed, as it was, to dissolve after its rental period had expired.

The man hadn't noticed Koestler's entrance. He just stared at the stereo tuned to its thunder rock station. He was clearly lost in a Chuckle fugue, eyes wide, pupils dilated, mind gone.

Koestler flicked on the lights as the LAPD crowded at the door. On the coffee table in front of the couch was a large mirror and several one-gram vials filled with a bluish-white powder. Off to one side was a small scale. Next to the scale was a two-kilo plastic bag of Chuckle, the same bags they had seen at Devil Dervish's mansion.

Koestler froze as the LAPD—Rux, Leone, and a dozen SWAT commandos—crowded in behind him. Rux tried to muscle through, but Koestler stopped him.

Amber Leone jerked to a halt as well. She pointed to McKimmie. "Jesus Christ! Look at his skin!"

Koestler had seen—and smelled—McKimmie's condition, and it was his turn to be terrified.

McKimmie's skin seemed to be undulating, moving about as if a thousand little muscles were straining against each other.

Something was alive and crawling just beneath McKimmie's skin across his upper body.

Koestler turned and pushed everyone back. *"Everybody, back into the hallway! Now!"*

With Leone's help they crowded back into the hall at a safe distance.

"What is it?" Rux asked.

Koestler glanced at Leone who had guessed the truth the moment she had seen McKimmie. She looked pale and about to be sick.

Koestler, breathing heavily, said, "He's got a colony of Chuckle worms inside his body."

"What?" one of the other officers asked, incredulous.

Louder, Koestler said, "McKimmie's producing Chuckle on his own and it's coming out of every pore in his skin!"

Koestler pointed to the open door to apartment #212. "There's a Chuckle outbreak in that room and it's the worst I've ever seen."

ELEVEN

THE SUN HAD JUST BEGUN its struggle to lift beyond the bloody eastern horizon when Alex Langley arrived at Eidolon Technologies. He had gotten no sleep the night before, having stayed behind in Los Angeles to give the police as much information as he could about his daughter's possible involvement with Jack McKimmie and the party McKimmie threw that led to his daughter's hospitalization. He was urged to file charges, at the very least, of reckless endangerment. The detective Rory Koestler suggested this. Langley and his wife were now considering it.

Langley never once mentioned to the detective that his expensive computer at Eidolon Technologies had come up with his name and that there was some connection with it disappearing. He was too distraught at the time and too taken up with the raid by the LAPD on the Cleargreen Apartments.

By the time he and his wife had arrived back at Simi Valley it was well after midnight. Langley was on the edge of nervous collapse. His wife, on the other hand, had her usual nightcap and several happy pills. She was still asleep when he left for work before dawn. Vivian might yet be asleep when he got back that night. Vivian was doing quite a lot of this lately.

But all Langley could do was take a shower and attempt to wash away the emotional detritus of the day in Los Angeles and leave for work. Rex had been on his mind the entire drive back. This was because Langley was now beginning to think that he knew why Rex might have disappeared.

Arriving at Eidolon Technologies just after dawn, however, did not put him in a better mood. He had to go through a newly erected security perimeter in the parking lot where several military vehicles with men at their gun turrets idled in the predawn gloom. Above him floated an antigravity sentry pod that watched every move he made.

Christine Myrland, he thought bitterly. This was her doing. Christine had made phone calls while he was away. Phone calls to her friends in Washington, not the least of whom was her father. Senator Frank Myrland, in turn, had called *his* friends in the military. The FBI and the CIA were undoubtedly already inside the building.

Once inside, Langley found security checkpoints had been placed at every hallway junction throughout the sprawling complex. His bar-coded ID badge got him through most of the checkpoints, except the last.

At the last security checkpoint Langley submitted to a breath analysis test, plus a scraping of skin from his gums and beneath his fingernails. Like every other employee at Eidolon Technologies, he had a DNA profile on record there. They went to check this. Three blank-faced guards remained. Just a few feet away from their station was the door to his own office. *So close, yet so far away.* God, was he tired.

Standing at the checkpoint with his briefcase, feeling dull and weary, Langley waited on permission to pass the line of soldiers who blocked him. From behind, however, he suddenly heard the militant march of boots on the tile of the corridor and he turned indifferently to see what the fuss was all about.

An army major loomed before Langley, brilliantly wide awake. His name tag said he was someone called Major Hannel. Hannel came at him with a bead on a kill.

"Compson!" Hannel said aside to the soldier next to him. This soldier carried an aluminum clipboard.

"Sir!" Compson said. The soldier gave the major the clipboard which bore the results of the tests Langley had taken just moments ago. The major studied the plaque's read-out, just to be sure his original assessment of its results were correct.

Hannel frowned at Langley. "According to this, Mr. Langley, you have been using Chuckle. Is that true?"

Langley watched as the guns carried by each of the seven soldiers in the hallway leveled in his direction.

Langley was no longer tired. He glared at the ice-blue—and *very* accusatory—eyes of Major Hannel. "Who the hell are *you* to ask *me* such a question?" he demanded. He stood within inches of Major Hannel's acne-scarred face.

Langley held up the clipboard. "This says that—"

"Shove it up your ass," Langley said. "Let me through. Now."

The major clearly was not used to being disputed. He stood even more erect. "This facility is now under military control. You are advised to behave according to military protocol."

"You can shove that up your ass, too," Langley said. He had far too much on his mind to consider the consequences of his actions now. He only knew that he did not have to take orders from this unctuous individual. In fact, there were few people on the planet he had to take orders from.

Behind Langley an elevator door opened with a friendly chime and Cecilia Garwin, the Eidolon Technologies board representative stepped out. Behind her was Eidolon's own security chief, Michael O'Mara. Garwin and O'Mara apparently had been watching this turgid little drama unfold on one of the many security cameras in the hallway.

"Good morning, Alex. What's the trouble?" Cecilia Garwin asked.

"This son of a bitch thinks I've been doing drugs, which I haven't."

"This is just a routine check, Alex," Garwin said with an attempt at placation. "We've all gone through it."

"Christine's put you up to this, hasn't she," Langley said. It was an accusation, not a question. Christine's fingerprints were everywhere here.

"Dr. Myrland had nothing to do with this," Michael O'Mara said. "This is a matter of national security now."

"And *I* have my orders," stated Major Hannel.

To Major Hannel, Garwin said, "This is Dr. Alex Langley, Major. He is one of our most important colleagues. Eidolon Technologies is nothing without him. If he says he doesn't do drugs, he doesn't do drugs."

"May I see that?" Michael O'Mara asked of the soldier holding the clipboard that held the results of Langley's tests. O'Mara was a thick-set, former Australian-rules football player. His nose had been punched and broken so many times, it was nearly flat. O'Mara studied the data sheet on the clipboard.

Major Hannel then said, "This man just might have a Chuckle worm and not know it."

Langley said nothing. Hannel had the look of a man who obeyed every order given him in his life, that an original thought was left to wither on the vine before it was ever plucked and considered.

O'Mara looked up from the clipboard. "This does show a trace of Chuckle in your system. Can you explain that?"

Langley sighed heavily. "I spent the weekend moving my daughter from L.A. When I was there, the police discovered that a resident, on another floor, was dealing Chuckle out of his apartment. Maybe it was in the air. Maybe I got some of it. I don't know."

"The fact is," O'Mara said, "you *do* have a trace of the drug in your system. Major Hannel will give you an antidote. Then you'll be free to pass."

"I do *not* have a Chuckle worm inside of me," Langley said, glaring at him. "I'd think I'd know if I was hallucinating."

"Not from what we hear," Major Hannel said.

"Alex, please," Cecilia Garwin said.

"Christ," Langley muttered under his breath. "Whatever. Give me your goddam antidote and leave me the hell alone."

"This way, then," the major said.

Langley picked up his briefcase and coat and followed the major.

He was ready to kill Christine Myrland.

"*This* is extraordinary," Christine Myrland said, dropping a massive print-out onto the conference room table.

A dozen top officials of Eidolon Technologies and several scientists from all around southern California had gathered that morning at 9:00 a.m. at her request. Present as well were three individuals from the Pentagon whom she had called the night before. They had hyperplaned to Edwards Air Force Base in the Mojave and had gotten there faster than most of the Eidolon employees who lived within five miles of the place.

To her displeasure, however, they had to wait on Alex Langley who was being inoculated for something or other. When Langley finally came in, his tie loosened and coatless, he was rubbing his upper arm and looked mightily annoyed. But that didn't matter. It was her show. He walked up to the head of the table and sat next to her on the right.

"What have you got, Christine?" Cecilia Garwin asked.

Next to Garwin sat Helen Cusack of the FBI and Jan Bork of the NSA, recently enlisted as part of the crisis team on Eidolon Rex's disappearance.

"As most of you know, Eidolon Rex handles hundreds of thousands of computer programs of federal and state agencies both here in California and across the country," Myrland said with excitement.

She tapped the print-out with a Kevlar-painted fingernail. "But with the cooperation of the NSA and Dr. Bork here"—Jan Bork, a stern woman nebulously in her late fifties, acknowledged her with a curt nod—"we tapped into other national data bases for other possible references to this Rory Koestler person and came up with another two hundred and eighty hits. Given the hundreds of thousands of programs, that might not seem like a lot, but, statistically, it is."

"What does it all mean?" Herb Lundquist asked. Lundquist was a programmer consultant brought in from JPL in Pasadena.

"I think it means that this man Koestler is at the center of some kind of widespread activity that Eidolon Rex picked up on just about the time he disappeared last week. Computers all over the country are finding his name."

"You've said before that your computer might have disappeared *because* of so many hits on this name," Lundquist said.

"That's exactly it," Myrland said tersely. "We now have corroboration, proof."

One of the many techs in the room said, "But how can a computer the size of a house *physically* disappear?"

Someone else said, "And how can it disappear because of one man's name?"

"We're working on that," Myrland said. "And we *will* find out why."

"So who *is* Rory Koestler?" another person asked.

Helen Cusack of the FBI stood up. This, Myrland knew, was her bailiwick. She said, "There are just three men with that name in the entire country. Only one resides in California. He's listed as an actor in Los Angeles. But there are no data trails after about ten years ago. Our guess is that he left the region before the quarantine and may be one of the other two in the country. We've got agents on it right now."

Graham Mishkula, one of the mainframe techs, spoke up just then.

Mishkula was elderly and wore suspenders. He had been at the company longer than anyone in the room. "Why Rex disappeared isn't nearly as important as *how* he disappeared."

Mishkula wore thick glasses with bifocals, rare for anyone in the middle of the 21st century.

"I think they're both related," Myrland said. "Once we find out who this Rory Koestler is, we'll know *why* Rex disappeared. After all—" She consulted the print-out with Rory Koestler's name. "Look at all these hits. For just three men in the entire country—"

"*Rory Koestler's a cop*," Alex Langley said.

Myrland blinked, then said. "What?" she asked.

"He's a cop in L.A. I met him yesterday. Nice guy, actually."

Myrland dropped the print-out angrily. "We don't have time for jokes, Alex," she said. "We ran the name through the smaller Eidolons at the FBI, the CIA, and the National Security Agency. We didn't come up with a cop in L.A. The other two are in Louisiana and South Dakota."

"I can't speak for what your friends found, Christine," Langley said. "But I met him at my daughter's apartment. He busted a big-time Chuckle dealer there. That's probably where I got tainted."

"Mr. Langley—" Helen Cusack of the FBI started.

"I'm sorry," Langley said, interrupting the woman. "And you are—?"

"Helen Cusack, FBI, Mr. Langley," the doughty woman said.

Langley dipped into his shirt pocket and withdrew a business card. He passed it to Cusack.

Myrland thought he should have passed it to her, since she was running the investigation. She flushed redly at the slight.

"That's his card," Langley said. "He gave it to me in case I found out any more details about the assault on my daughter. I'm sure it's him that you're talking about."

"Your daughter was *assaulted*?" Cecilia Garwin asked.

"She was," Langley said, rubbing his palms together, his elbows on the tabletop. "We're bringing her home as soon as she gets out of the hospital."

Myrland couldn't care less about Langley's daughter. "Let me see that card," she demanded. It was passed up to her. The card read simply: Detective Rory Koestler, L.A.P.D. - Santa Monica Division. It gave a phone number, a fax number, and an e-mail address.

Myrland felt bile in her stomach. Langley was always doing this; he was always preempting her.

"Well, Alex," she said. "It seems you have saved us a lot of time in trying to track this man down."

"That's why Mr. Koestler can't be found in any data base," Herb Lundquist said brightly. "If he's a cop, he probably has all of his data blocked, purged, or just encrypted."

Myrland flung the card onto the table where it spun a couple of times like a compass needle. "Then why is his name appearing in thousands of ordinary computer profiles around the country?" Myrland countered.

"That's what we're here to find out," Jan Bork of the NSA quickly interjected. Bork, a mousey woman, small and unassuming, made the perfect spymaster. She said, "The fact is that the man's name has come up in programs that link him to thousands of businesses and hundreds of thousands of people, all around the country."

"You think they're people he's arrested?" a young female tech, Derry Havens, asked from the back of the room. "I mean, maybe it's possible that all these names have something to do with criminal activity?"

"Derry," Myrland countered. "We're talking about hundreds of thousands of computer programs from all across the country. Local, state, federal, and private. Rory Koestler would have to be living simultaneously in thirty different states and hundreds of municipalities to affect that many people."

"Maybe all those people came *here*," Herb Lundquist said. "You know, as tourists?"

Several people started muttering their theories to one another until a dull roar filled the room.

"Look, people," Cecilia Garwin said loudly. "These are red herrings. All the Board's interested in is *why* Rex did what he did. They've got billions of dollars invested in Eidolon Rex and we have to make sure that it doesn't happen to him again. We can track down this Koestler individual later."

Myrland, however, was watching Alex Langley who was now twirling a pencil on the conference table before him like an impatient eight-year-old.

"Alex?" she asked. "You have something on your mind?"

He looked up. "Sure."

"Care to share it?"

"Okay," he said, leaning back. "I'd say that it's not the *man*, as such."

Michael O'Mara cleared his throat. "What's *that* mean?"

"It's not the man. And it wasn't the reoccurrences of the name 'Rory Koestler' that made Rex disappear. It was the very *act* of processing that particular name that sent Rex away."

"Go on," Cecilia Garwin urged.

Myrland felt dethroned. She fumed as all heads turned away from her, giving Alex Langley all of their attention.

"You're not going to believe me," Langley said.

"Try us, Alex," Myrland said. *We could use a laugh.* It was as if Langley was playing games with them.

Langley said, "In the first place, I don't think Rex went anywhere at all."

"Oh, give me a break!" Myrland threw up her hands in frustration. "We *both* were here when Rex disappeared! He had to go *somewhere*."

"You want to hear what I have to say or not, Christine?" he asked.

"Fine," she said. "Say whatever you like."

So he told them. It wasn't at all what they expected.

TWELVE

CHRISTINE MYRLAND GAZED DOWN at Alex Langley as if from a great height. Langley had the look of a man lost in a haze. She knew he was experiencing personal troubles at home, but that didn't matter to her. She'd let Langley hang himself with his dreamy theories. There were too many reasonable—and responsible—people in the room not to notice that Langley was on his way out.

So she let him speak.

Langley leaned his compact body forward. "I know the military wants a teleportation system so it can bomb China's billion-man army back to the Pleistocene if it decides to move on the rest of Asia. But *I'm* here to gauge Rex's general health, see that he's running right."

Already, she thought, Alex was out of step. Nicholas Holthaus of JPL said, "You make it sound as if Rex is human, Dr. Langley."

"Well, whatever Rex is, he's not human anymore. He's gone *beyond* human," Langley contended.

"Of course he's not human," Myrland then said. "He's a *machine*. What's your point?"

Langley looked up once at her, then looked away.

"My point is that a long time ago when people spoke of artificial intelligence, what they were really talking about was consciousness or, more accurately, *self*-consciousness. Rex has gone beyond self-consciousness. He's more than human. He's even more than *machine*."

Everyone there seemed to be paying attention, but she thought he was prattling. "Alex, really—" Myrland said.

One of the professors from Cal Tech cleared his throat. "Dr. Langley, you said this has something to do with the computer's 'act of processing.' What did you mean by that?"

Langley said, "Eidolon Rex's individual processors function at a molecular level, its switches are at the atomic level. These are several orders *smaller* than microtubules, the molecular 'processors,' if you will, in neuron cells of the human brain."

Myrland opened her mouth, but she was interrupted.

"Aren't you talking about Roger Penrose and his theories? Didn't he study how consciousness arises in brain activity?" the same professor said.

"That's right. Consciousness is the result of quantum-level electrical stimulation in microtubules. It's on the order of trillions of simultaneously activated particles, each generating its own charged field."

The man smiled. "I did my dissertation on Penrose's refutation of Majorana spin states," the man added.

Myrland rolled her eyes. This was getting them nowhere. "People—" she started.

Langley went on. "Levels of consciousness depend on how many microtubules in the brain's neuron cells are being stimulated at any one time. The greater the collective resonance, the higher the level of awareness. But it's not a question of a *bigger* brain. Whales and elephants have bigger brains than humans. It really comes down to the *degree* of quantum resonance throughout the brain."

"Alex—"

"But where the human brain has trillions of microtubule stimulations at any given moment, Rex has *quadrillions*. His cognition is now so concentrated in the central core that he has pushed his computations into a trans-quantum realm, something even Penrose didn't think possible."

"Alex, this is *highly* speculative," Myrland insisted. "We don't have time to fool around with graduate school speculations. The real issue before us is this man, Rory Koestler. *He* caused Rex to disappear. He's—"

Alex Langley suddenly leapt from his chair. The move was so sudden, so unexpected, that she had no time to react. He suddenly clamped his right hand over her mouth, holding her head with his left. Everyone gasped. It certainly woke everyone up.

"Can you just keep your mouth shut for two goddamn minutes, Christine?" he snapped. "Two minutes! That's all I ask. When I'm done, I'll leave the room and you can say whatever you want, for as long as you want. But I want just *two goddam minutes!*"

He let her go. Her mind had gone blank. She had no way to process this unexpected—and uncharacteristic—event.

Langley then added, "I am still the project director here and Rex is *my* responsibility until the Eidolon Board fires me. Not you, not your father. The Board. So just be quiet and let me finish!"

Langley returned to his chair. To the shocked gathering, he continued: "Look, people, just before Rex disappeared, he was doing trillions of computations per second. My guess is that he reached an energetic state at a level he had never experienced before. It was certainly a state that *we* had never seen before. And since Rex wasn't programmed to deal with it, he disappeared. But he *didn't* teleport. I want to make that clear."

Myrland, trembling from her humiliation, looked down upon him with barely controlled rage. "Then where did he *go*, Alex?" She mouthed each word slowly, carefully, and almost excruciatingly. Her face had gone red, her pulse raced madly. As far as she was concerned, Alex Langley's career at Eidolon Technologies was *over*. Witnesses she now had. What she needed next was something concrete, proof she could take to the Board to show that his mind had gone. This was part of the grudge she had to settle with him. It went all the way back to Santos Avionics and the disappearance of their massive computer, the Telemon Ajax 3000.

Before Langley could resume, Herb Lundquist said, "But, Alex, why the name 'Rory Koestler'? That does seem to be the trigger here. Christine's right. Rex went *somewhere*."

Langley shook his head. He seemed remarkably calm. "I don't think Eidolon Rex went anywhere at all. I *do* think the name 'Rory Koestler' was a trigger, but teleportation wasn't the result."

"Then *where* did he go, *Alex*," she said.

"He traveled in time."

She had him.

Several people in the room closed their eyes. A few shook their heads. Others simply sat there, stunned into rapt silence. Myrland couldn't believe it. She laughed. "You said *what*? That Rex traveled in *time*?" She didn't need proof. This was it. Alex would bury himself all on his own.

Langley seemed unperturbed by the reaction. He said, "If you look at the kinds of programs Rex was running, you'll see that they were for a wide range of industrial purposes. Some even included farming projections and all kinds of weather studies. I think Eidolon Rex *saw* enough of the future—at least the future as it related to him personally—that he simply 'jumped' up the line, to a creation point where his calculations ended with absolute certainty. I just haven't worked out the math yet, particularly where the propulsion factors come to bear, but that's what I think he did. He traveled ten hours into the future, almost to the second."

No one was laughing, but it was clear that in the eyes of some at the table, Alex Langley had made a colossal fool of himself. The military reps standing at the back of the room, however, had returned to looking simply bored. Myrland knew they had dismissed Langley's notions outright.

But she wanted to keep the heat on Langley. With any luck, she'd soon have his position. Their positions at Eidolon should have been merged long ago anyway.

"Time travel is impossible, Alex," she said. "It's a story-teller's conceit. There's no way it could have happened."

Langley frowned. He stared ahead as he thought. "Perhaps. But do you recall those four 'anomalies' we recorded last month and the one we had about a week ago?"

Everyone in the room but the guests and the military personnel knew about the incident to which Langley referred. She, particularly. A month ago, three brief, and certainly unexplained, disruptions registered in several very complex programs Eidolon Rex had been running at the time. The programs themselves were unaffected and they had written the anomalies off to a solar storm that was then taking place. Some even thought it might have been residual radiation from the India-Pakistan War that was still circling the earth. Others, however, (and Langley was one of these) claimed that Rex was too well-shielded to be affected by any kind of radiation. He had thought it was something different.

Langley now said, "I think those anomalies were moments when Rex leapt forward in time. They were leaps of mere nanoseconds. They happened so quickly that they wouldn't have even been noticed by anybody."

Cecilia Garwin, the representative to the Eidolon Technologies Board, propped her elbows on the table and sank her face into her hands, embarrassed or frustrated at this very unexpected development. Silence reigned everywhere in the room.

Garwin looked up. "Alex, do you know what the Board's going to think when you tell them that Eidolon Rex traveled in time?"

Langley seemed unperturbed. He said, "It's worse than you think. I don't think Rex traveled to the future. I think he *built* it. I think he found the most probable pathway from billions of probable pathways and step-by-step pulled himself there. I just haven't figured that out yet."

"Explain that," the two-star general said.

Langley turned to the man. "When all of Rex's calculations came together around Rory Koestler's name, Rex, I think, became a time machine. I mean, he became a time *engine*. Remember, he's got a self-sustaining and self-contained Amenta fusion reactor. What I'm trying to do now is characterize that probability threshold in stochastic mathematical terms. Otherwise, I don't think that—"

"Alex," Myrland said.

"I've got about sixty-percent of the math worked out," Langley continued. He reached for his briefcase.

Cecilia Garwin stopped him. "Alex, you can show us your math later. I'm sure the Board will want to see them. But some of us want to work on the teleportation angle. Rex did *disappear* after all."

Myrland quickly added, "And some of us want to find out more about this Rory Koestler. *He's* the one who made our computer disappear. And we can't use Rex until we know that he won't disappear again. Eidolon Technologies will have to shut down until we get Rex up and running again."

The two-star general, Dussex, stepped forward to the head of the conference table. Dussex was an old family friend and Myrland had phoned him specifically and told him about their meeting. "And *that* is more to the purpose of this meeting. We have given everyone here highest top secret clearance. We want results as soon as possible. With the unrest in China and the destabilization of Europe, the United States government is clearly interested in any military implications of your new technology."

The general stared at them all. He didn't need to stare at Christine. He said, "This is a *military* operation now. We've got authorization directly from the President, thanks in no small measure to the influence of Senator Frank Myrland. Your task is to find out exactly what happened to Eidolon Rex, find this 'trigger' that made him disappear, and get me a report of some kind in forty-eight hours."

He then left the room and the meeting was adjourned.

Everyone returned to their stations, including Alex Langley who looked as if he wanted to sock the general. Myrland wished he had. All the more reason to get Alex Langley out of her hair.

Still, the tensions she felt during the meeting reminded her so much of Ajax and Santos Avionics in South Bay. At the time, the Ajax 3000 was the most advanced computer in the world. Both she and Langley worked on it. One day, after calculating nothing more complex than wind-drift patterns for the residual radiation from the India-Pakistan War, Ajax disappeared. It baffled everyone and no expert alive had a theory as to what had happened.

Unlike Rex, however, he did not come back. It was a total loss and destroyed the company. No one knew where he went or why, and Santos Aviation collapsed before anyone could perform an "autopsy."

As it was, Eidolon Rex had the very same hardware configuration as Ajax. This was because Alex Langley had built both machines. Yet Rex had much more power than Ajax and had more random access memory. As Myrland thought about this, she knew that she was missing something. Were memory and power enough to bring a computer back?

And back from *where*?

The one thing she *did* know was that Eidolon Rex did *not* travel to the future. Time travel was *so* impossible that no physicist had seriously considered the prospect in fifty years. An American would be elected pope before that would happen.

And what about Rory Koestler?

Myrland spent about an hour looking through the hard copies of the various computer tasks that had come up with the man's name. They had thousands of such files. These were but a few.

Alone in her office, Myrland picked up the phone and got a clear, secure outside line. She pressed the numbers her father had given her the night before.

The party at the other end answered. "Yes?"

"This is Christine."

"Yes, go on."

"That matter we discussed last night."

"Koestler."

"Yes. Let's see what we can find out. Be discreet."

"We'll get on it right away."

She hung up the phone and returned to her print-outs. Whatever Rex had done, wherever he had gone, Myrland knew one thing for certain: She'd find out the Rory Koestler connection to her computer sooner than Langley would find his so-called time travel equations.

Maybe by then, Langley would have gotten fired. But whatever the case, his days there were numbered.

THIRTEEN

WHEN KOESTLER HAD DECIDED that acting did not pay well enough and took Edwardian Rux up on his offer to join the Protean Set, he began having a recurring dream. The dream came to him at odd times and he wrote it off to on-the-job stress. It had never bothered him before. But the dream often left him haunted and bleak for days following.

Lately he had been having the dream quite a lot.

Though there were subtle variations with each dream, its central motif was always the same. In the dream Koestler was a uniformed police officer in the LAPD, something he never had been in real life. Usually he is walking, but sometimes he is driving, in Canoga Park, at the far west end of the San Fernando Valley. Sometimes he is on Fallbrook; sometimes it's Shoup Avenue. And while it is always bright and sunny, wherever he's at, the air is quite cold. It's summer and winter at the same time.

Then Koestler is chasing after someone. He doesn't know who. He doesn't even know how it starts. But he is running. If the dream has him in his patrol vehicle, he has abandoned it. He is running, running, running. The police paraphernalia at his belt jangles and rattles. His gun is heavy, his boots weigh him down, his hat bobs comically on his head. He seems to be falling apart. But he *has* to catch the man he's after. If he doesn't catch him, he will lose his job, or lose his life, or something dire like that.

Suddenly the asphalt beneath his feet turns to mush and the black mush starts sucking at his shoes. Within seconds, he starts to sink. The more he moves forward, the deeper he settles. And his prey…he's just down the street and he is getting away.

With his silly hat, his bulky weapons, and his starched uniform, he can get nowhere. There are just too many encumbrances. He hates being a street cop. He's not free.

This is where he conceives a plan. Sal Briscoe once told him that if you can't control your life, take control of your dreams. So he does. He stops running forward and starts to run backwards.

Backpedaling, his shoes become unstuck and his legs move freely as he unslogs himself. As he does, he flings away his hat like a Frisbee disc, unclasps his belt. But he keeps hold of his gun. It's a real gun, a Glock. Not a Clobberer.

But now his prey has vanished.

He looks around. He's in a park now. Shadowland Park, a large, five-acre urban park surrounded by middle-class homes. There are swings and a merry-go-round and monkeybars and a large sand pit. There, a dozen or so children cavort beneath the shade of the sentinel eucalyptus trees that ring the park.

And Koestler wonders, *Has his prey fled into this park and is now hiding among the children?*

An *adult* among children? Yes! His prey can alter his appearance.

But who can do this? Koestler thinks, he thinks hard. *Bob Thermopylae.* That's the man's he's after. Bob Thermopylae!

Koestler stops near the swings, however. He's confused. *Hasn't he already captured Bob Thermopylae?*

He searches the park, the swings, the sandbox with its happy children. Bob Thermopylae's not there. Then Koestler wonders if he is after someone else.

Here Koestler sees the little girl. She is sitting on one of the swings, her bright red hair hangs low around her face. Koestler knows this girl. Her name is Vicki Celeste. She is not Bob Thermopylae. She is not his prey.

Suddenly—and it's always this way in the dream, regardless of its variations, regardless of its particularities—an unspeakable grief overwhelms him. It comes like a tidal wave from his deep past. He has done something to her. He stands there, cloaked in shame. He drops his gun into the sand. It lands without a sound.

He is the culprit. *He* is his prey....

"*Bad mans outside*," came a voice at the foot of his bed.

Koestler lurched awake, his heart pounding, his body covered in sweat. The image of Vicki Celeste was still in his mind, the sadness still gripping his heart.

However, little Stephie, clutching her BooBaby, was tugging at the big toe of Koestler's right foot and this brought him soundly back to reality. He heard the patter of falling rain coming from the bathroom.

"What?" he asked.

"There's bad mans outside," little Stephie repeated, softly this time, now that he was awake. She went back to sucking her thumb. Her eyes were wide and filled with worry. Who was in the shower? Susan? No, Susan was the night before last. It was Leslie. Leslie Manna, his financial counselor.

These lapses were becoming bothersome....

"Outside?" he asked. "Who's outside?"

"In a big car," little Stephie said. Stephie then turned and went back to watching Chalk Mules, or whatever it was on the wallscreen.

Koestler rolled out of bed and slipped into a pair of khaki shorts. He then irised a secret section of his bedroom wall and pulled his Clobberer from its recharge stand.

Leslie Manna, meanwhile, singing to herself, continued steaming her beautiful body in the shower, unaware that Stephie had woken him.

Koestler walked past the living room where little Stephie, her back to the foyer, was lost in her magical cartoons. He didn't want her to see his weapon, so he held it to one side as he made for the door.

Perhaps a normal cop—a cop such as Vincent Dunhill of Internal Affairs Division—would have been more circumspect before stepping outside to confront the "bad mans." But Koestler didn't think like a regular cop most of the time. Or maybe he was still in his "pursuit" mode from his doleful dream of Vicki Celeste.

Whatever the case, Koestler stepped out into a dense morning fog that hovered outside the Cove. To Koestler's left, about fifty yards down the street, was a dark sedan. Two people were inside. From the hood of the car, a parabolic listening antenna was pointing directly at his house.

Snoops.

Koestler, Clobberer in hand, started walking toward them in full view.

The parabolic antenna suddenly folded up like a Geisha's twirling fan and snapped back into the hood of the car. The windows of the sedan then turned a deep obsidian, becoming thoroughly opaque. The license plate numbers were already starting to change their identity.

The Chevy sedan wasn't a MetaMorph. But it was *stealth*. Only government agencies used stealth vehicles, so these weren't hired guns, local L.A. private investigators. Whoever they were, though, they had been braced. Koestler had clearly seen them, and that was not good for snoops, professional or otherwise.

The engine of the Chevy Stealth had been running all this time and it was nothing for the driver to drop the vehicle into reverse, pull a screaming backward U-turn, and make for the gated entrance of Paradise Cove before Koestler could get too close to them.

Koestler broke into a quick run. He had nothing to weigh him down, unlike his dream. He shot across the corner yard at the end of the street and hurdled a row of leafy rhododendrons as the car made its speedy retreat.

By the time Koestler got to the guard booth, the vehicle had pulled out into traffic and disappeared. Koestler stepped up to the booth, breathing hard from the run.

Old Mr. Gerard of Hateras Security had been reading a newspaper in his protective glass booth at the gate when the eavesdroppers had driven past. He didn't seem particularly bothered by their hasty exit. Koestler walked up to the booth and knocked on the window.

Mr. Gerard lowered his paper and squinted through his glasses. "Mornin', Mr. Koestler. Up kinda early."

Old man Gerard's voice came through a small speaker set in the bulletproof glass.

"Those people," Koestler said, trying to restore his breathing. "Who were they?"

"What's with the gun?" Gerard asked, looking down at the Clobberer. "Never seen a gun like 'at before. What is it?"

Koestler powered-down his Clobberer. "A special gun, Phil. Who were those guys? Did they show you any ID?"

Old Gerard leaned back in his chair, lowering his newspaper. "Los Angeles County Surveyor's Office. I didn't get their names. Didn't think to ask. Got their license number, though."

"Can I see it?"

"Sure."

Old man Gerard slid down the side window to the booth. He handed Koestler a slip of paper.

By the number of the plate, Koestler saw that the car belonged to some agency of the *federal* government, not county. He could run it and it would probably come up real, belonging to some anonymous agency who would have discovered that an unauthorized vehicle had been taken from their pool. He would run it anyway, see where it led.

"You know them fellers?" Gerard asked.

Koestler shook his head. "Not really."

Koestler wondered who they could have been. Internal Affairs would never use a federal vehicle in a stakeout; they had their own cars, none of which, as far as he knew, were MetaMorphs or Stealths. So who could they have been?

"If you ever see them again, call the police. They don't belong here," Koestler said.

Gerard looked at him over the top of his reading glasses. "Now you wouldn't be in any kinda trouble, now, would you, Mr. Koestler?"

86

"I don't know," Koestler said, wondering.

"How 'bout them private investigators your wife sent 'round about a year or so ago?" old man Gerard said. "They the same people?"

"We took care of that in court," Koestler admitted.

That was one ex-wife, however. He had two others. But yesterday he had squared his accounts at ChemSolar Bank, so it couldn't have been Arlene. But none of his ex-wives would have blown his cover just to get even with him. They all knew how dangerous his work was. If he got killed in the line of duty, their alimony and child-support payments would come to a halt. They didn't hate him *that* much.

So who *were* the men in the stealth car?

"Jim Barbour the night guard's told me you sure throw a party," Gerard said. "One o' your wives mighta found out."

Or his girlfriends, he realized. They were passionate and they were many. So far, he had managed to keep them unaware of each other. Leslie was in the shower. Susan Siebert was over in Century City. Sam Moore was still in Arizona. But Lana Lestikow and Genevieve Speich were actresses with quarantine passes and they were out of the state. One was touring with *Cats*. The other was filming a movie in New York. They were hardly ever in town. And it was easy enough to juggle Leslie and Susan. And so far, he wasn't in trouble with *them*.

"You're gonna have to choose one of these days, son," the old man said. "Life ain't a candy box, you know."

"So I'm told," Koestler conceded.

On his way back to his house, Koestler noticed that Mrs. Tenharkel had been watching from her window. She couldn't have seen the stealth car from her angle, but she had definitely seen him walking down the street wearing only his khaki hiking shorts with his Clobberer in his hand.

"They were trespassers, Mrs. Tenharkel," Koestler shouted at the woman.

The curtains closed quickly. He was going to have to reread the Paradise Cove charter to see if guns were allowed. If they weren't, he was going to have to own up to being a cop. And if he did that, they might ask him to leave.

"Rats," he said to himself.

When he got back to his house, little Stephie was still watching her cartoons in the living room, snacking on a Pop Tart. The interior walls of his house were now alive with their colorful commercial messages. A large red banner of a Coca Cola logo followed him into his bedroom, waving like a giant red flag.

Leslie was just getting out of the shower. She evidently wasn't aware that Koestler's urchin neighbor was sitting on the living room couch in full view of Koestler's bedroom. She came out of the bedroom stark naked, toweling her magnificent auburn hair, her breasts swaying slightly.

"What's with the gun?" Leslie asked, kissing him.

Koestler jerked his head toward the living room. "We have company," he said.

From the bedroom door they could see little Stephie eating her toast with both hands.

"Oh!" Leslie said, lifting the towel to cover herself.

Stephie turned and observed the two practically naked adults in the hallway. "Naughty!" she said. She then went back to her cartoons.

"How does she get *in* here?" Leslie asked as Koestler closed the bedroom door a bit.

"I haven't the slightest idea," Koestler said.

"Well, they *are* kind of cute at that age," Leslie Manna said. Her voice had a raspy quality to it, a smouldering huskiness from years of smoking Red Apple cigarettes.

"She's a very strange little girl," Koestler admitted.

Half an hour later, over breakfast and coffee, with little Stephie gone, Koestler was still thinking about the encounter with the Bad Mans in the government stealth vehicle. Leslie had already gone to work. Peace had settled around him.

But there wasn't peace anywhere else in the world, it seemed. An armada of poor people had now set sail for Europe from India and Southeast Asia. There were tens of thousands of boats involved, and heading for the blown Suez Canal. North of India, a billion Chinese males were anxious to find wives. Those billion happened to also be in the Red Army. They were drooling at Europe.

And President Katrina Larsen's migraines were getting worse.

Then deep inside his head, Koestler's Bailiff suddenly chimed: ATTENTION MISTER KOESTLER: MEXICO-PACIFIC BANK HAS NOW POSTED A DEBIT TO YOUR ACCOUNT OF THREE THOUSAND AND THREE DOLLARS AND FOURTEEN CENTS AS OF OH-NINE-HUNDRED HOURS PACIFIC STANDARD TIME. PLEASE CONTACT MS. NICHOLE KRUK, ACCOUNTS MANAGER AT MEXICO-PACIFIC BANK AS SOON AS POSSIBLE.

Koestler's coffee turned sour in his stomach. It had happened again and he didn't have the slightest notion how.

The day had begun badly.

FOURTEEN

A SMALL GOBLIN OF DISCONTENT whispered in the back of Koestler's mind regarding the bank overdraft at Mexico-Pacific. Two such incidents in less than a week's time was more than just unusual—it was downright alarming. But alarming in what way, he did not know.

The branch of the Mexico-Pacific Bank where he shared his account with Jill Parks was on 26th and San Vicente Boulevard in Santa Monica. He tried to get it straightened out over the phone, but they wouldn't do that. He had to do it in person. So Koestler put on another Face, programmed his driver's license to reflect that Face, then took his Sensei, now a modest Chevy sedan, into town.

As he drove, Koestler remained watchful as to vehicles or disguised traffic Eyes that might be following him. His on-board computer, a low-level AI, had already informed him that no one had placed a bug or a homing device on the car. No radio emissions or special-frequency signals were going out from his vehicle. That was of some reassurance. Still, the goblin was there.

Koestler made another vicinity check when he pulled into the Mexico-Pacific Bank parking lot in Santa Monica. He moved at a leisurely pace to the bank's entrance. *Just an ordinary day in L.A.*

Koestler tracked down Nicole Kruk. Ms. Kruk was an attractive blonde woman in her late twenties who wore her hair in a tight bun on the top of her head. She also had very large, and very natural, breasts. Koestler forgot all about the goblin.

"May I help you?" Ms. Kruk said, looking up from her keyboard when Koestler knocked at the open door to her office.

"I received a message today that the account I share with my ex-wife is overdrawn and it shouldn't be," he said. "The name's Koestler. Rory Koestler."

Ms. Kruk frowned as if confused. She said, "All our accounts have overdraft protection, Mr. Koestler. You're given a grace period to readjust your account and everything is usually fine." Ms. Kruk returned to her computer.

Koestler sat down in the chair before her desk. "You don't understand. It's an overdraft of three thousand dollars in a *savings* account, not a checking account."

"It wasn't a cash advance?" Ms. Kruk then asked.

"No," Koestler said.

Ms. Kruk sat back. Koestler noted the slight bounce to her breasts. She said, "Then it's a banking error."

Like ChemSolar's banking error.

"That's what I was thinking, unless you were robbed."

She leaned forward. "May I have your bank card, please?"

Ms. Kruk swiped the card into a slot on her computer keyboard. She followed that with a few typed commands.

"Hmm," she mused. "It says you have a debit with us of three thousand and three dollars and fourteen cents and it is a savings account."

Ms. Kruk stared at her monitor screen, clearly baffled. She said, "This has to be an error. If the money's not there, it's not there. And a cash advance is a credit card charge. It wouldn't show up on your savings account records anyway. Do you recall how much money was in the account when you last checked it?"

"I never check it," Koestler said. "This is the first time this has come up."

Ms. Kruk was typing. "I show four withdrawals this month. These are the dates."

On each of the four occasions, Jill Parks had withdrawn only modest amounts of money. Before the mysterious withdrawal, a little over two thousand dollars yet remained in the account.

"What happened to the remaining two thousand dollars?" Koestler then asked.

"Offhand, I'd say you were robbed."

"*Robbed?*"

Kruk stood up from her chair and adjusted her skirt. She said, "Let me run this past our comptroller. This doesn't look like any banking error I've ever seen. I'll be right back."

Koestler watched Ms. Kruk leave the office.

Out in the lobby, a person in an ancient diving suit, complete with metal helmet and lead boots, was standing, dripping water onto the lobby's marble floor. He had what seemed to be a paycheck and deposit slip in his hand.

Koestler pulled his phone from his belt. He punched Jill's work number. It rang once and she came on the line.

"Jill," Koestler said.

"There you are," she said. "Look. You're supposed to deposit the *full* amount of alimony on the first of the month, Rory. That was the agreement. I checked this morning and it's completely empty."

"I'm at the bank right now trying to straighten it out," he said quickly. "There were two thousand dollars in the account two days ago. It's some sort of banking error." He didn't want to tell her that she—*they*—might have been robbed.

"Banking error, my ass," Jill snapped.

"I'll get this straightened out. I promise."

"Too late. I've already filed a delinquency report. You'll be hearing from the courts soon. I want the money you owe me."

"Jesus," he said.

This was going to go on his credit report. And that would be another black mark against him.

"It's what you owe me for having three girlfriends while we were married," Jill said.

"But I only had two—"

She hung up.

Then he started thinking about IAD. If Vincent Dunhill found out about this, via his contacts with the court system, IAD would dog his every move. Edwardian Rux would not like that.

Now he'd have to straighten out the delinquency report. Then he'd have to go to TRW to straighten out the black mark on his credit file.

Koestler waited several long minutes, stewing in his own terror, thinking of the long lines down at the municipal court building. Finally, though, he got tired of waiting for Ms. Kruk with her wonderful breasts to return. He was beginning to suspect that something was up.

He found Ms. Kruk in a room with a sign on the door that said: R.P. Hargrave, Senior Comptroller. Ms. Kruk and several other individuals were bending over a single computer screen at the desk of one man. The men wore white shirts, black ties and no coats. The man at the desk wore a bow tie and anachronistic suspenders. Each looked frazzled.

"I take it there's a problem," Koestler said.

"Are you Mr. Koestler?" asked the man seated at the computer. This was R.P. Hargrave. Hargrave was in his early thirties, but he was balding drastically.

One of the other accountant types stepped past Koestler and closed the door.

Koestler said, "I just spoke with my ex-wife. I don't think she's taken any money out of the account lately."

Nicole Kruk stood up. "It appears that we've been hacked, Mr. Koestler."

"Hacked?"

"Actually, it appears that *you've* been hacked. We don't know yet if any other accounts have this problem, but we're looking." Ms. Kruk said.

Koestler blinked. The words almost didn't make any sense. "What do you mean *I've* been hacked?"

R.P. Hargrave, at his computer, spoke. "We don't know how it was done yet, but we can find no official withdrawal or electronic transfer of the last two thousand dollars in your account. Nor can we find any source request for the remaining three thousand three dollars and fourteen cents."

"So someone robbed you of three thousand dollars," Koestler said.

"And *you* of two thousand dollars," Hargrave said.

The gray accountant who had closed Hargrave's door said, "Which is an impossibility, at least the way our system is set up. All sorts of bells and whistles would have gone off and they didn't."

Hargrave said, "Whoever did this knew what they were doing. We've got the best encryption programs this side of the military and a firewall half a mile thick."

Ms. Kruk added, "The three thousand and three dollars and fourteen cents is a bogus figure and won't affect our own banking records at all. But the two thousand in your account really disappeared."

"Am I insured against this kind of theft?" Koestler asked.

"Of course," Hargrave told him. "But we've got to figure out what happened before we can credit your account."

"Why?"

"Because if it happened once, it can happen again. And if not you, then someone else."

"Or *everyone* else," Ms. Kruk said.

Hargrave said, "This could take several days to straighten out."

Koestler's next pay period was in one week. Jill could get by until then. That, however, was the least of his problems, if he understood what these people were saying.

"So someone targeted me specifically," Koestler said.

Everyone looked at him. Hargrave asked, "What do you do for a living, Mr. Koestler?"

So he told them. "I'm a police detective, here in Santa Monica."

"That could be the problem," Ms. Kruk said.

"I'd say that *is* the problem," Hargrave added.

Koestler merely nodded. He could almost hear Vincent Dunhill telling him: *Welcome to the world of* real *detective work, bucko. The Bad Guys are onto you.*

"I'm out," Brad Swiss said.

"What do you mean you're out?" Koestler laughed. He thought his partner was kidding.

"I don't think I can do this anymore," Swiss said. "Be a Protean. I'm an actor, not a cop."

After leaving Mexico-Pacific Bank, Koestler had put in a brief appearance at headquarters, mostly to mollify the elements of Internal Affairs who looked for any and all signs of dereliction of duty. Upon hearing that his partner, Brad Swiss, had been released from the hospital to the care of his wife, Koestler then decided to pay him a visit.

Brad Swiss lived in a comfortable, if modest, home nestled in the Hollywood Hills. When Koestler arrived, Swiss was sitting out in the sun in his back yard. Swiss's wife, Lilly, a high school teacher, was fixing an early dinner. The television was on in the kitchen. Its muffled cacophony could barely be heard where the two men were sitting in lawn chairs beneath a Chinese Elm out back.

Koestler had not seen Lilly so happy. At least not since their son had left for college. The winds of change seemed to be in the air.

Swiss poured Koestler a small cup of imported oolong tea then leaned back in his lawn chair. Even in the shade of the leafy tree, Swiss seemed pale and drawn from his dialysis treatments.

"This is a bad time to quit," Koestler said.

"We got Bob Thermopylae. He's all we've been after for the last decade. Now we have him."

"Bob's crew is around," Koestler pointed out. "And we still haven't found all of Thermopylae's worms. Rux thinks that there's someone out there pushing Chuckle not related to Bob's operation."

"You found him," Swiss said. "Borax. He was full of worms, wasn't he?"

"Borax was part of Bob's crew," Koestler said. "Rux thinks there's another vector loose in L.A. somewhere."

Swiss shrugged slightly. "Maybe. But time in the hospital got me thinking. With Bob and his crew out of business, Rux will put us onto the powder dealers, the big meth crews and the like. Remember, Dr. Pie is still at large. And his people eat their dead. We just aren't trained to go up against maniacs like that. We're *actors*."

"If we stay together as a team—"

Swiss raised a hand. "Fact is, cowboy, we can handle the exotics. The folks who traffic in exotics are mostly a non-violent bunch. Sure, some have guns, but most don't. The *real* bad guys have atomic bombs, Rory. And the ones who don't have atomic bombs use assassins no one knows how to find."

Koestler sipped his tea. There was more truth in Swiss's words than he wanted to admit.

"Besides, I've got to think about Lilly," Swiss said. "We've had people *disappear* in the Blight and Pasadena's a total graveyard anymore."

"But they weren't Proteans—" Koestler argued. "They had uniforms that had 'cop' written all over them."

Swiss shrugged this off. "And once the quarantine is lifted there's no telling how the drug culture will change in California. It'll get worse in ways we can't know."

Swiss seemed bleak, defeated. It wasn't the man Koestler had known ten years ago when the Protean Set had been formed. Each of the four actors who made up the Set had a love for drama and pretense, and each had a taste for danger.

On the other hand, none of them had ever gone up against the *urbanistas* in Pasadena or the Mexican mafia or any of the tribes in the Blight. And it was true: Dr. Pie was still at large and Dr. Pie *hated* the police.

The warmth of the handleless teacup seemed to be Koestler's only anchor to reality. It was no wonder that Internal Affairs, particularly Vincent Dunhill, thought so little of the Proteans. The Protean Set hadn't gone up against any serious crew their entire career. They hadn't shown their mettle.

Off in the distance, to the south, Koestler saw the *Fairuza Balk* heading out over the Pacific. The giant red airship was an astonishing sight. Koestler wished he were on board.

"You know we've pulled some dangerous busts," Koestler said. "Remember those JJ 180 freaks in Beverly Hills last year? Those guys were violent."

Swiss managed a slight laugh. "Lucky we had our Susan B. Anthonys. They danced a different tune, that's for sure."

"That's exactly it. We've got our own exotic weapons. Night drops, Pancakes, Spitwads. And then we've always got backup. Nobody goes in without backup and surveillance."

Koestler's pleas were falling on deaf ears.

Swiss shook his head somberly. "Lilly said there's a computer firm in Simi Valley that's invented a teleportation system," Swiss said. He was gazing distractedly to the south, following the *Fairuza Balk* in its lazy flight.

Swiss went on, "If some crew gets hold of a delivery system like that, we could get a bomb in our laps and not even know it."

"I saw the same report," Koestler said. "I don't think the government is going to let a teleportation system out of their hands."

"Yeah, well, Dr. Pie used to *be* military," Swiss pointed out. "That's where he gets all his equipment from. And we're just talking about *one* man."

"That *isn't* going to happen," Koestler said.

"Well, anyway," Swiss said diffidently. "Lilly and I have been thinking of leaving the state. With Tom in his third year at UTEP, we could move just about anywhere in the country. I can teach. I've got the credentials."

Koestler could see that Brad was already wedded to the idea of leaving. On the other hand, a few days' rest at home could bring him back around. He might just get antsy sitting around the house and doing nothing more than watching television and drinking his cleansing teas.

Lilly Swiss came out on the porch, drying her hands on a towel. Koestler and Swiss turned in their chairs.

"Senator Myrland's in the hospital. A maid, or something, found Myrland out on his veranda in the middle of the night. He's in some sort of coma," Lilly said.

"Myrland," Swiss sneered. "Remember when he came by the station a couple of years ago? Lucky us, we got to shake his hand. He probably got drunk and passed out."

"Actually, they said he's in some sort of very cold state," Lilly reported. "It's really weird."

"Did they say how it happened?" Koestler asked.

She shook her head. "No. Not yet, anyway."

The two men looked at each other.

"You think there's a connection here?" Swiss asked Koestler.

"Let's go see," Koestler suggested.

The two abandoned their lawn chairs and withdrew to the living room.

The *Fairuza Balk* had, by then, disappeared into the ocean haze in the distance.

FIFTEEN

A DAY LATER, while all of California was abuzz with talk of Senator Myrland's condition, Koestler went to see Sal Briscoe.

Koestler boarded the *Fairuza Balk* alone when Sal didn't answer the door to his seaside lair. If Sal wasn't in his home, he was usually in his ship. He rarely went anywhere else and had food and other necessities delivered to his home.

Koestler walked down the glowing corridor of the "engine room" in the stern of the fantastic, art deco airship. Giant luminous towers surrounded him on either side, dynamos of extraordinary proportions. They washed him in a gentle, crimson light. Beneath his feet, Koestler could feel a low, subsonic tremor. It gave the impression that the lower half of the *Fairuza Balk* had to be filled with powerful engines.

All this, Koestler knew, was an illusion. The real engines to the gigantic airship, the Zerwekhs, were about the size of a bathtub and were located far beneath the walkway, down where the anti-gravity plates were positioned along the flat "keel" of the ship. The engine "towers" were nothing more than frighteningly tall light panels: On board the *Fairuza Balk*, everything was for show.

Koestler found Briscoe at the far end of the corridor of glowing towers, working on a tower that wasn't glowing as mightily. Briscoe looked down at Koestler from his position at the top of a ladder.

"I let myself in," Koestler said.

"You always do," Briscoe said. He began to ratchet a light panel in place with a socket wrench.

Briscoe descended the ladder, replacing the wrench at his belt. "So what's on your mind?"

"If the quarantine lifts, how long would it take to fly down to New Zealand?"

"That again."

"I'm just asking."

"Your work is here," Briscoe said. "A warrior has to take responsibility for his actions. For you, that's right here."

"I'm serious."

"So am I."

They walked forward several compartments to one of the giant side viewing stations of the *Fairuza Balk*. This large viewing portal faced north. The Pacific Ocean beyond was a greenish color though the sky above was a gun-metal blue.

Briscoe poured himself a drink. He offered one to Koestler. Koestler took a seltzer water instead. Briscoe's drink was purple. Koestler had no idea what it was.

"So what's on your mind?" Briscoe repeated.

"I think my cover has been blown. They know where I live and they've got access to my bank accounts. Some of them, anyway. If it's some crew I've busted, I could be in really deep shit."

"You're *always* in deep shit," Briscoe countered. "You've just never owned up to it."

Even with his best friend standing in front of him Koestler felt remote. He said, "My son, Jon, ran away from home and he's got his mother's credit cards. He's also going around dressed as Elvis. That means thousands of dollars of royalties to the Presley estate. *And* he's eating like a gladiator at every good restaurant in town."

"Cancel the cards," Briscoe said.

Koestler stared at the former movie star. "The courts say I can't. I've still got to pay the bills. I've tried talking to his mother, but Annette thinks the whole thing is a great learning experience for Jon."

"And you as well," Briscoe said, sipping his purple whatever.

"You don't get it. If my cover is blown, I'm going to be out of a job," Koestler said. "If I go back to acting, like my partner wants to do, I'll have to go to New York just to get away from the crews I've taken down here."

"Okay."

"And even assuming I *can* get a job, the pay's still lousy. I'm in a bind, Sal."

"That's ridiculous. You could still be a regular cop. Give yourself a new Face, a new name. It's not as sexy as being an actor. But then again, being an actor is much overrated in this country, especially with directors who try to kill you and producers who don't care as long as you make them money."

Koestler stared out into the distance. "Being a Protean *is* like being an actor. I just thought I could have it both ways."

"No one has it both ways," Briscoe stated. "You get one or the other. Fudd's Law. No one's exempt."

"This wasn't what I came here to hear, Sal."

Briscoe put down his drink and walked over to the center of the viewing station. He began doing his strange movements again, as if invigorated by his concoction.

What Briscoe had said, however, was true. Sal had his magnificent ship, his Malibu digs, and his leisurely life in retirement. But to obtain that life, he had to "die" and lose a great movie career and a kitschy kind of immortality. No one had it all.

Briscoe began tapping the tips of his toes on the floor behind him, alternating each foot as he did. He then began twisting his feet from side to side. He spoke as he did his strange dance. "You need to get your priorities right. You can't get away with six wives, twelve girlfriends, and fifteen children and expect to *play* all the time."

"I don't *play*, Sal."

"You do *something*. And you're *always* in trouble."

Koestler watched Briscoe's sliding feet. Drowning on the set of a movie can do strange things to a man, he thought.

"One thing I can do," Koestler then said after a time, "is start carrying a gun."

"I thought you carried a gun."

"A real gun. A Glock. Maybe a Tech-Nine. With hollow-tip bullets."

Briscoe stopped and stared narrowly at him. "Does this have anything to do with that odd little girl you live with?"

Koestler was surprised at the question. He suddenly felt an unexpected tightness in his throat and his eyes became moist and warm.

Finally, he said, "Stephie, yes. That's part of it. If anything happened to little Stephie—"

"Then you'd be your own worst nightmare."

Koestler nodded.

"I'd say it's time you made a few choices in your life," Briscoe then said. "If not, they'll be made for you. They were for me and you don't want that. Trust me."

"Why don't you just lie to me now and then? Tell me what I want to hear."

"You know the answer to that."

Briscoe continued with his inane movements until it was time for Koestler to head on to work.

Several hours later, Koestler found himself in the staff lounge at head-quarters in Santa Monica, stirring a cream mixture into his coffee. Without Brad Swiss there, he felt like a stranger in a strange land. Koestler recalled that when Frank Myrland, then campaigning for senator, had visited the station, he had promised all kinds of money for departmental needs. None, of course, had materialized. Perhaps if they, the Protean Set, had their own offices, instead of a War Room, Koestler would have felt more like a cop, a *real* cop who belonged there.

Koestler was only minutes musing over his coffee when Vincent Dunhill of IAD darkened the door to the staff lounge.

"Well, now, detective. This is the most I've seen of you in the last three years," Dunhill said, grinning like a Tyrannosaurus.

"Lucky you," Koestler remarked, tasting his coffee.

"You know, I rented one of your old movies last night."

In his life before the LAPD, Koestler had made a handful of films. They were less than memorable. They showed mostly in Asia and he got zip in royalties. Sal still made millions.

Koestler said nothing. Dunhill was like a fart in the room. Koestler was just waiting for him to go away.

"I can see why you became a cop," Dunhill then added. The man's bristly flat-top haircut made his head look like an aircraft carrier.

"Strange how things turn out," Koestler moved past him.

"Chuckle's *still* out there, detective," Dunhill said loudly as Koestler walked away. "And you're either with us or against us!"

What did *that* mean?

Two other officers of Internal Affairs—Cabot and Kashkashian—had been watching the exchange. Koestler didn't like their predatory expressions either. It made Koestler wonder what, if anything, IAD knew that he didn't.

Koestler walked down the corridor, rounded a corner, and reached the War Room. There he found Kip Dixon and Edwardian Rux. The only ones missing were Brad Swiss and Amber Leone, and Brad was now MIA forever.

"Where have you been?" Rux asked him. He seemed more impatient than usual. "I've been calling you for the past hour."

Koestler pulled his phone from his belt and looked at it. "Goddam it," he said, angry with himself. "It's not buzzing me again."

He shook it violently. The page LCD screen indeed registered the call Rux had placed to him, but the phone had not rung. Koestler pressed the ringer function. It rang.

"I'll get it fixed then," Koestler said.

"Or get a new one," Rux said. "Things are happening fast around here."

"What things?" Koestler placed the phone back on his belt.

"Bob Thermopylae's come out of his coma," Kip Dixon said from where he sat at the long table.

Rux added, "I want you two to get over to the hospital and see what you can get out of him before his lawyers show up and muzzle him."

"How did you find out?" Koestler asked.

"Dr. Helms contacted me. Thermopylae woke up an hour ago and, according to the doctor, seems alert enough to speak."

Koestler frowned, taking a final sip from his now-lukewarm coffee. "I would have thought Helms would have called Thermopylae's lawyers first, instead of us. At the least, members of his family."

"That's the funny part," Kip Dixon said, rolling his broad shoulders slightly, an unconscious mannerism Dixon did when he got excited. "Thermopylae *specifically* asked to see us."

"Us?"

"Us," Dixon said. "The police."

"Then let's go talk to him," Koestler said. "I hate dealing with lawyers."

Rux grabbed Koestler's arm as they headed for the door.

"Captain?" Koestler queried.

"Make sure Thermopylae hears his rights and *ask* him if he wants to see his lawyers first," Rux said gravely. "By the book, detective."

"By the book," Koestler said.

The bulldogs of IAD had been watching their brief meeting through the large glass wall of the War Room. Koestler had seen them as well.

When they stepped outside into the hallway, Edwardian Rux said to them, "Go somewhere else, fellas."

"Not likely, Ed," Dunhill responded. "You know that."

Even Edwardian Rux was not immune from IAD.

By then, however, Koestler and Dixon had become ghosts and had slipped out the back.

Snarled traffic on the 405 forced Koestler and Dixon to take a helicopter west, out over the ocean where a southeasterly route provided them the most direct way to Manhattan Beach. Koestler and Dixon were out of the craft the second it had landed.

Once inside the Aaron Stively Medical Center, they went directly to the detention ward where Dr. Randall Helms was waiting.

"How is he?" Koestler asked.

"He's awake and seems alert and normal," Helms told them.

"How did he come out of it?" Koestler asked. He was thinking of the other victims of the strange hypothermia. "Was it something your people did?"

"Not at all," Helms reported. "Mr. Thermopylae just woke up and asked the nurse for some water."

"What about Billy Styvesant?" Kip Dixon then asked as they walked past the last security checkpoint. Koestler and Dixon showed the guard their identification.

"I checked on Mr. Styvesant and Ms. Connors before I called your captain," Helms said. "They are the same. Stable, but the same. I think Ms. Connors will wake up soon. She's simply suffering from exhaustion. But Mr. Styvesant is still in his hypothermic coma."

Koestler paused just outside the door to Bob Thermopylae's room. To the doctor, he said, "We have to do something before we talk to Mr. Thermopylae."

"Right," Dixon said.

On the spot, Dixon and Koestler changed their Faces. Dixon became Sal Briscoe and Koestler went back to Robert Redford. What was missing were the aviator costumes they had worn the night of Devil Dervish's shindig. But all Koestler and Dixon really needed were the Faces Bob Thermopylae would recognize from the night of the bust.

Dr. Helms watched the transformation of the two Proteans. It only took a few seconds.

Koestler pushed open the door to Bob Thermopylae's private room.

Koestler was momentarily taken aback when he saw the beautiful blonde woman on the bed. But then he knew that this was Bob Thermopylae, not the young and attractive Madonna Ciccone.

"I'm Detective Koestler of the LAPD and this is Detective Dixon," Koestler said. "We'd like to ask you a few questions."

The Madonna nodded, eyes wide, clearly alert.

"First we have to inform you of your rights based on the Geneva Protocols and your right to have your attorney present, including members of your family, if you wish."

Thermopylae held up a small hand, stopping him. "I know what my rights are. Go ahead. Ask, and you shall receive."

Koestler and Dixon exchanged looks. Dixon shrugged. Something in Bob Thermopylae's voice had definitely changed. The vocal softness of the historical Madonna Ciccone seemed to have merged with Thermopylae's real voice. It was faint, but present nonetheless.

But it was more than that. As Koestler thought about it, in some bizarre way, Bob Thermopylae—the old Bob Thermopylae—was *gone*.

Koestler knew that his first series of questions should be about Thermopylae's remaining worm factories. Questions about his crew and his distribution network should have come second and third.

Instead, Koestler asked the question that had been on *his* mind all this time. "Do you remember Devil Dervish's party?"

"Of course." Thermopylae's voice was musical, even when he was just speaking words.

Madonna, Koestler thought. *This is Madonna.*

Dixon seemed fascinated as well.

"The person who took you down was not a member of the Los Angeles police department," Koestler said. "Do you have any idea who it was?"

"We're wondering," Dixon interjected, "if it was a rival gang, somebody out to get you."

The voice was almost sweet, the smile sweeter. "*I* did," Thermopylae said.

Neither detective knew what to say.

"I don't understand," Koestler said. "*You* did?"

"Mmm," Thermopylae muttered. "Well, I brought it all on myself. It's all my fault. But, I'm glad it happened."

Thermopylae raised his—*her*—delicate hand, with its IV drip. The fingers were slender, just like the fingers of the historical Madonna Ciccone who had died the year Koestler had turned ten, the year of the Winter Summer. He remembered it well. *He was still living in Canoga Park, with Vicki Celeste and Shadowland Park just down the street and around the corner....*

Kip Dixon leaned over slightly. "Bob, does someone else have Chuckle worms? Are there any other crews, besides yours, working the streets?"

"Whoever has Chuckle, has the worms," Madonna said quietly. "My crew, your crew."

"But not everybody's got a factory or the distribution network you have," Koestler said.

She sighed, smiling enigmatically.

"We're not making ourselves clear, Mr. Thermopylae," Koestler said.

"My name's Cleveland. Cleveland Evers. I made up the name Bob Thermopylae when I created my band. I wanted to be in show business, you know."

"Cleveland Evers?" Dixon said, looking at Koestler. "Or Chloe," the woman on the bed told them with a half-smile. "I think it's going to be Chloe for a long time now."

"Okay, Ms. Evers," Koestler said. "We're after this assailant of yours. Now if you could—"

"Don't you want to know about my factories?" the new Chloe Evers asked.

"Yes, we do, but we need to capture your assailant," Koestler insisted. "He, or his friends, can do a lot of harm. To you, and to us."

"Not as much as Roger Grafman," Chloe Evers said.

The two Proteans looked at one another.

"Roger Grafman?" Dixon asked.

Chloe Evers smiled. "Lovely Roger. Who would suspect a happy fat man with rings on his fingers and bells on his toes, ho, ho." She laughed softly.

Koestler knew the name. He turned to Dixon. "Roger Grafman's a film producer. He even backed one of the movies I was in about fifteen years ago."

"No kidding? Which one?"

"*Kid Charlemagne*," Koestler said. "It didn't do well here, but was boffo in Indonesia. Grafman's got all kinds of connections in this town."

"Would he still know you?" Dixon asked.

"Probably not." Koestler looked at Chloe Evers. "Is Roger Grafman your point man in Hollywood?"

Chloe Evers nodded.

"And where is your main factory?" Kip Dixon asked.

"In the basement of the Sunset Palms Hotel. Downtown," she said. "It's been there a while. People come and go, talking of Michelangelo."

Dixon turned to Koestler. "The Sunset Palms. That's just off Beverly Glen Boulevard."

Koestler, though, wanted to get Bob Thermopylae back onto the subject of his assailant, the player. But Chloe Evers had closed her eyes and had fallen back to sleep.

The three men stepped out into the hallway. Koestler turned to Randall Helms. "Look," Koestler said, "if Bob wakes up, try to keep him from a phone for at least an hour. If he does get to a phone, let us know. We've got to get warrants to search the Sunset Palms hotel and that could take some time."

"Let alone mount the damn raid," Dixon furthered.

Dr. Helms nodded.

Out on the helipad, Koestler and Dixon changed their Faces once again. On the way back to Santa Monica, via the same ocean route they had taken to Manhattan Beach, Koestler said he'd go after Roger Grafman and Dixon could have the raid on the Sunset Palms Hotel.

With any luck, the Bob Thermopylae affair might be over by sundown and the Rottweilers of Internal Affairs would have to look elsewhere to feed.

SIXTEEN

WHILE KOESTLER AND DIXON were in transit back to the station, Koestler filled in Captain Rux on the meager details of Bob Thermopylae's confession. When they landed, Kip Dixon went about setting up an assault team for a raid on the Sunset Palms Hotel. Rux had already begun assembling SWAT personnel and several plainclothes detectives were also getting ready, every one of them eager to finish the Bob Thermopylae affair.

Koestler went directly from the helipad at the Santa Monica police station to the staff parking garage where his Sensei was waiting. There, he changed his Face and made several adjustments to his wardrobe. A jaunt to Beverly Hills would require a more appropriate Hollywood attire. His pants became bellbottoms, his jacket filled out with a high collar and thick, expansive sleeves. His amplified Adidas running shoes with their hidden servomechanisms, however, remained the same. The princely white running shoes had never gone out of style in Hollywood.

As Koestler eased his Sensei into traffic, he paged Amber Leone through his mastoid implant. She was evidently out in the field somewhere because she didn't immediately respond. But traffic was sluggish as usual and he didn't mind waiting for Detective Leone to check her messages.

Amber finally called Koestler from somewhere in Westwood. She had been at a health club following a lead they had picked up from one of the confessionalists they'd arrested at Devil Dervish's party. Koestler told her what he and Kip Dixon had learned from the now-awake—and now Chloe Evers—Bob Thermopylae. Leone said she would meet him at the Highwayman Restaurant in half an hour. She needed to change and adjust her wardrobe.

Koestler took Santa Monica Boulevard northeast. When he crossed under Interstate 405, he marveled at the heavy traffic in the anti-gravity lanes above the 405. Giant, lozenge-shaped cargo ships moved through the air gracefully above the interstate, heading northeast to Fresno and Bakersfield. It was a sight Koestler hadn't yet gotten used to…like the Eliminator towers lining the craggy Santa Monica Mountains to the north.

His mind began to wander, as it always did when he was stuck in traffic. Thoughts about the Highwayman Restaurant kept coming back into his mind, an echo of some earlier information deposit in his brain. The Highwayman…the Highwayman…why was that so important?

Then he remembered. The Highwayman was where Carol Langley had worked part-time as a waitress.

He thought about this. It seemed far too coincidental for there *not* to be some sort of connection. Yet Carol Langley's father, Alex, had been quite emphatic about his daughter's clean drug history. So, too, his daughter's stern Mormon roommate. But Mormons were human, too. Their children where just as susceptible to the wayward lures of the world as anybody else's children. Maybe the Langleys, Julienne Clements, her other roommates *all* had something to hide.

Still, why didn't the player take out Jack McKimmie when he had the chance? Jack McKimmie seemed as likely a candidate for hypothermia as anyone Koestler had dealt with so far. They had found three pounds of Chuckle in McKimmie's apartment. The player, or players plural, seemed to be targeting Chuckle dealers.

Was Frank Myrland a Chuckle dealer too? Politicians had all sorts of skeletons in their closets. Perhaps some of Senator Myrland's skeletons were still alive and doing business in the Washington/Baltimore region…

Koestler powered up his Clobberer. There was a lot to be learned at the Highwayman.

Koestler pulled his Sensei into the south parking lot of the Highwayman Restaurant just after 2:00 p.m. The lunch crowd had undoubtedly thinned out by now. Koestler saw that the parking lot was two-thirds empty. This was good. The fewer civilians caught in the mix, the better.

Detective Leone's MetaMorph—a '22 Mazda sedan—pulled into the parking lot about five minutes later. Leone was wearing a Face Koestler was familiar with. She was also wearing her work-out togs and a big, bulky sweatshirt that had TENSEGRANAUT written on it. The shirt hung down to her hips, easily concealing her array of weapons, including her small Clobberer.

The two Proteans rendezvoused behind a wall that separated the parking lot from the entrance to the Highwayman. The wall provided an excellent blind where they could confer.

"Did you tell Rux about this?" Leone asked.

"Kip's on it as we speak," Koestler said. "But I did call for backup. They should be here in about ten."

"Then let's wait," Leone suggested.

But Koestler was feeling anxious. If there were aspects of his life that he couldn't control—such as the spending habits of his teenaged children or the overdrafts of his ex-wives—there were some aspects of it he *could* control. This was one of them.

"Let's take him ourselves," Koestler said. "I want to personally walk Grafman in handcuffs right past Dunhill and his pet squirrels."

"What's the rush? Let's do this thing with backup, casual-like. Walk in, walk out. Live happily ever after."

Koestler squinted in the weak rays of the early spring sunlight. The ink was barely dry on the arrest fax his Sensei had cranked out just before he had arrived at the Highwayman. "No. When Thermopylae's crew gets wind that their ringleader is awake and blabbing, they'll bolt. Grafman has connections all over the world. He could go anywhere if we lose him. We've got to grab him now."

"Okay," Leone said. "It's your call. How do you want to do this?"

"You go in and get seated. I'll follow in about three minutes."

"How do you know he's here?"

Koestler pointed to a late-model solid gold Cadillac in the parking lot. The license plate of the heavily-armored vehicle said KATYLIED.

"That's Grafman's car. I'd know it anywhere."

Leone nodded.

"Grafman has his own table in back on the north side of the restaurant. You'll recognize him easily. He's huge. Weighs at least three-fifty."

"Okay."

"There are restrooms near the kitchen," Koestler went on. "Walk to the restrooms and stand in the alcove. We'll brace him, see if we can get him to leave without a fuss. By then the cavalry should be here. In and out, like you said."

"All right."

Leone slung her tote bag over one shoulder and headed for the entrance. "What's the news on Brad?" Leone asked.

"Brad might be resigning."

Leone looked startled. "He's *quitting*? Rory, we need him. We've got to be a quartet."

"I know, I know," Koestler said. "Rux will just have to recruit someone else."

Leone shook her head. "I don't know about this, Rory."

"Let's get this done and we can figure out Brad's case when it's over."

"Sure."

Detective Leone disappeared inside. She wasn't at all happy about the news about Brad Swiss.

Koestler waited, mentally checking off the time in his head.

Two patrons came out of the restaurant about a minute later. Clark Gable and Carole Lombard. The Gable masquer wore a thin khaki suit with an authentic, pre-World War II yellow silk tie. The Lombard wore a knee-length red suit with a green archer's hat with a jaunty feather. Right out of the 1930s. They were excellent ringers.

Koestler's mastoid implant chimed suddenly and broke his thoughts.

An unfamiliar voice sounded out in his head. *"Detective Koestler?"*

"I'm here," Koestler subvocalized. "Who's this?"

"This is Madden and Chung, Hollywood," the voice returned—Madden or Chung, Koestler didn't know which. *"Our ETA is five minutes. What's your situation?"*

"Detective Leone is already inside the Highwayman Restaurant," Koestler subvocalized. "She should be seated by now. I'm going in. We'll be out in the parking lot with our man by the time you get here."

"Need a black and white?" Madden or Chung asked.

"If one's near," Koestler said. "We're trying to do this quietly. No fuss, no muss."

"Copy that. Out."

Koestler finally entered the restaurant.

Once inside, he let his eyes adjust to the gloom. The major wheeler-dealers who used the Highwayman Restaurant had gone for the day and only a few wannabes remained. The only masquers he saw were an Oliver Hardy and a Stan Laurel grumbling over burgers and fries. The Stan Laurel might have been a woman, given the width of her shoulders. They had probably come from a reading or tryout.

A young man, very effeminate, came up to Koestler. He was dressed in a tuxedo but without the coat. He cradled several menus. "May I help you?" he asked with a flourish of studied superciliousness.

Koestler shook his head. "I'm looking for Roger Grafman."

"Do you have an appointment to see him?"

"You take *appointments* to see him?"

"If you don't have an appointment—"

"He'll be glad to see me," Koestler said. "I was in one of his movies a long time ago."

The young man wasn't impressed by this information. He probably saw dozens of celebrities every day of his life. He scowled with contempt.

"Please don't do that," Koestler said. He pulled out his badge by the chain around his neck. "Why don't you go out and smoke a cigarette or something? Take a break."

The young man blanched at the sight of Koestler's badge. He didn't see one of those every day. The young man put his menus down and headed for the door.

Koestler tucked his badge back beneath his shirt and proceeded casually through the restaurant. As he went, he loosened his jacket a little so he could better reach his Clobberer.

He passed Amber Leone's booth.

Leaving her large tote-bag, Leone rose from her table and headed for the restroom. But she stopped in the small hallway before the kitchen. She awaited Koestler's signal.

Roger Grafman, true to form, was at his private table in the back along the north side of the restaurant. A brick wall rose up behind him. To his right stood a large window made of thick, obsidian-colored glass.

Important-looking papers lay strewn about the table. Film scripts were piled on the seat beside him. A portable computer and phone were the only electronics on the table. Directly in front of Grafman was a tray of delectables. Pudgy fingers sampled the tray constantly.

Though Grafman was currently speaking in an animated manner into his phone, Koestler couldn't hear a sound. The restaurant's management had placed two tall and very narrow sound baffles discreetly before Grafman's table. Grafman could conduct business in this manner with only the slightest mumbles getting through.

Koestler walked up and tapped the button on top of the baffle on the left, shutting the entire system off. Roger Grafman's pig-like eyes considered him. He wasn't pleased that his concentration had been broken.

"Can't you see I'm on the phone?" Grafman asked. The phone was the size of a domino tile.

Koestler waved the arrest warrant.

Grafman spoke into the phone. "I'll call you back. I've got a situation here." Grafman set the phone down and folded the meaty fingers of his hands together on the tabletop.

Koestler said, "Bob Thermopylae's in the slam and he's just spilled the beans." Koestler pulled his badge out by its chain and left it in place. "And you're one of the beans. Call a forklift, Grafman. We're going downtown."

Roger Grafman's natural pallor was a pasty white. He never lounged around pools. He never golfed at Palm Springs. He spent most of his time inside making deals. Koestler watched as the man's face lost what little color it had.

"Thermopylae's named you as a co-conspirator in the manufacture and distribution of Chuckle. We've got warrants to search your person, your home, and your vehicles."

A thick-fingered hand reached for the phone. But Koestler stopped him. "You can make your call downtown. You have the right to remain silent—"

Grafman had a small mouth. It was working now like that of a fish out of water, gasping for air. And the man's eyes had changed focus.

Koestler keenly watched Grafman's eyes and noticed that he wasn't staring at him any longer. Instead, Grafman was looking past Koestler, over his shoulder.

Koestler sensed movement behind him and to his right. That would be Amber Leone, stepping from the alcove.

Grafman's eyes lit with fear and the man started to rise from the booth, inching up backwards. His feet were suddenly on the seat, his hands out before him defensively. Grafman shouted, *"No! Don't!"*

Koestler felt a chill surround him as a fierce breeze whistled behind him.

He turned, expecting Amber Leone. Instead, he saw a goblinesque figure race around him, skirting him, moving to his left. It forced Koestler to look first one way, then the other.

But by then, the assailant had already frosted Roger Grafman.

And it took less than one second for all of it to happen.

The assailant was only a blur. Koestler felt a wash of arctic air from the player's weapon as it swept Grafman's booth.

Koestler jerked around to his left. Incredibly, the player, still something of a blur, passed right *through* the obsidian window. It passed without breaking it, without moving aside a single molecule of brick, mortar or paint in the wall that held the window in place.

At the same time, all three-hundred-plus pounds of Roger Grafman came crashing down onto his table, launching papers, scripts, and nibbles toward the ceiling.

Amber Leone stepped out from behind the wall that separated Grafman's section of the restaurant from the restrooms. She had her Clobberer out. And so, too, did Koestler. And this time they did not hesitate. They aimed at the window where the player was drifting through as if it were nothing at all. The Clobberers spoke in unison.

Glass flew as lightning and thunder smashed a large section of the wall of the Highwayman Restaurant to pieces. Brick shards, glass, and debris violently flew onto the sidewalk beyond. The sound was deafening.

Koestler then vaulted out of the man-sized hole in the wall the Clobberers had made. But by the time—just two seconds later—Koestler had stepped out onto the sidewalk, the spectral assassin was gone. Only a breeze remained.

"I saw him, Rory!" Amber Leone said, wading through the debris, joining him on the sidewalk. "I saw him come right out of the partition next to the kitchen! The partition's just inches thick! That sonofabitch was *real!*"

But Koestler wasn't listening. He was staring at a car that was illegally parked across the street that ran perpendicular to Beverly Glen. It was a '38 Chevy Stealth sedan, the very same one that Koestler had chased out of his neighborhood in Paradise Cove. It had been parked on the street with its eavesdropping antennas aimed at the Highwayman Restaurant.

What were they doing there? How could they have followed him from the station to here? After all, he had on a different Face and his Sensei wasn't the same one that had left the Cove that morning. *Unless they were after Grafman.* It was a day for too many goddamned coincidences. Koestler clearly saw both the driver of the Stealth car and the woman sitting beside him. He focused on the woman. She had long dark hair, sultry eyes, and a very startled expression on her face.

Strangely, he had gotten less of a good look at the driver. Though it was only an impression, but he felt that the woman was the one in control of the operation, not the man. He was just a lackey, a chauffeur.

Quickly, though, the driver punched the window command and the windows shot up and became liquidly opaque. The eavesdropping antenna once again folded up and snapped back to its hidden cranny.

The Stealth vehicle then leapt from its spot with screaming tires and burned rubber. Wheeling around the corner, it disappeared to the north on Beverly Glen.

"Who was that?" Leone asked, clutching her Clobberer. Leone had only taken notice of the Stealth car when it had made its noisy retreat. She had been searching for some sign of Roger Grafman's ghostly assassin.

"Another player, I think," Koestler said.

The two Proteans turned back to the hole in the wall of the Highwayman Restaurant to see after Roger Grafman. They were not surprised to find that he was the latest victim of the strange hypothermia.

They weren't surprised when, later that day, it made the news.

SEVENTEEN

THE HIGHWAYMAN RESTAURANT had been officially put out of business.

The physical damage Koestler and Amber Leone had done to the restaurant as they had tried to stop the entity that shot Roger Grafman could easily have been repaired in a few days. However, a crime scene investigator unearthed security tapes in a storage locker that showed Grafman conducting some of Bob Thermopylae's business there as well as his own. The audio on the tapes was particularly incriminating.

The same crime scene investigator also came across the security tape that recorded the "frosting" of Roger Grafman. Captain Rux set up a playback on scene and the tape detailed Koestler's professional mien and Detective Leone's skilled backup. It also showed the blurred image of the player emerging impossibly from the thin partition and skirting past Koestler. The player's "exit" through the dark windows of the restaurant was also the clearest image they had yet of this remarkable ability.

As the crime scene investigators tore apart the Highwayman, the LAPD was busy on another front. Kip Dixon and a platoon of SWAT personnel led a by-the-book assault on the Sunset Palms Hotel. In the basement of the hotel they captured seven space-suited workers and confiscated two hundred pounds of Chuckle.

The greater discovery, however, was the trays of Chuckle worms. They found several cultivation trays seething with Chuckle worms. The trays had automatic skimmers and these were slowly raking up the bubbled residue from the surface of the nutrient-rich growth habitat. The residue was then automatically funneled onto flat trays where it dried and was later ground into powder. None of this, however, made the news.

All in all, it had been a good day.

What remained was the paperwork. This flowed over into the next day and Koestler, Dixon, and Leone were given small cubicles on the third floor of the Santa Monica headquarters which housed the precinct's administrative wing. This was a good thing, for it was two floors away from the Internal Affairs Division. In fact, Vincent Dunhill et al. probably did not even know they were in the building.

The Protean Set, however, got an unexpected visitor shortly after one o'clock that day. Koestler had just returned from lunch and was ensconced in his cubicle when he heard someone ask: "I'm looking for a Detective Koestler."

This person had spoken to the receptionist whose desk was in front of the elevators on the third floor.

Koestler stood up and saw Dr. Bert Bender from the UCLA Medical Center. Bender was dressed, this time, in casual Levi's, deck shoes and a work shirt.

Koestler left his cubicle and searched his memory for the Face he had worn when he had visited Brad Swiss for the first time. As he recalled, it was his default face, the one he wore now.

"Dr. Bender," Koestler said, shaking the man's hand. "You have something for us?"

Bender glanced around the busy office area. "Is there somewhere we can talk?"

At this point, both Kip Dixon and Amber Leone had risen from their cubicles to see what was going on. Koestler waved them over. "This is Detective Dixon and Detective Leone," Koestler said, by way of introducing them. To the Proteans, he said, "This is Dr. Bender. He looked after Brad in the hospital."

Amber Leone found an office not in use. "We can go over there. That's the vice squad conference room."

They repaired to the room where Dr. Bender pulled out a folded piece of paper from his shirt pocket.

"I did what you said about contacting Randall Helms at Aaron Stively concerning our mutual 'hypothermic' patients," Bender said. "Helms and I brainstormed on how to go about setting up a hot line to see if there were any more of these hypothermia cases in the area."

"What did you come up with?" Koestler asked, taking the paper.

The sheet detailed several cases recently in California, Arizona, Utah and Colorado.

"Dr. Helms called me last night," Bender said. "He found three in the Washington, D.C., area, and two in New York. Manhattan, to be specific. But then, it's always cold back there, so those could just be coincidental."

"Senator Frank Myrland was found in a hypothermic coma just the other day," Kip Dixon said.

"Yes," Bender acknowledged. "But he was nowhere near the Atlantic where you can still freeze to death."

"How did you set up the hot line?" Amber Leone asked.

"It's mostly an e-mail dump," Bender said. "Dr. Helms and I sent queries to every physician we have on our list server categories. We're asking them to send out queries on their list servers and so on. Like a chain letter. This is the list I printed off last night." He pointed to the list Koestler held.

Koestler passed it to Dixon. Dixon then said, "This doesn't make sense. Can all these people be related to the Chuckle trade?"

"Is that what this means?" Bender asked.

"We don't know yet," Koestler responded. "It would help if we had names."

Bender frowned. "There are privacy issues here. I can't go beyond the actual occurrences."

Koestler nodded, saying nothing. At the moment looking into the list of names would present a logistical nightmare. There wasn't enough people-power in the Santa Monica division of the LAPD to undertake such an investigation.

Koestler nodded. "It's probably just as well. Right now we've got enough to handle. Just let us know if you come across any more of these. That would be the biggest help."

Dixon pointed to Bender's unusual garb. "Is this your day off, doctor?"

Bender nodded. "Yes. I'm going fishing. As far out in the Pacific as I can get."

"At least it's safe out there," Amber Leone said.

"That's the whole point," Bender said.

Twilight had flowed over the eastern mountains when Koestler finished the last of his paperwork and done his filings. It had been a long day and he was exhausted. He really felt the need to unwind.

Before he had left the station, he had called one of his girlfriends, Genevieve Speich. Genevieve was a playful, black-haired imp, another actress, and was sometimes a bit more trouble than she was worth. But she was one of his few girlfriends who happened to be in town and she said she would meet Koestler later at his house. Dinner and whatever sounded fine.

Koestler had only pulled out onto the Pacific Coast highway in his Sensei, heading west toward home, when his phone chittered. The sound snapped his thoughts in half.

He pulled the phone from his belt. "Hello?" he said.

"*Help me! Help me!*" came the cry of a little person. "*Help! Help! Help!*"

"Stephie?" Koestler said, looking at the phone. "What are you doing—"

"*They're here! They're here! Help!*"

The line at Stephie's end went dead.

Little Stephie, in the short time Koestler knew her, had managed to get into just about everything he had. But she had never used the phone before. Furthermore, he had no idea how she had managed to dial his number. But then he remembered that his kitchen phone had all his important emergency numbers stored in it in case one of his many girlfriends wanted to call *him*.

Even so, how did Stephie know to press the correct button that would reach his cell phone?

With chilling certainty, he realized that little Stephie must have speed-dialed *every* number he had on the kitchen phone until she got him.

Christ, he thought. Now everybody knew something was up. One of those numbers was to Edwardian Rux's cell phone. One was to Brad Swiss's. Another to Sal Briscoe's phone. One was even to his sister's home in the valley. *That* would take some undoing and not a little bit of unpleasantness.

Koestler immediately streamlined the Sensei into a Ford Forty Nine with afterburners. Police lights emerged from the hull and its siren started to wail. Koestler dove into the center lane that threaded the Pacific Coast highway and rocketed straight for his home in Malibu. Moments later, he just missed colliding head-on with an Oscar Meyer Weinermobile making a left hand turn in the center lane.

When Koestler pulled screaming into Paradise Cove, the exit gate had been demolished and their night watchman, old Jim Barbour, lay unconscious—or perhaps even dead—on the ground outside it. There were, however, no bullet craters or laser-melted holes in the glass of the booth. That was a good sign.

Koestler sped around the corner to his house.

Standing across the street from his house was grim Mrs. Tenharkel.

She had a broom in her hand and a condemnatory frown on her face. Koestler bounced the Ford Forty Nine onto the driveway and shut the siren off. Clobberer drawn, he headed for the front door.

The door, he found, was wide open. The lock had been broken by brute force from the outside. All of the lights in the house were on.

Koestler leapt through his front door. "*Stephie! Where are you? Stephie!*" he shouted.

Koestler moved through the hallway. The living room furniture had been overturned. His framed posters knocked askew, his bedroom a mess.

He found little Stephie hiding in the kitchen pantry. She was singing to her BooBaby and playing with her fingers in a distracted manner. Koestler felt a universe of relief.

"Stay here," he said, shutting the pantry door.

Koestler moved through his condominium, all of his senses alert. Each of his three bedrooms had been ransacked; so, too, the two bathrooms. Even so, the stereo unit, his three laptop computers and kitchen appliances had not been taken. He checked the hidden crannies in the walls where he cached his weapons and those, evidently, had not been touched either.

Little Stephie came out from her hiding place, sucking her thumb, cradling her BooBaby.

Koestler was so relieved. She might belong to someone else, but he felt an overwhelming devotion to her. In fact, this was the first time he felt this way about *any* child, including his own.

Koestler knelt down to her. "Did you see the people who did this?"

Her thumb still in her mouth, she nodded.

"How many were there?" he asked softly.

"Three," she said. "They were *bad*."

"Was there a woman with them?" Koestler asked.

Stephie nodded, her ponytail bobbing up and down.

He then took little Stephie by the hand and led her out of the house. Glancing up to the third tier of the Cove, Koestler spied the mighty Erendira, fists on her ample hips, frowning in a cone of golden light from the streetlight overhead. *How had she known Stephie was in trouble?*

The answer to that question came from the wail of sirens and the flashing blue-and-yellow orbs of the Malibu Police. One of the buttons on the phone automatically dialed 911...or perhaps nosy Mrs. Tenharkel had called the police on her own, having seen the strangers enter Koestler's home. In any event, the whole Cove seemed to be rousted.

Three police cars came screaming onto Koestler's street, one stopping before Mrs. Tenharkel's house, the other two braking before Koestler's.

Little Stephie broke free and ran up the wooded path at the end of the street. Erendira took her by the hand and swiftly disappeared, leaving Koestler to the Fates.

By now other neighbors were out in force to see what was going on.

Even a helicopter had been called into play, its bright platter of light searching the vicinity for miscreants, but always somehow coming back to Koestler.

For the next hour Koestler took the police through his home as LAPD forensics took pictures, fingerprints, and video tapes of the crime scene.

Koestler told the Malibu police everything he knew except the part about little Stephie. He'd do everything he could to prevent this from getting back to her. He had never felt so protective…and grateful that she was still alive.

The head detective from the Malibu division was a tow-headed blonde child named Detective Joel Bisby. He was half Koestler's age.

"Who could have done this?" Detective Bisby asked, baffled. "They didn't *take* anything."

Koestler pulled the youngster aside and revealed his identity and his role as an undercover narcotics agent in Santa Monica. He then said, "I saw a Chevrolet Stealth car here a couple of days ago with government plates. They got past our gate with forged credentials. I saw them again yesterday during a takedown in Beverly Hills. This could be them."

Detective Bisby looked around, arms out, indicating the disheveled living room. "But this looks like a *panty* raid. They *had* to be after something."

Perhaps they were. Koestler stopped short. He stared at the walls of his living room. "Rats," he said.

"What is it?" Detective Bisby asked, also looking around.

"My walls," Koestler said. "They're display walls. AdScans. They're supposed to activate when I'm at home. It helps on the mortgage."

Koestler stepped into the hallway. He opened a hidden panel in the wall. Behind it was a control box with a row of red lights that showed that it had been tampered with. He never touched it and he didn't think little Stephie knew that it was there. If he eliminated his girlfriends as suspects, then that left only professionals. *Snoops.*

Koestler tried the reset button several times, but the system wouldn't come back on.

On a hunch, he took out his money clip. He removed the folded bills and put the metal clamp up against the panel. The clip stuck.

Detective Bisby looked on, perplexed.

"They magnetized the whole system," Koestler said. "They fried its circuitry. Damn."

"But how did they know you had an AdScan?" Detective Bisby asked.

"Unless one of my girlfriends told them," Koestler said. Which was always a possibility. Especially if one of the more jealous ones—and Genevieve Speich was in that category—had found out about his other girlfriends and ratted on him.

But ratted to whom?

And why attack the AdScan system? Why not just take a sledgehammer to the place? That's what Jill Parks had done when she had found out about his outside affairs three years ago.

Then something else had occurred to him. Koestler noticed that he hadn't heard from his Bailiff all day. In fact, its five o'clock report hadn't come through yet.

Koestler pressed the pressure-sensitive plate behind his ear. Detective Bisby looked on curiously. The Bailiff did not respond.

Koestler said, "I've got a court-appointed Bailiff. It's not broadcasting. Something's really wrong here."

"So what kind of trouble are you in anyway?" Detective Bisby asked.

"Apparently quite a lot," Koestler said.

If it could be proven that *he* had tampered with his Bailiff he could go to jail. Clearly someone was out to get him.

EIGHTEEN

CHRISTINE MYRLAND LAY NAKED, MEDITATING over a cigarette. Above her hung a cloud of smoke, acrid and bitter as her thoughts. The bed belonged to the man who happened to be in the bathroom, Trent Andreesen. Andreesen was a California field supervisor for the National Security Agency, an on-and-off-again lover. Sated with sex, she fooled idly with the remote for Andreesen's wallscreen television, scrolling impatiently through its sixty thousand channels. Andreesen got every known video feed from around the world, both public and private, one of the perks he received for working at the world's most efficient eavesdropping agency. The sound was on mute.

"We almost had him," Myrland said.

Andreesen slid his naked body back into bed.

"That's not quite accurate," he said. "*He* almost had *us*, Christine. And he blew bricks all over my car. My commander isn't going to like the repair bill. You know what Stealth vehicles cost? The paint alone costs fifteen thousand dollars."

Tall, blonde and, to Christine, fabulously gorgeous, Trent Andreesen was one of the best friends she had in high places. She had met him through her father when he got the NSA to farm out several low-security jobs to Eidolon Technologies. As such, the NSA had a powerful interest in Eidolon Rex's health.

"It's all Alex Langley's fault," she muttered, crushing out her cigarette. "I could kill the son-of-a-bitch. I wish I could just fire him and be done with it."

"Langley? His profile says he's practically harmless. Family man and all of that. I think you're overreacting." Andreesen pulled the sheet across the flat plain of his stomach.

"No, I am not. Alex misled us. And I think he did it intentionally."

"And how did he mislead you?"

"For one thing, Rory Koestler didn't look at all the way Alex described him. He didn't even look like the guy we were watching at his supposed home in Malibu."

"And why would Alex Langley lie?" Andreesen asked, still skeptical.

Myrland lit another cigarette, pulled a heater, then blew out a long nimbus of smoke. "We have a difference of opinion about Eidolon Rex," she finally said.

Andreesen rolled over and propped his head on one elbow. He might have been handsome, but he wasn't malleable. Her moods didn't rattle him as it did her other lovers. This might have been why Andreesen lasted so long.

"You know," he said almost playfully, "I haven't seen you this angry in a long time."

"It happens."

"This wouldn't have anything to do with what's happened to your dad, would it?"

She glared at him. "Hell, no. This is about Alex Langley and what *he's* trying to do to *me* at Eidolon."

"And this guy Koestler."

"That's right," she said, tapping an ash into the ashtray on her stomach.

"And what's Koestler *really* done to you?"

"He made my computer go away."

Andreesen fell back onto his pillow with a frustrated sigh. "Christine, he doesn't even know you exist. It was just an accident, what happened to Rex."

"It wasn't an accident," she said.

The fact was that she still hadn't been able to link Eidolon Rex's disappearances—major and minor—to anything either Alex Langley or Rory Koestler had done. She did know that Alex and his team had been present when Eidolon Rex disappeared. Yet, subsequent hardware checks and software scans showed nothing out of the ordinary.

However, they had yet to do an operations systems check. And *that* she didn't look forward to. She'd rather keep after Koestler, see what she could ferret out on her own without using Eidolon's facilities. That's what Trent Andreesen was for, and something he was very good at.

As it was, there would be billions of lines of code in Rex's software that would have to be painstakingly examined before an operations check. Fortunately, large clusters of those lines of code *she* wrote, having imported much of it from Telemon Ajax. Langley, however, had a hand in writing large sections of the operating systems. Such a detailed examination of code would take up valuable time and use precious resources she didn't want taken up and used.

"The fact is," she went on, "the person we tracked from the police station to the restaurant didn't look at all like the man Alex originally described to us."

"That doesn't mean Alex has been lying to you," Andreesen said. "You might have gotten the description wrong."

"Whose side are you on?"

"Christine, I've called in a lot of favors to help you get at Koestler. I've got to be the devil's advocate here. What if Alex Langley hasn't done anything wrong? And what if your computer *is* traveling through time as Langley says? That's a terrific discovery, an important discovery. So what if *he* stumbled across it. You said so yourself. You function as a team or not at all. Right?"

"Eidolon Rex is *not* traveling in time," she countered forcefully. "I've got as much corroborating data for my theories as he does for his. More, in fact. I think Langley's trying to pull a fast one."

"You've got the best minds in the computer sciences in the country working on Rex. Langley's not going to fool all of them."

"I still don't trust him," Myrland finally said. "I know he's up to something and whatever it is, it isn't in the best interests of Rex or Eidolon Technologies."

Andreesen didn't say anything for several seconds. He then looked at her. "What we can do is plant some bugs in Langley's home, perhaps in his car. I can have him tapped by mid-afternoon Friday. This guy Koestler might be able to disappear on us, but I can guarantee you that Langley won't."

"I've already got him bugged," she said distractedly.

Andreesen raised an eyebrow. "You have?"

Myrland pondered the middle fingernail of the hand that held her current cigarette. "I got clearance from the FBI to do it last week. I claimed a possible security breach at Eidolon. Michael O'Mara and Major Hannel backed me up."

"And your father, of course."

"Well, yes, he helped."

Andreesen sat up and crossed his legs before her. He looked like a sleek, athletic Buddha. In a former life, she thought, he must have been an African cat. "If you're not careful, Christine, you might get slapped with a harassment suit. It won't matter if the tap was justifiable for national security reasons. He still has his rights."

"I know his rights," she said. "And I know mine."

"Besides, without documentable evidence showing probable cause, whatever you learn from a wiretap would be inadmissible in court. I'm half-tempted to put an end to all this myself. I don't want to be part of a vendetta."

"It's *not* a vendetta. Besides, you'd have to call the FBI and the CIA and one private detective agency in Los Angles to stop the *whole* thing. I'm going to *get* this Rory Koestler and I'm going to pin Alex Langley to a wall like a bug if he gets in my way."

"Jesus, Christine—"

She stared levelly at him. "I'm going to find out what both of these men are doing, especially Rory Koestler. You can either help me or you can back out. This *is* a national security issue. It could lead to one of the greatest scientific discoveries of all time. Certainly a great weapons system."

While she had been speaking, Myrland had been scrolling lazily through the news channels. She focused on the KTLA news channel.

"Here we go," she announced.

A perky field reporter for KTLA was presently standing outside the Highwayman Restaurant with the gaping hole in the back wall Detective Koestler and a colleague had earlier made that day.

Above and to the right of the screen appeared an LAPD departmental snapshot of a man with dark blonde hair and an actor's rugged good looks. Beneath the photograph was the name: Detective Rory Koestler.

"What?" Myrland exclaimed. "That's not Koestler!"

The reporter was in mid-sentence, saying, "—*sources identify the officer in question as Rory Koestler of the Los Angles police department, a twelve-year veteran in the narcotics division.*"

"You're right," Andreesen said, sitting up.

They listened as the reporter continued. "*With Detective Koestler was an unidentified undercover policewoman. They were apparently attempting to serve a warrant on a film producer named Roger Grafman when an unidentified third party assaulted Mr. Grafman before the arrest could be effected. This large gap in the wall you see behind me was the outcome of the ensuing altercation between the two detectives and the unknown third party.*"

Myrland crawled to the end of the bed to get a better look. She was interested in seeing if several phone calls she had made right after the debacle at the Highwayman were about to pay off. As competent as she knew Andreesen to be, he would not cross certain lines. However, she knew of others who would.

Andreesen seemed puzzled. "I don't get it. How did they get a photograph of Koestler? That kind of information is never revealed to the public. Under any circumstances."

Myrland smiled. "Santa's elves."

"What?" He stared at her, baffled.

She ignored him as the reporter on the screen detailed the incident. They showed an aerial view of the Highwayman as it was cordoned off by the police after the assault on Grafman. The video was from a hovering police Eye. Myrland was impressed. This, too, would have not been released to the media. She would have to add a bonus to her pay-offs at Fetterling and Associates, who did her dirty work.

The clip ended and the reporter came back on screen. She said, "*The police are not commenting at this point on the investigation, only to say that it was related to a series of recent drug busts in Hollywood.*"

Myrland played it back.

Andreesen said, "You know, KTLA's going to have to do a lot of explaining to the police and the district attorney. A tape like that shouldn't have been released to the media."

"It wasn't. It was stolen. Then it was leaked."

He looked at her. "And how do you know that?"

"The people I hired. The private detective agency I mentioned."

Andreesen got out of bed and wrapped himself in his bathrobe. "Christine, I can't help you if you keep going behind my back like this. You can do some things in the cause of national security, but you can't do anything you want. Violations of this sort end up at the Supreme Court and lots of people in high places lose their jobs because of it."

Myrland was not listening to him, however. She was thinking. "I *know* there's some connection between Koestler and Rex's disappearance."

"I don't see it, Christine. Given everything you've told me, I just don't see it. He's a cop and we may have compromised an operation he was conducting. If they ever track us down—"

"They won't track us down," Myrland said. "I'll see to that."

Andreesen merely raised his eyebrows.

She said, "I'll have him so busy in his life he won't have *time* to track us down. Maybe by then we'll know where he fits into this."

Myrland leaned back onto the pillows. "Let's turn the heat up on this guy, see where he goes, see what he does. Rex *knows* something about

Koestler and it made him disappear. Since I can't get into Rex to find out, the next best thing is to go after Koestler."

"What do you have in mind?" He stood in the hallway door, apparently heading for the kitchen and the coffee pot. "I mean beyond what we've done so far."

She looked up at him. "What would *you* do in the name of national security? I mean, how far would you go?"

"Not so far as to jeopardize my job, Christine," he said grimly.

"It's a little too late for that, don't you think?"

"Okay," he said, surrendering to her with a sigh. He closed the bedroom door and returned to the bed where she was smiling impishly. "What do you have in mind this time?" he asked.

"It's big." Andreesen closed his eyes and shook his head. She told him. And it was big.

NINETEEN

ALEX LANGLEY FELT LIKE a wad of taffy in a glass-enclosed confectionery case being pulled three different ways by forces over which he had no control.

He had before him on his desk at Eidolon Technologies pages culled from scholarly journals about time-travel theories going back at least sixty years. He also had his assistants dig up essays where they could regarding the relocation of matter in space. He also had dug up his own mathematical scratchings, his Kantian shirt-cuff jottings, all the Post-It notes he had lying around the house. He also got his assistants to scrounge up the design schematics to Eidolon Rex, at least those assistants who had top security clearance. He was on the cusp, he felt, of describing a genuinely new and genuinely *feasible* theory of time travel....

But he wasn't able to concentrate. His wife was losing herself to the soporific fog of alcohol and drugs. His daughter was still in a coma that may or may not have something to do with drugs. And to make matters worse, there now seemed to be as many soldiers filling the hallways of Eidolon Technologies as there were Eidolon employees. Indeed, balloon buildings and other temporary military structures had sprouted in the Eidolon parking lot. There was now a heliport and giant Sikorsky SkyCranes were bringing in crates of materiel around the clock. He could feel the vibrations of their rumbling blades coming up through the floor.

The only blessing in this mix was that Christine Myrland had been gone the last several days. That, however, might have had something to do with her father's condition in Washington, D.C. He'd had a stroke of some kind and Langley guessed that Christine had gotten permission to pass through the quarantine to visit him.

Langley secretly wished that Christine would *stay* in Washington with her father. Those two were peas of a pod. On the other hand, there was no telling what kind of damage Christine could do while she was there. She had all sorts of government contacts, as many as her father, and she could still cause him and Eidolon a lot of misery. The woman had a wild hair up her ass, some proverbial axe to grind, and he wished she'd just disappear so he could find out what Rex had really done.

Christine's main flaw was not her intelligence—which Langley freely admitted was exceptional—but her impatience. Rather than mathematically work out the causes of Eidolon Rex's disappearances, Christine sought the easy route: Find out who this man Koestler was, then follow him, harass him, until he comes clean.

Absentmindedly Langley pulled out an ulcer tablet and popped it into his mouth. *So much on his mind, and only one brain to work with...*

One of his assistants, Cameron Banse, a young post-doc in Computer Science from Cal Tech with short blonde hair and large green eyes filled with intelligence, came in with a detailed photo-print of a Benthorpe processor. It was two feet by four feet and young Banse laid it across Langley's desk. Benthorpes had replaced the aging Pentium Twenty series with their impossibly microscopic quantum pathways. Benthorpes had been designed specifically for use at Santos Avionics in Telemon Ajax. The Benthorpe Mark Twos were the heart and soul of Eidolon Rex.

"They've got soldiers guarding the copiers now," Banse said. "You know that? I had to sign for the goddam thing."

Langley passed a hand over his nearly bald head. "They're in the johns as well and *they* flush the toilets."

"Christ," Banse said, shaking his head.

Langley studied the photograph of the chip, following its intricate lines with the tip of a pencil. He recognized which particular chip Banse had photographed. "You couldn't get any closer to the core than this?"

"I didn't have your level of clearance to get at the Dallas series in the core itself," he said. "I thought this would be close enough. Dr. Tansman's team scanned it for damage right after Rex disappeared. It's undamaged. Since it's one of the routing chips in the series, I thought it'd be just as good."

"It should be good enough," Langley said. "The Mark Twos are just a few microns away from the Dallas series. Anything that would have affected the Dallas chips would affect the Benthorpe Mark Twos."

Eidolon Rex had thousands of Benthorpe processors. Each one was half the size of a grain of salt. Langley believed that within each Benthorpe lay the keys to the time-travel process. He *had* to put his worries about his wife and daughter behind him. He *had* to focus.

"Do you still think Rex is moving through time?" Cameron Banse was one of Langley's sympathizers within Eidolon Technologies. He was certainly young enough—twenty-eight—to still harbor new and innovative ideas, ideas that every corporation needed to stay ahead in the world.

Langley nodded. He said, "We've known for a while now that 'time' is an activity of pure consciousness. But the billions of connections each Benthorpe chip makes during processing goes beyond the mere mimicry of synapses in the human brain. They're more akin to the quantum energy events that take place in cellular microtubules in the neuronal tissue of the human brain."

"Penrose," Banse said. "I took a seminar from Tim Brookshire at Stanford on Roger Penrose's theories of quantum-generated intelligence."

Langley nodded again. "Right. Penrose thought that microtubules were the sites where quantum energy events took place in brain cells. The flux of energies inside the billions of microtubules cause the alpha and beta tubulins to act as on-off switches. These components are much faster than simple synaptical firing."

"Right," Banse said enthusiastically. "But if Rex is doing human-level quantum exchanges, why hasn't he achieved human-level consciousness?" Banse asked. "Why hasn't Rex started talking to us?"

"Because Rex's gone *beyond* human-level consciousness," Langley said. "Remember, we were running Rex at his highest level of computation abilities when he disappeared. It went *way* beyond what we do in our brains. I think what Rex did was transcend human consciousness and reach *time-consciousness*."

"And you think this was done by an overload of the quantum flux forces at the molecular level in the Benthorpes?" young Banse asked.

"The Benthorpes, the Dallases. Remember that Penrose thought that consciousness arose from a *global*, or system-wide, energy event in the brain. That event had to reach a critical threshold before consciousness could arise in the brain. Computers at the turn of the century couldn't do that. Ours can. At least Rex can."

Late in the 20th century Miguel Alcubierre had shown that it might be possible to build a space ship that "shrank" space in front of it in order to "pull" it toward its proposed destination target. The Alcubierre warp engine would create a spatial discontinuity, a black hole, in front of the interstellar vehicle in order to get it to accelerate. The focused mass of the black hole would "pull" the ship toward it, accelerating it to superluminal speeds. To slow down, the ship would create another discontinuity behind it. What Eidolon Rex had done was to create a massive time discontinuity. Through its extraordinary accumulation of predictive details, Rex's energetically compressed data simply "pulled" the future to its current moment in time by creating the future. He leapt.

Banse rubbed his chin, thinking. "You know, that sounds as if this might be the next stage in evolution. *Homo sapiens chronos.*"

"Except that Rex got there first," Langley said.

"But *how*? That's what I don't get."

"The name 'Rory Koestler' must have allowed Rex to extrapolate enough of the future *around* that name, that he was able to move forward, *occupy* the farthest moment he could project himself into. He'd been making similar leaps nanoseconds at a time these last three weeks but we never noticed it."

"So maybe Dr. Myrland is right about this Koestler person being the key to everything," Banse said. "By the way," Langley then asked. "Where is she? Did she fly to Washington to see her father?"

Banse shook his head. "No. She's gone after Koestler himself. The rumor is that she wants to bring him in. *Here*, at Eidolon."

"What else have you heard?" Langley asked.

"Just that the Board is giving her free rein. She's on a real tear, Alex.

"I think she's gone a little bit crazy."

Knuckles rapped at the door just then.

"Come on in," Langley said loudly.

Cecilia Garwin stepped in. Behind her was the very tall Michael O'Mara, Eidolon's security chief. Behind O'Mara appeared Major Hannel. Two soldiers remained in the hallway beyond.

"What can I do for you folks?" Langley asked.

"Hard at work, I see," Cecilia Garwin remarked diplomatically.

He nodded. "Dr. Banse and I were just checking a detail in the Benthorpe design. We think we've found an unexpected side-effect of an increased energy gradient that we may have overlooked during Rex's design stage. I think it might be responsible for his disappearance."

"Are you still working on your time-travel?" Garwin asked. The woman was frowning and not making much of an effort at hiding her disapproval.

Langley said, "We're just following your orders, or I should say, the *Board's* orders. We're trying to figure out how Eidolon Rex disappeared. The time-travel theory is relatively incidental to what actually happened. We'll get there."

Garwin said, "Alex, we're here to tell you that the Board has decided to focus all our efforts on Christine's teleportation theories."

The taffy machine was churning once again. "Look, Cecilia—" he started.

Major Hannel closed the door. His demeanor was, even for him, unusually grim. "Mr. Langley. Satellite photos have confirmed that the Chinese are now massing in the western Gobi. The Pentagon thinks China is preparing for a push into Central Europe and southeast Asia. President Larsen has been informed of this and she wants us, I mean Eidolon Technologies, to work on a practical teleportation system."

Langley ignored Hannel's presumed authority in the room. He looked instead at Cecilia Garwin, the only authority *he* recognized and even then it wasn't much of a recognition. "So Christine got all the way to the president this time. I'm impressed."

Young Banse stood off to one side, eyes wide with terror.

The Eidolon Board representative smiled, but there was no kindness in her smile. "The fact is, Alex, that Christine *has* met President Larsen, but, no, I don't believe they are friends. This directive comes from the Joint Chiefs and the Secretary of Defense. President Larsen has merely signed off on it."

"Rex did *not* teleport," Langley said. He tossed the pencil he held in his right hand onto the schematic before him. "And we'd be wasting our time trying to prove that, let alone build a weapons system capable of wiping out the Chinese army."

Cecilia Garwin frowned. "Alex, the Pentagon's own scientists have reviewed Christine's assessment and think that her math suggests that teleportation is possible."

"What? Christine hasn't been here long enough to work *out* the math," Langley said. "She's been in Los Angeles for the last three days harassing a police detective. Why don't you drag her ass in here and tell her what you're telling me? She should be *here*, not in L.A."

"Be that as it may, Alex," Garwin said, "we're shifting all our efforts over to making teleportation work."

"The fact is," Major Hannel went on, "we're turning this into something like the Manhattan Project. We've secured the vicinity surrounding Eidolon Technologies and are building living quarters for everybody. We'll be moving the entire staff here inside of forty-eight hours."

"You're joking," Langley said.

"We're all involved, Alex, not just you," Garwin said, this time a little more softly. "My son's moving in as we speak."

"You're all crazy," Langley said, astonished.

Young Banse stood against the side wall watching, like a prisoner awaiting his execution.

"Alex—" Garwin pleaded.

"This is illegal," Langley said. "You'll be in front of the Human Rights Court in The Hague inside of a year for this. All of you. I'll see to it personally. And I've got witnesses." He indicated young Banse, whose eyes had indeed witnessed the whole thing, if perhaps with great trepidation.

Major Hannel seemed to take some delight in Langley's outrage. "The president just signed an emergency decree allowing us to do this. It's all legal and above-board."

"Then I'll make sure that Larsen will be there with you," Langley said. "This is illegal and unconstitutional."

"Not if the rest of the world goes to war with China," Major Hannel said. "And if the world does go to war, the United States will lead it. And it's going to need the help of every one of its citizens. This means you and every other person in this building."

Langley heard boots marching in the hallway outside his office. *Guards were being set in place throughout Eidolon Technologies. Not just in the high security areas, but everywhere inside the building and beyond.*

Langley glared at them. "Somebody's going to pay for this, Cecilia. I'll see to it personally. I don't give a rat's ass what's going on in China, Christine Myrland does *not* run Eidolon Technologies!"

"As long as we get a teleportation system out of this, it won't really matter," Major Hannel concluded.

"And what if we can't deliver?" Langley countered, stepping in front of the man.

In a more ameliorative tone, Cecilia Garwin said, "Alex, I think you can come up with something. If you can rise above your personal differences with Christine, we can demonstrate that Rex went *somewhere*. Even the *threat* of such a system might get the Chinese to think twice."

Outside the complex a giant United States Army VTOL troop carrier settled onto the asphalt of the western parking lot.

Garwin looked out the window. "We'll leave you to your work, Alex. We've got other rounds to make."

"Are you moving Christine in here, too?" Langley asked.

"Of course," Garwin said. "We're all caught up in this, even Christine."

The trio removed themselves from Langley's office, leaving him with his rage and young Banse with his terror. They'd just been enlisted. *Drafted* was the better word. And in the Army, desertion or dereliction of duty brought serious consequences.

Langley popped another anti-acid tablet into his mouth then handed the small jar to Banse, who helped himself to one as well.

TWENTY

A NEW GUARD in a newly-fortified security booth at the entrance to Paradise Cove was there to greet Koestler when he returned in his Sensei later that day. The guard's name tag said MAYBERRY and he resembled a retired professional wrestler. He was so big he could barely fit into his booth. He also wore armor and this time carried an automatic weapon. Koestler also noticed that several new security cameras had been installed around the entrance to Paradise Cove. They craned their necks watching him from tall posts like buzzards perched on tree limbs.

Koestler had reconfigured his Sensei and his license plate numbers to their more familiar forms so he could pass the recognition systems-check. He also made sure that he was wearing his default face. All this had to be done for the new guard, Mayberry. Koestler didn't want to get into any more trouble than he was already in.

Inside the bullet-proof enclosure the new guard frowned as he wrote down the time of Koestler's arrival. He then touched a button, commanding the newly-rebuilt gate to lift. He then spoke into his microphone. "You're clear to proceed."

Only then did Koestler notice the two horizontal slits in front of the booth. They were clearly gun ports. This did not bode well. The cameras followed him as he headed for the first tier.

Koestler eased the Sensei down his street. A quiet ocean fog had drifted over Malibu and all Koestler wanted to do now was relax in front of the television with a drink and a girlfriend.

That would have to wait, however: A cluster of cars and one atomic bike had gathered before his condominium and standing before his doorway was a crowd of people, some bearing briefcases, others carrying manila file folders, stuffed, it seemed to him, with important papers. One bore an ominous-looking envelope which was being tapped with stern impatience against a thigh.

Koestler's spirits sagged. Earlier that afternoon, an ultimatum had come from City Hall that the Protean Set was to suspend all operations until further review of the damage done by the release of Koestler's name and photograph to the media. IAD was looking into *how* Koestler's picture got released in the first place. Vincent Dunhill had accused Koestler of doing it himself in order to gain notoriety and a cheesy tell-all book contract. Koestler almost hit him. Rux, however, approved administrative leave for Leone, Dixon and Koestler until the investigation was complete. Everyone needed time to cool off.

Koestler pulled into the driveway and climbed out. He counted twelve people before him, a perfect jury, with Mrs. Tenharkel, the judge, sitting on her front porch across the street in a rocking chair.

"All right," Koestler said. "Who's first?"

"I am," said a hefty young man. This was the minion of a lawyer. He unceremoniously plopped an envelope into Koestler's outstretched hand.

The man behind the server was clearly his partner. On the partner's shoulder crouched a camera making a video record of the delivery.

"What is it?" Koestler asked.

The two men merely walked away. Their duties had been executed. What did they care?

"Mr. Koestler," said the next man in line impatiently.

Koestler held up his hand, stopping the man as he took out the letter. It was from a law firm. The missive told him to reestablish his account at ChemSolar Bank or they would initiate the appropriate action for dereliction of child support payments and alimony on behalf of his ex-wife, Arlene Palfrey.

The amount he owed Arlene was a mere twelve thousand dollars. He had forty-eight hours to correct the situation. This couldn't be right. There *was* money in Arlene's bank account. Or at least there *should* be. There certainly was the last time he checked. *But all this for twelve thousand dollars?*

The day had been long and Koestler hadn't gotten around to finding out why his Bailiff had gone silent. In fact, he had forgotten all about it. Now that oversight was going to cost him. *Unless this, too, was another banking error.* If not, he was going to have to shuffle around some of his mutual funds and stock investments in order to get money into Arlene's account.

Koestler looked at the next person in line. He was a college student in hood, goggles, and riding leathers. He'd come in on the atomic bike. "Are you Koestler?" he asked.

"What do *you* think?" Koestler snapped.

"This is for you, then," the goggled young man said. "Sign here."

"I'm not signing anything."

The letter was a summons for an immediate IRS audit, telling him in no uncertain terms that he needed to come to the Santa Monica office of the Internal Revenue Service in ten days, with or without his accountant. He also had to bring his tax records for the last seven years. The letter was vague in details but clear in its threats.

This puzzled him. He had always had his taxes scrupulously done by the largest tax accounting firm in the country and never once in his life had he been audited. Even when his marriages collapsed and dozens of divorce lawyers became involved in stripping the carcass of his meaty finances did the IRS ever once come calling.

And never once did they *hand-deliver* their demand for an audit.

And besides that, it was March. The IRS was never a year late on an audit. The IRS had the fastest computers in the world. Eidolons, they were called. *The New York Times* had made a big stir about super supercomputers in the hands of the government. This didn't make any sense.

Koestler looked up. The messenger on his atomic bike had fired up his machine. He swung around and headed down the street.

The next person in line cleared his throat. He was a fastidiously dressed man and had swept-back brown hair and hawklike features. "I guess this is your day for bad news," the well-dressed man said. Two other individuals were with him. Back-up singers, Koestler thought. Diana Ross and the Supremes. They ought to be in sequins.

Koestler snatched the papers from the man's finely-manicured hands.

As he did, the man said, "My name is Cal Maples and I represent Financial Acquisitions of Sherwin Oaks," he said with evident pride. "What you have in your hand is a copy of the lien notice placed on your residence by your wife."

"What's the matter with the mail these days?" Koestler asked. "I thought you guys sent these things in the mail."

"These are special circumstances," Maples said. "We were told to make sure you received the notice personally." The two men flanking Maples were tough-looking characters and looked as if they were armed.

They then turned away and returned to their vehicle, which, Koestler noticed, wasn't a Stealth car. However, there were no other vehicles parked along the street and that meant that the remaining group of people had to be from the Cove, his erstwhile neighbors.

Koestler had never seen any of them before, especially down here on the first tier.

A small, prissy individual stepped up to Koestler. At least the man didn't have a fistful of papers in his hand.

"Mr. Koestler, I am Eugene Harrold and I'm the president of the Paradise Cove Home Owners Association. We need to have a long talk, Mr. Koestler."

Help.

By the time Koestler finally entered his home, an hour had passed and Mrs. Tenharkel across the street had long since gone to bed. The show in Koestler's front yard had come to a dramatic end with his eviction. The angry villagers had just forced the mad scientist to take his monstrous behavior elsewhere. He had thirty days to vacate his condominium.

Koestler tried to plead his case but neither Harrold nor his boyfriend or any of his neighbors on the second and third tiers of the Cove would hear of it. Koestler's identity and his occupation had been made public and that meant that Koestler had lied about his job on his membership application. Technically, he still *was* an actor, but the residents of the Cove weren't persuaded. Besides that, strange vehicles had been seen prowling the streets of the Cove and a valued security guard had been gassed because of him. Add these factors to Koestler's wild nights with his many girlfriends, and you had a formula for dissatisfied neighbors. Koestler was told to take his troubles and his lifestyle elsewhere.

Once inside, Koestler made himself a drink and sagged onto his couch. The television wasn't on. No music played. The wall screens were operating with their colorful ads, but Koestler forced them out of his mind. How had all this come about? He and his team had captured Bob Thermopylae. They even had located Bob Thermopylae's main Chuckle factory and confiscated what Thermopylae said was the bulk of his worms. They also had Thermopylae's crew under arrest. And the last Koestler heard, there was even talk in Congress about lifting the quarantine because of the Thermopylae take-down. He and the rest of the Protean Set should have been hailed as heroes. But they weren't. Especially him.

Instead, he was being probed, followed, sued, harassed, investigated, and now evicted.

Then there was little Stephie. Koestler had secretly hoped that the imp would have been in his living room watching her Chalk Mules show. For the last month her presence had actually been the only stable factor in his life. He had four children of his own, but given the vagaries of his life, he had never grown up with them. His marriages had always broken up before the kids arrived, and when they did arrive, they came as virtual strangers. The courts did their best to keep him away.

He guessed that the Housing Association had gotten to Stephie's mother and told them what a bad man Koestler was and that little Stephie should stay away from him.

"System," Koestler said aloud.

"SYSTEM ON," said a female voice from the ceiling.

"How much money do I have left?"

The System said, "SPECIFY WHICH ACCOUNTS: ALPHA, BETA, DELTA, or GAMMA."

The Alpha account, the one which his wives tapped through their own sub-accounts, was his main savings. It was in arrears and garnisheed. He knew that. Delta and Gamma held his tax-sheltered annuities and his police pension which no one could tap into, not even himself. The Beta account was his secret, untouchable account. It was for emergencies only.

"Beta," he said, not wanting to hear the answer.

"TWO HUNDRED AND FIFTY DOLLARS AND SIX CENTS," the System said.

"Good Christ," he muttered.

They had even gotten to that. Whoever "they" were.

It was time to go for a drive.

The evening fog drifted over the Pacific Coast highway as Koestler's Sensei headed north. He passed a Batmobile heading south in a hurry. It shot by too fast for him to see if Batman was inside or some Chucklehead who *thought* he was Batman....

Bankruptcy was a possibility. Brad and Vivian Swiss owned a small group of apartments in Santa Monica. He could hole up there for a while. They might even cut him a deal. Since he still had his job, he could provide for himself and his many wives, but only marginally. The bottom line was, however, that he would no longer afford his high-maintenance girlfriends or any of the other luxuries that came with the higher salary of a Protean. That life was over.

But that created another problem and it made his palms sweat. If the LAPD eventually disbanded the Protean Set and remanded him back to being a mere detective or demoted him to street cop, would he get a concomitant lower salary? Koestler could feel the sweat ooze from the pores of his skin and his heart began to palpitate.

He was in very deep shit.

Fortunately, Sal Briscoe was at home. The *Fairuza Balk*, at her mooring station, hovered majestically just a few feet over the water, her long lines illuminated by every light in the strange vehicle. Since Briscoe, by law, was prohibited from flying the *Fairuza Balk* at night, he nonetheless left its lights on all night for the passersby on the Pacific Coast Highway to see.

It was a spectacular attraction. Koestler parked his Sensei in the empty lot behind J. J. Moon's surf shop. But as he descended the wooden steps that led to Briscoe's house, he found Sal sitting on a wooden bench by the pier admiring the display the *Fairuza Balk* made. Briscoe clutched a cup of hot chocolate that wafted its curl of steam into the night.

He stood for a moment in silence, staring up at the brilliant airship. He then said, "I'm in trouble, Sal."

Sal Briscoe, swathed in Arctic gear and high leather boots, turned away from his fantastic toy. Briscoe's furred collar riffled in the breeze. "You knew it was bound to happen," the big man said. "Your past was going to catch up with you sooner or later."

"Karma," Koestler muttered. He zipped his own jacket against the cold and thrust his hands in his pockets. His heart still raced, his forehead beaded sweat. He felt as if he was having an anxiety attack.

"Explain this to me, Sal. I pay my bills, I pay my taxes. I keep all my accounts up to date. And I catch a major bad guy. Then suddenly I'm being audited, followed, and sued. It's a statistical impossibility that all of it should happen now. I think someone's out to get me."

"Maybe you're out to get yourself," Briscoe said.

Koestler glared at Briscoe. "My life's a little different, Sal. It's not like yours."

Briscoe nodded. "You told me a story once. You were ten years old and you beat up an eight-year-old girl. In case you *don't* remember it, it was the very *first* thing you told me about yourself when we met."

Koestler couldn't remember the exact occasion when he had told Briscoe about Vicki Celeste, but lately he could think of nothing else *but* Vicki Celeste.

But who was out to get him? It couldn't be Lieutenant Dunhill or anyone else in IAD. Despite his faults, Dunhill wasn't a stupid man. Besides that, he didn't think Dunhill had contacts with the IRS. Squealers themselves were often audited.

This was more than just someone squealing to the IRS and his ex-wives. It was certainly too calculated to be a retributive gesture from some crew he had taken down.

The two walked along the deserted dock bathed in the luminance of the indomitable airship. Briscoe appeared as if he'd just been reading Koestler's dismal thoughts. "So what about that little girl?" he asked.

"I didn't beat her up, Sal."

"You punched her in her mouth and cut her lip. She fell down and hurt her head."

"I was just a kid. I didn't mean anything by it."

"I'll bet that's not what *she* thinks," Briscoe said.

Koestler stood at the mooring lock for the *Fairuza Balk*. All of his problems seemed to diminish before the enormity of the airship...and what he had done to Vicki Celeste. The beautiful little girl with long red hair had only come over to play in his back yard.

He caught himself mid-thought. *Beautiful.* The word had appeared in that description and he now realized that the brutish ten-year-old had found little Vicki *beautiful*. He had never thought about it until now.

"Jesus," Koestler whispered. "What did I do?"

"I don't know, old friend," Briscoe said. "But whatever it is, you're paying for it now."

"In spades," Koestler added.

TWENTY-ONE

THE FOLLOWING DAY KOESTLER got something of a break. A woman from the municipal courts downtown called Koestler to tell him that his Bailiff was going back on-line precisely at eleven that morning. Koestler was to be forewarned because the sign-in could be quite startling. She wanted to make sure Koestler wasn't a brain surgeon or an ambulance driver in the midst of some crisis. The sign-on could have catastrophic consequences.

However, the nice lady from the courts did mention that something had been amiss with Koestler's link to the Bailiff system but, by law, could not disclose the exact nature of that particular malfunction. While he would be cleared of any charges of tampering with his Bailiff at his end, it still did not explain *how* the system went off-line or *who* had caused it to do so.

Even so, this meant that it had been a coordinated attack, timed to the break-in of his home.

So Koestler prepared himself. Since he was on administrative leave, he could now concentrate on his stalkers. He called his many wives and asked them—*begged* them, actually—not to dip into their accounts for at least forty-eight hours. He was honest and more forthcoming with them than he had ever been, even when married to them. He wasn't acting or lying. He meant it.

However, his next series of phone calls were much less positive. He called the IRS and they told him that they, indeed, hand-delivered all kinds of notices to scofflaws. But those were often deemed special cases. As it was, she said that their computers—massive Eidolons—did not make mistakes. Their computers were indefatigable, invincible and, if provided the precise information, infallible.

Eidolons. Koestler had never heard of them before his recent troubles began, but they were starting to surface quite a lot. Someone, he realized, was after him and that someone might have access to Eidolon computers.

So Koestler armed himself with a new Face, reconfigured his Sensei into a Plymouth junker and tucked his Clobberer into its shoulder holster. He set out to discover who was pestering him and why.

Koestler leaned over the desk of the manager of the Wells Fargo bank where Maria Coontz kept her account. He did it in such a way as to expose the butt of his Clobberer in its shoulder holster. He had just come from a successful foray over at the ChemSolar bank branch where Arlene Palfrey's account was kept. He hadn't gotten Arlene's account settled, but he did get the bank to admit that something fishy was going on. They discovered that Arlene's account had indeed been tampered with, and tampered with from the outside. Koestler left them making desperate phone calls to the home office. The Wells Fargo branch where he kept Maria Coontz's account was only down the street. A pattern was beginning to emerge and he didn't like it.

Koestler said, "I can have the California state bank examiners here by three o'clock this afternoon and my lawyers here by four. If you guys don't play straight with me, I'll have you strung up by your heels."

On his belt his badge hung like a golden tongue.

Hank Carrew was the manager of the Wells Fargo bank branch. He was a big man who wore expensive suits. But judging from the look on his face, Koestler could see that Mr. Carrew wasn't used to being confronted in this, or any other, matter. Carrew was virtually speechless.

"Last week," Koestler began, "I had over eighty-two thousand dollars in a special account monitored by the municipal Bailiff system, all for my ex-wife, Maria Coontz. The money is no longer there and I did not remove it nor did she. I want to know what's going on."

"I can assure you, that—" Carrew stammered.

"I don't want your assurances," Koestler said. "I want you to locate the problem *and* the person who caused it. I'm not leaving here until I get some results."

"All right, Mr. Koestler," Carrew said. "Please have a seat."

"My wife's name is Maria Coontz," Koestler said, sitting at the chair. He spelled Maria's name and gave him her account number. Carrew began typing the information into his computer. Two of Carrew's associates, a man and a woman, were now standing at the door.

Koestler added: "Several days ago the account was drained. Completely. My wife says she had nothing to do with it and *I* certainly had nothing to do with it. I don't think it's a simple banking error, either. I have two other accounts at other banks and it's happened to them as well."

The secretary and the vice president, who were standing in the doorway, were joined by two other office workers. Quite a crowd had gathered. Koestler felt like he was again on stage.

When the screen brought up the information Carrew sought, Carrew looked puzzled. "You still have the money, Mr. Koestler."

"What are you talking about?"

Carrew swung the screen around. "You transferred all the money from your account here to your account in the Cayman Islands."

"*What?*"

"Your account in the Caymans," Carrew repeated.

"That's ridiculous!" Koestler stammered. It was almost funny. "I don't have an account in the Cayman Islands. I don't even know where the Cayman Islands are."

"Not according to this," Carrew said, pointing to the screen.

The line, glowing in bright yellow on the blue screen, indicated a massive withdrawal of $84,013.18. There was, however, no indication who or what agency had authorized the request.

"I did not make a wire transfer of *any* account," Koestler said.

"Let me see this," said the woman at the door behind Koestler. She moved to Carrew's side with some authority. She had severe black hair and very black eyebrows and smelled of cigarettes. She examined the screen. She then said, "It's true, Mr. Koestler."

"I did *not* do this," he reiterated.

"Somebody did," said the woman.

One of the other men walked over to examine the screen. Carrew said, "This is Pete Pulborough, detective," he said. "Pete's our accounts troubleshooter."

Pulborough nodded vigorously. He was in his late twenties but looked much older. He had the agitated mien of a hyper-alert rodent...or someone who drank far too much coffee.

Pulborough pointed to the screen. "We have several safety protocols that would prevent any unauthorized individual from getting at your wife's account, Mr. Koestler. But the money went out and was accepted. You *do* have an account in the Caymans."

Koestler thought about this. "Then it's an account that someone set up for me."

"And that could be trouble," the woman with the eyebrows said.

"How so?" Koestler asked.

"The Caymans are where a lot of people in the U.S. hide their money from the IRS. Usually in the form of bogus companies or small incorporations that can't be traced."

Pete Pulborough nodded. "But your account is in *your* name and that's the weird part."

"What's weird about it?" Koestler asked.

The squirrely Pulborough said, "The only reason for anyone to set up an off-shore account is to hide money. That's why they do it in dummy corporations. But yours is in your name and that makes it *very* easy for the IRS to see whose account it is."

And Koestler was already in trouble with the IRS. "Then I was set up," Koestler said.

"It looks like it," Carrew said from his chair.

"How can I find out who did it?" he asked.

"You can't," said the woman with the eyebrows.

"Can I get that money back?"

Carrew nodded. "Certainly. We can initiate a wire-transfer immediately to reestablish your account here for your ex-wife."

"But that doesn't get the IRS off your back," Pulborough said. "No way."

"Why?"

Pulborough said, "Because it'll look like income to the IRS. I'd say they're already alert to the deposit in the Caymans and are pulling your file as we speak."

"I *am* being called in for an audit," Koestler admitted.

"That could be it," Pulborough said.

"Then how can I convince the IRS that I didn't set up an overseas account to hide my money?"

"That's what lawyers are for," said the woman with the eyebrows.

Mr. Carrew added, "Whoever it was, though, had to have been familiar with our codes and our programming procedures as well as those in the Cayman Islands."

"But we do none of that here," said the woman.

"Where's it done?" Koestler asked.

"San Francisco. We just do banking here. Only Pete here knows how to do any real programming at this branch."

"But you know," said a younger man standing in the door. "It *could* have been someone who knows how to deal with our computers. I mean the actual hardware, not the software."

"What kind of computers do you use?" Koestler asked.

"Eidolons," Carrew said.

"Eidolons," Koestler said. "The other banks use Eidolons *and* so does the municipal court system."

They looked at Koestler, not following him on that last remark. So he clarified it. "I'm on their Bailiff system. I have an implant and I talked with them this morning. They use Eidolons as well."

Pulborough then added, "I know the IRS uses Eidolons and so does the FBI."

Mr. Carrew looked at Koestler. "Do you think someone at one of those places has targeted you for some reason?"

"I'm already being targeted by the IRS," Koestler said. "But they're just reacting to something someone's told *them*. No. It's someone else."

"But why pull money out of your wives' accounts?" the woman with the eyebrows asked. "What about your personal accounts? Do they still have money?"

"Barely," Koestler said. "But the way things are going, it might not last for long."

"Then you'd better get a lawyer," the woman with the eyebrows said, this time somewhat softly.

Koestler felt marginally better when he left Wells Fargo. At the very least he could now establish for the courts that he had nothing to do with the drained accounts, that all along he had been acting responsibly. But that still left unexplained the people and reasons behind the thefts.

Standing in the parking lot before his junker, Koestler scanned every parked car in the lot and across the street in search of Stealth vehicles or suspicious persons who might be eyeballing him, for he knew that he *was* being watched.

At that moment, the phone at his belt rang. He answered it.

"*Hey, cowboy.*"

It was Brad Swiss.

"Better be good news," Koestler said. "I could use some."

"I don't know about that, but I've just left Bert Bender at UCLA."

"And?"

"You remember that girl who got zapped in her dorm the night we took down Bob Thermopylae?"

"Carol Langley. I spoke to her father and we got the guy who sold her the Chuckle. Why?"

"Bender told me that she came out of her coma about an hour ago. I was in for a post-operative check-up and ran into him. I think he's called her parents already."

Koestler stood beside his Sensei in the bright sunlight thinking. Just like Bob Thermopylae, she came out of her coma.

"*You there, cowboy?*" Swiss asked.

"I'm here."

"*Well, I thought you'd be interested,*" Swiss said.

"I *am* interested. Look, Bender's set up a hospital hotline to gather information about other cases of hypothermia around the country. Do me a favor and tell him to notify us when other victims come out of their comas."

"You think that's happening?"

"Bob Thermopylae came out of his and I'll bet you dollars to donuts that Billy Styvesant's awake as well. He's at the Aaron Stively Medical Center in Culver City."

"*Hmm,*" Swiss mused. "*That's possible.*"

"I could use your help on this, man."

Swiss hesitated. "*I know. But this is the best I can do right now. And then there's Lilly, you know.*"

"I know. She's worth it. Just make that call to Bender and I'll keep you posted on what comes from this." He hung up.

Koestler slid into his junker and recalled the Face he wore the day he met Alex Langley and his wife at the Cleargreen Apartments. He then pointed his vehicle west and headed for the UCLA Medical Center.

TWENTY-TWO

IN HER OFFICE AT EIDOLON TECHNOLOGIES, Christine Myrland fumed. She desperately wanted a cigarette but couldn't afford the time to step out onto the lounge balcony for a smoke. She had just made a discovery, the implications of which baffled her and this bafflement had apparently over-ridden her body's addictive impulses.

At her desk, she had three flatscreen monitors facing her. She also had before her a long print-out taken from a recent analysis of Eidolon Rex. Taken together, the data suggested something she couldn't explain.

She had explained them to security chief Michael O'Mara and, for as little as he understood, *he* found them peculiar. Myrland had called O'Mara in when she had made the discovery because he was interested in all things pertaining to Alex Langley as well.

A gentle tap sounded on the door and both O'Mara and Myrland looked up. Cecilia Garwin entered the room.

"I got your message, Christine. What's all the fuss?"

Garwin quietly closed the door, blocking out the sounds of a small platoon of soldiers marching by. They were just changing the guard at the intersection just down the hall.

"I found something very strange in my analysis of Rex's base programs," Myrland said in a husky voice. She must have smoked four hundred ciga-rettes in the last forty-eight hours in her efforts at rattling loose some an-swers from Detective Rory Koestler's life. Nothing seemed to be working on that front, however.

"What have you found?" Garwin asked, concerned.

Michael O'Mara looked up from the print-out. "It looks like Christine's found evidence that Alex Langley might have sabotaged Eidolon Rex," he said tersely.

Myrland said, "We've found an anomaly at a very basic programming level, something our initial damage scans didn't find."

"I don't understand," Garwin admitted.

And Myrland said, "Rex uses a unique programming language, which Alex and I wrote. I wouldn't have made a mistake like this. Only he could have done it."

"What, specifically, did he do?" Garwin asked.

Myrland took a deep breath. As much as she admired Cecilia Garwin and respected her rank, the Eidolon Board rep was *not* a computer scientist.

There was no way she could broach technicalities to the woman, at least insofar as Garwin would understand them. She said, "I think Alex planted lines of code below Rex's subroutines. Disruptive logic schemes that sabotaged Rex's cognitive processes. They slipped past me. But they're definitely the source of Rex's catastrophic malfunction."

Garwin was wearing a brown suit and pants outfit that gave her a military bearing. She frowned heavily and said, "Christine, I thought you were working on your teleportation theories. You know Alex is already under review for Rex's strange disappearance. The Board needs you to focus on the teleportation angle right now. Which is what I *thought* you were doing."

Myrland glared at her. Sometimes the woman could be *so* dense. "What do you think I've been doing these last three days? I just came across this"—she tapped one of the flatscreens emphatically—"by accident."

Garwin countered. "You haven't *been* here for three days, Christine. If you'd let this Koestler person go, you might get some work done."

Myrland stood up. She was easily seven inches taller than Garwin. "Since we can't risk Rex running through the same programs with Koestler's name—the same programs that made Rex disappear—I've been trying to find out on my own who Koestler is and what connection he has to Eidolon Rex. But *everything* I do here is about Rex *and* the teleportation project."

"Then what's this about Alex?" Garwin asked, clearly impatient.

"I found several clusters of code in the main operating system that only Alex could have written," Myrland said. "I know they're his because they are the same operating codes he used in programming Telemon Ajax over at Tuttle Systems five years ago."

"Can you prove that?" Garwin asked, crossing her arms.

"I might. If we subpoenaed Santos Avionics we could get the specs Alex and I drew up for Telemon Ajax. I'm sure someone's got them somewhere."

"That would happen only if it involved litigation of some kind," Garwin said. "I don't think their lawyers would yield them without a fight."

Myrland said, "If that's what it takes. Alex and I were the programmers at Santos Avionics. These lines of code are *exactly* the same sequences we used. I'd recognize them anywhere. But when I came here, I made damn sure that I wouldn't make the same mistakes on Eidolon Rex. I rewrote the new sequencing codes from scratch. They were not like these."

She indicated the long print-out O'Mara was leaning over.

She went on, saying, "But when I saw *these* sequences, I knew that only Alex could have written them. They're the *same* codes that were in Telemon Ajax."

Garwin seemed momentarily speechless.

Myrland sat back down. "Here's the wrinkle. As you know, Telemon Ajax melted down. But part of him *did* vanish, just like Rex. There's *something* here"—she indicated the flatscreens with a nod—"that apparently *does* cause teleportation."

Garwin now looked confused. "I thought you said Rory Koestler made Eidolon Rex disappear. Did Koestler's name appear in his subroutines?"

Myrland shook her head. Sometimes talking to Cecilia was like talking to a seven-year-old. "The subroutines are all lines of computer code. It's not specific to any name. These routines allow the computer, *all* computers, to operate whatever software is placed over top of them. It's all mathematics and programming logic."

"The point is," Michael O'Mara interjected, "these subroutines point directly to Alex Langley. Only *he* could have written them."

"Then what about Rory Koestler?" Garwin asked.

"Koestler's name was merely the trigger for Rex's disappearance," Myrland told her. "We have yet to understand how the two are connected. The discovery of Telemon Ajax's codes here was just an accident. That's why I called you in."

Garwin thought about this. She then said, "Did Telemon Ajax disappear because of Rory Koestler's name?"

It was Myrland's turn to blink. She looked up at Michael O'Mara then back to Garwin. "I don't know that," she admitted. "We never did a damage assessment on Telemon Ajax. We thought he merely suffered an overload of some kind. Certainly what was left was impossible to take apart. He was all fused, melted."

"The Ajax computers were supposed to go in the new B-5 bombers," O'Mara said. "They would have been about the size of Rex, right?"

Myrland nodded. "But when McDonald-Douglas canceled their contracts with Santos Avionics, the company folded. I left immediately and started looking for another job. But Alex stayed. He was one of the very last to leave Santos Avionics."

"Maybe *he* did the damage assessment on Telemon Ajax," Garwin said. "Maybe he knows something."

"Maybe he brought it here," the ever-suspicious O'Mara added.

"Then perhaps bringing our lawyers in on this would be a good idea," Garwin finally admitted.

"I say we should have a long talk with Alex," Myrland told them.

Garwin said, "Alex has taken the day off. He's picking up his daughter from the hospital at UCLA. She's apparently able to come home."

"*That's* convenient," Myrland said.

"I wouldn't be surprised if he never came back," O'Mara groused.

"Why wouldn't he come back?" Garwin asked. "His wife's already here. She's overseeing the transfer of their things to their new quarters in the alpha compound. I saw her this morning, in fact."

Myrland looked up at O'Mara. "I'd make sure that Mrs. Langley doesn't leave the lot, under any circumstances. She can tell the Army haulers what to bring from her home. But I think she should be kept here."

O'Mara nodded. He then left the room.

Garwin watched him go.

"Don't you think that's a bit extreme, Christine?" she asked.

"The Chinese are marching west," she said. "And every one of them is carrying an atomic grenade. This project is too important to the security of the United States and I'm going to use every means possible to get some answers."

When Garwin had left, Myrland picked up her phone and engaged its scrambler. She then dialed Trent Andreesen who was in Los Angeles dogging their evasive detective.

The connection came alive with Andreesen's voice. "Christine. I was about to call you," he said.

"Where are you? Exactly," she asked.

"I'm heading north on San Vicente Boulevard following our primary subject," Andreesen said. "He's on the move again. At least I *think* it's him. It looks like he's got a dozen disguises, but we've got a tracer in his vehicle, which we found out is a MetaMorph. I've got a man tracking down the plates registered to the LAPD for the vehicle, but that's assuming they're registered to the LAPD. If they're registered with him or some other civilian, it'll be more difficult to track them down. But that's how Koestler's been eluding us."

She didn't care about that. "How far are you from the UCLA Medical Center?" Myrland asked, reaching for her cigarettes and lighter.

"About twenty-five, thirty, minutes. Traffic's light. Why?"

"Slight change of plans," she said.

"But Koestler's up to something. We found out that he's been put on departmental leave and he's headed somewhere in a hurry. I can't let him go."

"We've got to bring Alex Langley in first. We can follow Koestler later," Myrland insisted.

"What about your secondary target? What about that part of the plan?" Andreesen asked. "Are you still going to go through with it?"

"Yes. It's all set."

"Who—"

"Never mind," she said. "What you don't know can't be traced back to you in case anything goes wrong. But it may be our only trump card with Koestler if we can't learn anything from him directly."

Andreesen sighed audibly at his end. *"Jesus, Christine. I can't talk you out of this?"*

"No," she said, cigarette dangling in her mouth. "It's done. And it's necessary. In the end we're going to have a technological breakthrough that will protect us from our enemies and send us to the planets. In this case the end does justify the means."

"All right, then," Andreesen said. "Is there anything else?"

"Just bring Langley in."

She hung up.

She then left her office and walked to the lounge where, on the open-air balcony, she would be able to smoke. And think. She had a lot on her mind.

The lounge, it developed, was empty, though there was a young Army private guarding it. She saluted him by hoisting her right hand with the cigarette lighter. He got the idea. She walked through the door and headed right for the balcony.

She was relieved to see that no one else was out there. She had no desire for human company at that moment. She certainly didn't want to exchange inanities with anyone. What mattered to her now were the millions of lines of code that she had discovered in Rex's subroutines. They had come from Telemon Ajax and they *only* could have gotten into Rex by Alex Langley's hand. There was no other explanation.

She lit up and inhaled deeply on her cigarette. She *had* him. He was history at Eidolon Technologies. Nothing could come between her and the articulation of a genuine theory of teleportation.

Adrift in thought, she heard a sound behind her. She turned to see a figure in a shining green uniform and steel helmet emerge from the wall in a muzzy blue light.

Cold suddenly suffused every molecule of her body. Her cigarette dropped from her stiff fingers as she fell onto a small coffee table. The table flung the ashtray at the other end into the air and it came down with a resounding crash.

This caught the attention of the young Army guard inside who was standing watch over the lounge. He came to see what all the noise was about.

Otherwise Myrland would have been out on the balcony all day, practically frozen solid.

The last thought in her head was a memory, the sound of her father's voice as she and girlfriends raced off in a car they had stolen from one of their boyfriends: *One of these days, Christine, one of these days....*

TWENTY-THREE

KOESTLER DROVE HIS SENSEI, now a sleek, sand-colored Hyundai with fresh plates, down San Vicente Boulevard, taking a more circuitous route to the UCLA Medical Center. He did this partly to see if anyone was following him. It also gave him time to think through his situation.

As he went, Koestler saw the legacy of Bob Thermopylae everywhere. Chuckleheads and masquers lined the streets, all of them thoroughly lost. But this would soon end, he knew. Bob Thermopylae's worms were now in the hands of the Army and Bob himself was in the slammer, singing like a canary. The Chuckleheads of L.A. were soon to be extinct.

But it wasn't over yet. The player attacks were related in some way to Bob Thermopylae, but Koestler hadn't figured out just how just yet. It didn't help matters any that a fax sheet had just dropped from his dashboard from Kip Dixon. On it was a list of seven more hospitals nationwide reporting new cases of the sudden hypothermia. One hospital was in Great Britain, the first overseas. The attacks were spreading.

Koestler eased his disguised vehicle into the public parking lot of the UCLA Medical Center, heading for the main entrance. He had arrived not a moment too soon.

Alex Langley's car was parked in the hospital's sheltered drop-off zone. The door to the passenger side was open and the lid to the trunk had been popped open as well. A small suitcase waited on the sidewalk near the rear bumper, Carol Langley's things.

Koestler saw the squat, balding Langley standing in a rumpled suit and loosened tie in the doorway as his daughter was escorted in a wheelchair by a giant black male nurse wearing hospital greens. Though clearly awake, Carol Langley still appeared shaken from her ordeal. She also had the look of a world-weary, middle-aged woman now, not the ebullient twenty-one-year-old she was supposed to be. The pallor of her skin was that of sickly mushrooms.

"Dr. Langley!" Koestler called out, jogging up to him.

Alex Langley had just placed his daughter's suitcase into the trunk of his vehicle. Exhaustion was written all over the man's face.

Koestler reached the sidewalk. "I'm sorry to barge in on you like this, but I need to ask you and your daughter some questions before you go. If you don't mind."

The large male nurse who had escorted the Langleys to their vehicle considered Koestler with extreme hostility. He stepped forward, like a nightclub bouncer, to intervene.

Koestler took out his badge. "I'm a cop," he said. "Go away."

Langley turned to the nurse. "It's all right, son. We can take it from here. Thank you."

The male nurse glowered at Koestler, then headed back to the center, leaving Carol Langley in her wheelchair, which, apparently, they were taking with them.

Langley stood beside the open trunk. "How can we help you, detective?"

Carol Langley watched the two men from her wheelchair.

"Didn't you tell me that you worked for Eidolon Technologies?" Koestler asked. He put away his badge.

"I'm the project director there," Langley said. "Why?"

Koestler said, "I have direct evidence that the city's Eidolon computers have been tampered with. Their security features have been broken into or penetrated somehow, but I don't think it's being done by anyone within those agencies or by a lone hacker on the outside."

"What computers specifically?" Langley asked, interested now. "I mean, where are these computers?"

"The municipal court system, for one. Several different bank branches in Santa Monica also have the same problem. They use Eidolons as well."

"Are they networked?" Langley asked.

"I don't think so. They're separate institutions."

Langley passed a thick-fingered hand over his bald pate. He seemed more exhausted than his daughter as he thought this through. "Mr. Koestler, are you asking me if all these Eidolon computers have been penetrated in an attempt to cause *you* harm?"

Koestler jerked his head back slightly, surprised. "You know about this?"

Langley scanned the entrance area of the medical center. With people coming and going, with nurses and attendants helping people into and out of their vehicles, it could have been a hotel instead of a hospital. Langley looked squarely at Koestler. "What I'm about to tell you is privileged information, Mr. Koestler. But we're having some problems with our main computer at Eidolon Technologies in Simi Valley and one of our experts believes that *you* are the cause of those problems."

"Me?"

Langley took a deep breath. He had come to a decision. "About two weeks ago, while we were running several million programs at the same time, our main computer…malfunctioned."

"What do you mean by that?"

"It disappeared."

"Excuse me?"

"It vanished. Into thin air. I was there, but didn't see it myself. But my colleagues did. And we're still trying to figure out what happened. But Eidolon Rex was gone for about twelve hours, then it came back."

"I still don't get it. What does this have to do with me?" he asked.

"When Rex returned, our main programmer did an analysis of the factors common to the programs Eidolon Rex was running at the time he disappeared. Your name emerged as the only common factor in his disappearance. It came up in hundreds of thousands of separate programming tasks Eidolon had been given by tens of thousands of state, local, and federal agencies."

Koestler didn't think such a thing was possible. "There's got to be some mistake. How could my name make a computer disappear?"

Langley shrugged and hitched the belt of his pants. "At the moment, no one knows. But this programmer of ours, a woman, is determined to find out. We can't risk Eidolon Rex disappearing again, so she's called on friends of hers who happen to be in very high places to smoke you out. She's Senator Myrland's daughter, Christine Myrland, and she thinks you're some sort of national security threat."

"That's preposterous."

"Of course it is. But your name *did* come up. There's no mistaking that."

The day was bright and sunny, rare for that time of year. The wind balmy and clean, thanks to the presence of a nearby Eliminator tower. And far to the west and very high in the sky the *Fairuza Balk* hovered out over the Pacific Ocean. Just an ordinary day in Paradise.

Langley closed the lid to the trunk. "I wish I could tell you more, Mr. Koestler. But there are real issues of national security involved and I can't go into them. But I will tell you that I'm completely opposed to what Christine's doing. Personally, I think she's a loose cannon. But there are some technological ramifications here that could be very important and those I *am* interested in."

"But you think she's the person who's been tampering with the Eidolons at city hall?" Koestler asked.

"Christine can manipulate any Eidolon computer anywhere in the world from her *desk* at Eidolon Technologies," Langley said. "For all that, *I* can do it from *my* desk."

"Would you be willing to tell this to the district attorney?"

"That I can tamper with Eidolon computers?"

"No. That Christine Myrland's the one who's been doing the tampering."

Langley nodded, if slowly. He then said, "Everyone at Eidolon knows Christine's after you. We even have a woman who sits on the Eidolon Board who's in on it. You could take them all down. The Board, the Army, everybody."

For the first time in days Koestler felt his spirits lift.

"In fact," Langley went on, "I was in on one meeting where the FBI and the NSA were present when Christine suggested that they investigate you. We could indict them, too."

"What about the IRS?" Koestler asked.

Langley nodded. "This Eidolon Board liaison, Cecilia Garwin, told me later on that Christine called her father, Frank Myrland, to see if he could pressure the IRS to get to you."

"This had to be before her father was shot," Koestler said.

Here Langley looked puzzled. "Shot? We weren't told that he was shot. He got drunk on the balcony of his townhouse and passed out. He nearly froze to death."

Koestler shook his head. "That's not the real story. We don't know exactly what's going on, but whatever happened to Frank Myrland is the same thing that happened to your daughter here."

Carol Langley had been silent through this. She said, "The senator was engineered. We both were engineered."

"Who told you that?" Koestler asked.

"The man who slowed me down." Carol Langley's voice was dry, hoarse. The words seemed individually phrased, spoken with some care.

"Are you talking about Borax?" her father asked. "The drug dealer?"

"No," his daughter said. "It was someone else."

Koestler faced Langley. He said, "What we know is this. All around the country people are being put into extreme hypothermic comas by an unknown group of assailants. We don't know who they are or why they're doing what they're doing. But I've personally seen them at work. Twice up close. I think your daughter was the victim of such an attack."

Alex Langley's brow furrowed with worry. "Carol was *shot?*"

Koestler nodded tersely. "We don't know what kind of weapon it was. But the same thing happened to Frank Myrland back east."

"But *why?*" Alex Langley asked.

"We don't know that, either," Koestler said. "But we're trying to find out. However, *I'm* being harassed by this Christine Myrland and I can't get any work done."

Despite his exhaustion, Alex Langley had suddenly taken on a look of profound determination. "Well, I can help you there. Christine's impeding *my* work as well."

"Daddy," Carol Langley then said from her wheelchair. The two men looked over to where Carol Langley was sitting. "Who's that?" she then asked.

At the far end of the parking lot, facing a turn-off to the main boulevard beyond, sat a Stealth vehicle. A parabolic listening antenna on its hood was focused on them. It was the *same* Stealth vehicle Koestler and Amber Leone had spooked outside the Highwayman Restaurant.

Nonchalantly, Koestler turned to Langley. In a low voice, he said, "I'm going to contact the district attorney and tell him about our talk today. We'll need an affidavit with everything you've just said in order to stop this woman. But right now, get your daughter into the car and get out of here."

"I don't—" Langley started.

In a lightning-fast action, Koestler spun around on his heel and raced toward the Stealth vehicle as fast as his feet could carry him. He had fifty yards to cover and he had to cover it quickly.

Fortunately for him, his eavesdroppers were sitting with their vehicle's engine off. The few seconds it took for the driver to start his car were enough for Koestler to close the distance between them. He wasn't going to let them get away this time.

The vehicle came alive, its rear tires smoking as it shot backwards, in reverse. The driver then swung the car into a roaring one-hundred-and-eighty degree spinabout and aimed for the exit.

But Koestler was close enough.

From his jacket just beneath his right armpit, he pulled out a roll of Susan B. Anthonys. Normally one would do the trick, but here he needed the weight and momentum of the whole roll.

He wound up and threw the entire roll of Susan B. Anthonys at the fleeing vehicle with all his strength.

His aim was good. The roll dropped in a powered arc, falling in the street in front of the Chevy, setting free its one hundred coins. They flashed silver in the late afternoon light.

The vehicle soared right over them. As it did, the one hundred anti-gravity discs engaged. The car suddenly lurched in the air and did an ugly somersault. It came crashing down loudly, rolled a couple of times, finally settling on its roof. By then, the coins were dead, their energies spent.

There was no need for Koestler to run now. The folks in the vehicle weren't going anywhere. Koestler pulled out his Clobberer, armed it, and walked up to the wreckage.

Koestler found the driver, upside down, blood oozing from a nasty cut on his forehead. The man was unconscious, draped with the remains of his quickly deflating airbag. Koestler didn't think he needed Clobbering.

The man on the passenger side was very much conscious and was struggling with his seat belt, trying to untangle himself.

Alex Langley had walked up to the wreckage. He seemed to recognize both eavesdroppers.

"Mr. Koestler. That woman I was telling you about?" he said.

"Christine Myrland."

"Yes," Langley said. "These are friends of hers."

Koestler looked at the distant Eliminator tower sucking pollutants from the air above Los Angeles. He then pondered the wreck in the street.

"Well," he said, "Looks like we're starting to make some progress."

TWENTY-FOUR

"DO THESE GUYS HAVE NAMES?" Koestler asked Alex Langley, standing beside the wreck.

The driver of the overturned vehicle had a gash on the top of his head that was going to need medical attention. He was now awake and crawling out of the driver's side window. Shattered bits of glass fell from his shoulders like diamonds, dancing onto the asphalt.

"I don't know who he is," Alex Langley said, referring to the driver. "But that's Trent Andreesen. He's with the NSA, so I assume the driver is, too."

Andreesen squirmed on his back, struggling to extricate himself from his side of the car. The suit he wore had been torn in a dozen places.

Andreesen finally gained his feet and his right hand went into his coat for his gun.

But Koestler had his Clobberer in the man's face before Andreesen could draw his weapon. "I wouldn't," he said.

Koestler removed the man's weapon and gestured to both men. "You two. On the sidewalk. Sit!"

"You don't know how much trouble you're in, Koestler," Andreesen snarled as he lowered himself to the sidewalk. "You've assaulted two federal agents and destroyed a government vehicle. And now I can nail you for illegal search and seizure *and* illegal detention."

"Whatever," Koestler said.

Several individuals who had just emerged from the UCLA Medical Center had gathered on the sidewalk to see what was going on. A white-coated intern was now on his way over. His coat flared out like two white wings.

Not letting his eyes leave his two captives, Koestler addressed Alex Langley. "What kind of computers does the NSA use?"

"Of course. They use Eidolons," Langley said. "The NSA bought our top-of-the-line model four years ago. You can thank Christine Myrland for that."

"I see."

"And the NSA has also been watching you. Also thanks to Christine Myrland," Langley added. Andreesen had stone-cold blue eyes. He glared at Langley from where he sat. "You've just violated your national security oath, Mr. Langley. You're going to jail for this."

Alex Langley did not seem bothered by the man's threat. To Koestler, Langley just seemed spent, exhausted by all the tomfoolery generated by this mysterious Christine Myrland.

Koestler peered down at the two NSA agents. "Look, friend. I don't think the NSA charter allows you to harass decent Americans." Koestler then leaned over the man. "And since when does the NSA carry *guns*? Do you have a permit for that thing?"

Andreesen simply glowered at him.

The intern with the white coat finally came up to the site of the over-turned car. "Is there anything I can do here?"

Koestler gestured to the two agents sitting on the hard asphalt. "These men need medical attention. They're both under arrest, however."

The medic appeared stymied, not quite knowing what to do. Koestler's expression told him that Koestler did not want the intern around. At least for the time being.

"All right. I'll get a stretcher."

The young intern hurriedly ran back to the entrance of the UCLA Medical Center.

Overhead, a newschopper drifted into the vicinity. This was followed by an anti-gravity Eye. The Face Koestler wore was the one Alex Langley was familiar with, not his default Face. Therefore, whatever appeared on the six o'clock news wouldn't be traced back to him.

Now, if he could just keep his name out of the papers.

"Down on your stomachs. Both of you," Koestler said.

The two men complied.

From his belt Koestler pulled out two plastic handcuff-cords and deftly tied the two NSA agents.

He turned aside to Alex Langley. "You'd better get on out of here."

"And get a good lawyer while you're at it, Langley!" Andreesen said, face-down in the street.

Off in the distance Koestler heard sirens. But these were fire trucks. Someone had apparently put out a 911 call. No doubt the local police had also been alerted to the fracas.

But what Koestler needed was his own people on the scene, friends, not foes.

He pulled his phone from his belt and buzzed Edwardian Rux.

"*Rux here,*" the captain responded.

"This is Koestler. I've just taken down two men who have threatened me. The Westwood police are about thirty seconds away, but I need you here to back me up. I've also got proof that several individuals have tampered with city hall computers and that they've broken into the computers of several banks and stolen money. The two guys I've got here are linked to them."

"*Where are you?*" Rux asked.

"UCLA Medical Center," Koestler responded. "I also want an arrest warrant drawn up for someone named Christine Myrland. She lives in Simi Valley. She's the mastermind. We're going to have to bring the FBI in on this. She's—"

"*Let the Westwood police take care of everything. You can do more good here than there,*" Rux said. "*Come on in and tell me what you've got.*"

Koestler stood stock still, his Clobberer in one hand, his cell phone in the other. The sirens were getting louder, heading their way...and Koestler was thinking.

Rux didn't sound right. His voice had been almost musical—the beguiling actor, not the stern cop. Rux never spoke that way unless others were in the room with him. That meant that something was amiss.

"Hold on, captain," Koestler said. "I've got another call coming in."

Which was a lie. He put Rux on hold and speed-dialed Brad Swiss.

When Swiss answered, Koestler asked, "What kind of trouble am I in?"

"*Jesus! Where the hell are you?*" Swiss said in a hushed whisper. Lilly must have been nearby.

"I'm at the UCLA Medical Center with some bad guys. I just called Rux. He's acting funny."

"That's because the FBI's after you. Word is that you've kidnapped somebody. They came by the house about half an hour ago. Lilly's freaking out."

"They came to your house? Why?" Koestler asked.

"I'm your best friend and they thought I knew where you were."

"If they come back, don't tell them anything."

"I don't plan to."

Koestler switched back to Captain Rux. "So who the hell am I accused of kidnapping, captain?"

"Detective, you need to come in."

Then a new voice came over the line. Someone down at headquarters *had* been listening in. It *had* to be the FBI. "*You harm that little girl and you're dead meat, Koestler.*"

"Who is this?" Koestler demanded.

"Groppenbacher, FBI. We don't know what you're up to, Koestler, but bring Stephanie Kost back to us unharmed and we might go easy."

Koestler couldn't have been more shocked. "*What?* Little Stephie has been *kidnapped?*"

"*You ought to know,*" Groppenbacher answered.

"Wait. You think *I* kidnapped her?"

Koestler was still trying to grasp the notion that Little Stephie had been kidnapped at all.

But, then, he *hadn't* seen her for a couple of days.

"*And what's this about a one-billion-dollar ransom?*" Groppenbacher blasted. "*Just who do you think you're dealing with here? the* Kennedys? *We'll crucify you, Koestler!*"

The Bad Mans had got little Stephie.

Standing behind Koestler, Alex Langley cleared his throat. He had not gone back to his car as Koestler had told him.

"Did I overhear correctly that someone's been kidnapped?" Langley asked.

Koestler nodded. "A little girl in my neighborhood. They're trying to pin it on me." Koestler then read something in Langley's face. "Do you know anything about this?"

"Langley!" Trent Andreesen shouted from the sidewalk, his voice muffled somewhat by the rough concrete.

Langley ignored him. "Yesterday, the whole southwestern wing of Eidolon Technologies was shut off from the rest of the complex. Then a special helicopter landed there. I remember Christine saying that she would do just about anything to get you to reveal whatever it was that made Eidolon Rex disappear."

"There's nothing to reveal," Koestler stated flatly. He still held the cell phone with its open line.

"*I* know that. But Christine's convinced everyone at Eidolon that you're the center of some sort of vast conspiracy that made our computer disappear. I think Christine might have kidnapped the little girl."

Koestler stared at the two NSA men lying on their stomachs in the street, their wrists wrapped in stiff nylon snares.

"What do *you* know about this?" Koestler said, dropping to one knee beside Andreesen.

"Bite me," Andreesen said resolutely.

Koestler stood up. Sirens were everywhere, but traffic had been blocked by the gathering crowds, so Koestler had a few seconds' advantage. He holstered his Clobberer and his phone, which automatically broke the connection to Edwardian Rux.

"Get away from here as fast as you can," Koestler said to Alex Langley. "We'll worry about the affidavits later."

Langley retreated to his vehicle where his daughter was waiting. Carol Langley had closed the trunk and gotten into the car on her own. The wheelchair was now abandoned on the sidewalk.

Koestler then took out a Spitwad from his belt and crushed its brittle shell, just enough to activate it. He flung it at Andreesen's feet. It exploded into a brownish goo that expanded to the size of a medicine ball as it mixed with the air. It glued Andreesen firmly to the sidewalk. Unless they had the right kind of solvent—which Koestler guessed they did not—the police and fire personnel would have a hell of a time freeing the man. They would be here for hours.

Koestler ran back to his Sensei and when he left the scene by the only available exit, he threw a console switch and several spiky caltrops fell from his bumper. Police cars, fire trucks, and any other pursuit vehicle would have their tires blown out if they tried to follow him.

Several had. And several did.

Koestler knew that his home in Paradise Cove would be watched by everybody from the FBI to the Los Angeles police, from Mrs. Tenharkel to little Stephie's fearsome *au pair* Erendira on the third tier. As Koestler lost himself in the streets of Westwood—he went through a car wash and morphed his vehicle again—every friend and acquaintance he had was probably now being interviewed by the FBI. This would include Sal Briscoe. Undoubtedly the FBI would be searching the nooks and crannies of Briscoe's magnificent vessel, the *Fairuza Balk*, for either Koestler or the missing five-year-old.

What Koestler needed was a safe house, someplace no one would think of to come looking. He needed time to plan his next move.

As the afternoon waned toward evening, Koestler drove his Sensei, now configured as a sensible '22 Subaru with Oregon plates, north on the San Diego freeway, over the hill to Sherman Oaks. That late in the day the traffic was heavy and it was easy for Koestler to hide from the highway patrol or the Eyes of the LAPD that were roaming the skies. They couldn't be everywhere in a city of forty million, and that was to Koestler's advantage.

After a while, Koestler found a particular street in Sherman Oaks and the one house where he knew that, for the time being, he would be safe. The courts had ordered him long ago to stay away from his three ex-wives, regardless of circumstances, or he would go to jail. Rux knew this and undoubtedly wouldn't think of looking for Koestler at Maria Coontz's house in Sherman Oaks. If Rux never thought of it, so, too, the FBI. No one would think he would turn to one of his wives at a time like this.

A Jeep SUV was in the driveway and the lights of the house were on inside. This brought Koestler an infinite sense of relief. Maria's place had a sense of *home* about it.

Maria answered the doorbell when Koestler rang.

"Hi," Koestler said sheepishly.

Maria just stood there, speechless for several seconds.

Koestler had on his default face and the expression of sincerity he wore was absolutely real. "I'm in a little bit of trouble. I need your help."

Maria's dark hair was longer than Koestler remembered, and she was a bit heavier, but she was still beautiful.

"What kind of trouble are you in?" she asked hesitantly. "Gang trouble? I won't have you bringing gang trouble into my house."

Behind Maria in the living room came the sound of cartoons. *Chacmools.*

"No, it's not gang trouble," he said. "Can I come in? I don't want to be seen."

Maria, still skeptical, stepped aside.

Koestler eased past her, moving into the foyer of the house that, technically, he still owned.

Maria confronted him and spoke in a low voice. "Why are you here?"

They both were whispering now, not waning their young son, Elric, to hear what was being said.

"I'm in trouble with the police. And the FBI."

"What?"

"They think I kidnapped a neighbor of mine, a little girl. But I didn't," he said. "I swear I didn't."

Maria seemed to believe him and relaxed a little. She then said, "What about our bank account? Did you straighten that out?"

"That's part of it," Koestler said. "But, yes, I did straighten it out. Or it will be in a couple of days when the smoke clears."

"What does *that* mean?"

Koestler took a deep breath. "Someone who knows about computer systems has drained all my bank accounts, including yours. I've gotten the banks to reinstate the lost funds, but right now, I need to lie low. I've got to figure out who's doing this to me and get them to stop."

The mix of emotions in Maria's eyes told him that some part of her had accepted what he was telling her.

Suddenly in the hallway appeared a little boy. He had brightly-dyed red hair and was dressed up as Batman's Robin. He had a long, yellow cape and swung a lasso with a Batarang on the end of it.

"Hey, small size," Koestler said. He lowered himself to one knee. "How are you doing?"

Elric walked up to his father, his face brightening. "Daddy!"

Holding his son awakened something deep inside him that he had thought had long ago died.

"You're getting big," Koestler said, looking at him. "Someday you'll be as big as me. Maybe bigger."

"Are you going to live here now?" Elric asked in a very musical voice.

Koestler rose to his feet. "I'd like to, but I don't think I can."

"Why?" Elric asked with a frown.

"Because I'm a policeman and I don't want you or your mommy to get hurt."

"Are you like Batman?" Elric asked, swinging his lasso with its flapping bat.

"Sometimes."

"I can be Robin!" Elric then turned and ran with a squeal back to the living room and the Chalk Mules.

"Get ready for dinner," his mother shouted after the boy. "And turn off the television!"

She then faced Koestler. "Have you eaten?"

"I haven't eaten all day," Koestler said.

"Well," she said, "come on in and have dinner and you can tell me about all the trouble you're in."

Koestler almost wanted to weep.

TWENTY-FIVE

THE FOLLOWING MORNING KOESTLER had a vision. It happened while he dressed for the day in the spare bedroom of Maria Coontz's Sherman Oaks house after Maria had left for work and Elric had caught his bus for school.

As it turned out, the FBI had come in the night to see if Koestler might have gone there to hide. Young Elric was long asleep and Maria, ever the actress, steered the surly agents away with her natural charm and grace. To put icing on the cake, she also expressed her open hostility toward her ex-husband, telling them that if that son of a bitch ever darkened her doorstep she'd have the police there in a New York minute. They were not to worry.

What the FBI did not know, however, was that Maria Coontz was a former, and very able, actress. Koestler would forever be in her debt.

After Maria had left for work, Koestler ate a breakfast of instant eggs, instant toast and instant coffee—lots of coffee. After he cleaned up, he watched the news. Several reports of mysterious hypothermic comas were coming from all parts of the country now. From Seattle to Miami, Boston to San Diego, all the news stations told of eyewitness accounts of the attacks that defied credulity. Koestler knew that if Christine Myrland had her way, *he'd* get blamed for them. But all he wanted at the moment was to get little Stephie back. He'd sort through the rest later.

Breakfast over, Koestler stepped into the garage through a connecting door to the kitchen. A long time ago he had left several footlockers in storage at Maria's house. Maria never knew what was in them nor did she seemed to care. Certainly no attempt had been made in all this time to get past the palm-print locks for a look-see. But had Maria examined the cache, she would have discovered an arcane assembly of police weapons that only members of the Protean Set were authorized to use. Koestler had kept them for a rainy day. *This* was that rainy day.

Koestler plunged a mild, timed-release amphetamine booster into his skin and grimly began sorting through the items. Almost everything he needed was there: his thin, Kevlar vest, a Snowball cylinder filled with Snowballs, a Night Drop launcher filled with hundreds of BB-sized Night Drops. He found Pancakes and three energy packs for his Clobberer. There were no Susan B. Anthonys in the cache, but Koestler had stowed away two rolls of Tonya G. Hardings. They would do.

The vision came when he stepped into the kitchen. There, Koestler noticed for the first time the colorful drawings Elric had done in school which Maria had clamped to the refrigerator with magnets of the Chac-mool girls, Rene, Nyei, and Kylie. The stick-figure drawings were of happy boys and girls cavorting beneath a smiling, beneficent sun. They all had bright red hair....

The vision came right at that moment he'd glimpsed the drawings, with the wind outside idly nudging the swings in Elric's swing set back and forth, back and forth. *Red hair.* Vicki Celeste and *her* red hair....

He recalled how Vicki only wanted to play in his sandbox that afternoon during the summer of the Little Ice Age, the Winter Summer. She liked the large set of swings Koestler's father had built for him and his big sister, Rebecca. In fact, it had been Rebecca who had invited little Vicki to come over and play.

Koestler had ignored them both until Rebecca went inside the house to do something and Vicki came over to play with him. Was it because little Vicki seemed so happy that day? Was it because she was Rebecca's friend and not his? Or did he do it because he really *was* a shit and hated flirty little girls?

All he remembered was that he got up and punched her in the mouth, knocking her backward out of the sand box, where she hit her head on the ground. She had started to cry and away ran home. She never came over again after that and eventually she and her parents moved away from Canoga Park.

Strangely, Koestler's memories of his life seemed to begin with that one moment of childhood brutality; all else before that time was nebulous and vague. It was as if he had only then come awake to his life, stunned by a sudden infusion of guilt and shame from that single event.

Now, another little girl was in jeopardy because of him. And while he couldn't undo what he had done to Vicki Celeste, he could undo whatever it was that provoked Christine Myrland to abduct Stephanie Kost from the safety of Paradise Cove. In fact, it changed him. Turned him into something he had never felt before. Forced him to see something he had never seen before *in* himself. He saw his path. He saw what he must do.

So he made a Face, retrieved his Sensei from an apartment complex on the other side of the block where the FBI would never have thought to look, and drove west on the Ventura freeway in the clear bright air of the San Fernando Valley. He then turned south on Las Virgenes which wound west and south through the Santa Monica mountains. This was the back-door route into the community of Malibu.

Koestler had a back-up plan wherein he needed Sal Briscoe, the only other person in the world he could trust. But he would have to be careful. The FBI would be watching Sal Briscoe's seaside lair and the *Fairuza Balk* itself. He would have to be very circumspect.

Koestler changed his Face and the configuration of his vehicle—as well as the license plates—several times before he got to the Pacific Coast Highway. He did see two anti-gravity traffic Eyes, but one Eye was watching a forest fire to the west which had sprung up around a giant Eliminator tower. The Eyes did not seem to be searching for him specifically.

When Koestler reached the Pacific Coast highway, he turned west. Minutes later, he could see that Sal Briscoe was not home: the *Fairuza Balk* wasn't at her mooring station and Koestler could not see the bright crimson airship anywhere in sight. Sal had probably cut out after the FBI had interviewed him.

However, Koestler didn't need to get to Sal directly in order to insti-gate his plan. Instead, Koestler pulled into the parking lot of the Moon Dude Surfing Outfitter's Shop, Briscoe's immediate neighbor. Before get-ting out of his car, Koestler checked his Sensei's sensory systems to see if there were any eavesdropping laser pinpricks dancing on his vehicle's metal skin. There were none detected. Nor were there any vehicles in Moon's parking lot filled with FBI agents looking down the steep wooden stair-case at Sal's small seaside home.

Inside the outfitter's shop, Koestler found the venerable J. J. Moon, standing behind the counter. The shop had just opened and there were no other customers in the store and old man Moon was reading the morning newspaper.

"Cold mornin', ain't it?" the sun-baked Moon said, looking up at Koes-tler as he entered.

Koestler had his light coat zipped up clear to his chin. This was to cover his vest and conceal his Clobberer. "Sure is," he said.

"What kin I do for you?" Mr. Moon asked.

Moon was a spindle of a man, a walking, talking mummy of a man. Freckles covered his body and he had the scars of excised carcinomas on his forearms, nose and neck. He lived for the sun and it would probably kill him one of these days.

Koestler pulled his tracker from the clip on his belt and handed it to the old man. "Could you do me a favor?"

"Guess I could," Mr. Moon said. "Depends."

Koestler pulled out his badge to allay any fears he might have had. "It's nothing illegal," he said. "I need you to deliver this device to the man who lives down there."

Moon took the device and turned it over in his hands. It was about half the size of a cell phone. He then looked to see where Koestler had indicated.

"The man who lives down there?" Moon said.

"Sal Briscoe, yes. Tell him that a police detective gave it to you. He'll know what it's for. But get it to him as soon as he comes back."

"The guy who lives there," Moon repeated.

"That's right."

Koestler scanned the shop. Besides the usual equipment for surfers, the shop also carried a selection of clothing and swimming apparel. Koestler went through the racks and found a sleek, army-green raincoat with sheep's wool padding and excellent stitching. The weather was supposed to change to rain later that day and Koestler knew that he'd need a raincoat. He might as well go in style.

"You know that coat's a Zolezzi," Moon said. "Pretty expensive, hereabouts."

He took the coat to the counter. "I'll take it. What do I owe you?"

Moon rang up the purchase and said, "That'll be two hundred and eight dollars and forty-five cents."

Koestler pulled out a money clip and peeled away three hundred-dollar bills. "Keep what's left. For delivering that." He pointed to the tracker.

"For the guy who lives there," Moon said, jerking his head in the general direction of where the *Fairuza Balk* would have been had it been moored that day.

"You got it."

"Okey-doke."

Moon deposited the bills in the cash drawer and softly shut it.

Koestler donned the raincoat, checked his equipment, then went to his Sensei. It was time to visit Simi Valley.

For a pair of prisoners, Alex Langley and his daughter were being given the royal treatment. The day after the two had returned from the UCLA Medical Center, Major Hannel, the supervisor of the military lockdown at Eidolon Technologies, had come to escort Langley and his daughter from their home to Eidolon Technologies personally. He pulled up to Langley's Simi Valley home in an armored limousine and made sure that Langley and his daughter were ready to go.

Carol had slept on the long trip from L.A. Langley worried the whole time that she might have slipped back into her coma. But a quick call to Dr. Bender had informed him that coma victims actually recovered the more they slept. The brain needed time to heal and he thought Carol was going to be all right.

A day later, father and daughter rode alone in the armored limousine, with Carol still bundled up. For reasons nobody understood yet, Carol was still suffering a low body temperature. She was dressed in a pant suit outfit with her heavy leather coat and sheepskin gloves. Sitting beside her, Langley could feel some of the radiant chill she gave off. It was most peculiar.

Carol looked at her father as they pulled away from their suburban neighborhood, a Hummer leading the way and an armored riot-control vehicle bringing up the rear. Major Hannel was in the Hummer, having left Langley alone with his daughter in the back seat of the limousine.

"Why are they taking us to Eidolon?" Carol asked in a soft voice.

Langley smoothed the hair on her forehand, matted from so much sleep. He had told his daughter very little about what had been going on at Eidolon. Or in the rest of the world.

"The government thinks we have some answers to their problems and they want everyone to work on them. They thought it would be easier if all our families were there and we didn't have to go home at the end of the day. You know, like the Manhattan Project?"

Carol stared through the glass partition that separated them from the driver of the limousine. The world outside drifted past them in absolute silence.

"I can help," she said weakly.

Langley smiled at her. She could have been ten years old again. "You're helping already. We're just glad you're okay, glad you're healthy." *Glad you're alive*, he said to himself as a kind of prayer.

The gentle rolling of the limousine down the highway did a lot to dispel the tensions he'd felt working under the baleful stares of Christine Myrland and Cecilia Garwin. But now he could concentrate on his work. And the more he thought about it, the more he realized that it wasn't a bad idea that the Army was moving everyone to one location.

He cradled his daughter, never wanting to let her go. Ever.

Carol stared ahead. "You know what they told me?" she suddenly asked.

"What did they tell you?" he said, humoring her.

She closed her eyes. Her eyelashes were like small brown butterflies, delicate. The limousine had reached the guarded gates of Eidolon Technologies. She said, "They told me that you're the father of time travel."

"Me?"

She nodded. "But I'm supposed to help you."

"How?"

The limousine was now moving through a row of Quonset huts and balloon buildings in the south parking lot.

His daughter held up her thumb and forefinger and said, "By making it shrink."

She had fallen back to sleep by the time they arrived at their quarters.

Strangely, Langley thought he knew what she meant.

TWENTY-SIX

KOESTLER ABANDONED HIS SENSEI in a parking lot of a Ralph's Supermarket up the coast in Oxnard, disguising it as a battered '25 Chrysler Crossfire which no one would think out of the ordinary. He'd seen far too many police Eyes patrolling the Pacific Coast Highway and knew that he was going to have to find another means of travel. The Sensei had far fewer morphing resources than he did. It only had eight possible configurations; he had over a hundred. By now, Rux would have given the FBI the eight descriptions his Sensei could take on and, while that would cause them to look harder, with enough effort the FBI would eventually find his vehicle.

This was only a minor glitch, however. Down the street from the Ralph's Supermarket was an inland anti-gravity bus terminal. Once it attained its cruising altitude five hundred feet above State Route 34, he would be able to avoid any prying Eyes and ride the entire way to Simi Valley in comfort.

In the terminal restroom Koestler drew up a haggard Face, one he hadn't used in years. He boarded the next bus, finding a seat in the rear of the pilotless craft. There had been a private security guard at the Oxnard terminal, but he did not appear to be looking for anyone in particular. He merely sidled along the platform beside the hovering bus, fulfilling his duties…as Rux and Dunhill would be fulfilling *their* duties. Koestler was probably the most sought-after man in the state right now.

Koestler knew that he could have gone to Rux and explained the situation to him. He also knew that in the end Alex Langley would probably finger Christine Myrland as little Stephie's kidnapper and Trent Andreesen as the man who broke into his house. Certainly Mrs. Tenharkel would be able to identify Andreesen's Stealth Chevy as being the one in the Cove the day his condo was ransacked. Rux probably would have understood.

However, Rux wouldn't be able to keep the FBI and IAD off his case. The FBI undoubtedly would place Koestler under immediate arrest on federal kidnapping charges as they looked into little Stephie's disappearance. At the same time, Internal Affairs would be rigorously looking into the matter from their own perspective. Koestler would probably be suspended without pay for the duration and thus his bank accounts would dry up and this would turn his ex-wives against him right when he needed them most.

Then there was Christine Myrland. She would still have to be dealt with. The problem was that Koestler didn't know what this Myrland woman was capable of, let alone what she was after. If she was anything like her father, she could without a doubt cause him all kinds of trouble.

As the bus rose to its cruising altitude and its passengers settled in for the buoyant ride, Koestler activated the television screen on the back of the seat in front of him. Every local news channel was running with the story of little Stephie's kidnapping. POLICE DETECTIVE WANTED IN KIDNAPPING was the lead for one story. RORY KOESTLER—ROGUE DETECTIVE—FUGITIVE FROM JUSTICE were the words plastered across the screen of yet another.

Christine Myrland was doing this, he knew. She'd have the clout, thanks to her father. For Koestler knew that the FBI would never release the details of any ongoing case to the public, not even if they were desperate for leads. Certainly the LAPD would never release the name of one of their detectives to the press, particularly the name of an *undercover* detective. That would be tantamount to a death sentence.

This showed the ruthlessness of Christine Myrland, whoever she was.

Koestler wiped the moisture from the back of his hands, the only real part of his skin exposed to the air. The heavy raincoat he wore and the Kevlar vest with its weapons also contributed to his discomfort. But through the window he saw that rain clouds of a surly gray color were gathering over the Pacific. He was glad he thought of the raincoat.

Koestler pondered the denizens of the anti-gravity bus. Most were sitting up front, but only he and an off-duty soldier occupied the rear of the vehicle. The soldier had short blonde hair and wore a brown beret. His head lolled upon his shoulders as he drifted in and out of sleep.

It was so rare to see soldiers or sailors these days. So he asked himself: *What was a soldier doing on a bus headed east toward Simi Valley?*

The dozing soldier opened his eyes as the anti-gravity bus whipped along at a hundred miles an hour. He looked at Koestler. He noticed the heavy-duty raincoat and saw that Koestler was sweating.

"Nervous, huh?" the soldier asked.

Koestler yielded a wan smile. He plucked at his raincoat. "I may have overdressed a bit."

The soldier sat up and looked out the window. The bus made no noise whatever as it soared along the invisible highway in the sky. "I've never gotten used to these things myself," he said. "They should have wings or something. At least a parachute."

"I hear that," Koestler said.

Koestler covertly glanced at his watch which contained an embedded Sniffer chip. The number 3 on the dial face was blinking. The chip sensed a trace of Chuckle in the air of the bus. The soldier, though, didn't seem a likely user of Chuckle. Koestler couldn't say the same about the other passengers. Bob Thermopylae's legacy was still present.

The bus made several stops as it headed inland. Eventually, it lost most of its passengers except Koestler and the soldier who slept nearly the entire trip. That was fine with Koestler. He had a lot to think about.

Using the computer embedded in the seat before him, Koestler found a street map of Simi Valley. He studied this for a moment, then called up a couple of photographs of Eidolon Technologies. He was a bit worried as to how he was going to get into Eidolon Technologies itself. He could find nothing but public information photographs on the net and these did not immediately suggest a possible means of entry to the sprawling complex.

Then Koestler considered the soldier sitting across the aisle.

He reached into his inner pocket and pulled out what would look to the average person like a candy bar. He broke off a piece. At the same time he held his breath. If the soldier wasn't fully asleep now, he would be soon. And he would be out for quite some time. The candy bar contained a powerful, fast-acting anaesthetic gas.

Koestler held his breath for a full minute, until the soldier started snoring loudly.

Breathing again, Koestler then removed a six-inch rod from a vertical pouch in his boot. He activated the scanning rod and carefully drew it down the young man's face. A horizontal blue reading-line followed the contours of the soldier's face, from his forehead to his chin, from the right cheekbone to his left. The data went straight to Koestler's Face cache in the small computer in his belt. From there it went straight into Koestler's new Face.

Koestler then took the soldier's ID badge as well as the identification papers from his inside coat pocket. Koestler placed the soldier's beret on his own head where its low-level AI chip automatically adjusted the cap to the shape of Koestler's skull.

The bus began its descent to the Simi Valley terminal. Koestler began to get a bit nervous. Loath as he was to admit it, Vincent Dunhill had been right about the Protean Set in at least one regard: The Proteans had never gone undercover in a truly dangerous situation. They had never gone into the Blight. They had never faced the serious cocaine or heroin cartels that ruled much of southeast Los Angeles. For Koestler, most of his duties as a Protean had been a cakewalk, an actor's dream.

Now he was going up against a mysterious woman, the United States Army and God knew what else. Koestler wondered what Dunhill would have to say about *that*.

Still, this was about little Stephie, not Vincent Dunhill or Edwardian Rux or even the FBI. It wasn't even about *him*. This was about little Stephanie Kost who was, right then, at the very center of Koestler's universe.

In the main conference room on the second floor of Eidolon Technologies in Simi Valley, several grown-ups were shouting across a long table at each other. All the while a five-year-old girl in her jammies sat at the other end of the conference table, furiously sucking her thumb and holding tight to her BooBaby. Outside, it was getting dark as heavy rain clouds approached.

Eidolon Technologies Board representative Cecilia Garwin was in a panic.

Garwin had learned only that afternoon that Christine Myrland had "borrowed" the little girl from her home in Malibu as part of a plan to coax the secretive Rory Koestler out into the open. No one could use Eidolon Rex until the mystery of Rory Koestler was solved and this was Christine's last-ditch effort to make that happen.

They had a problem, however. Christine was now in the hospital suffering from some sort of malady that strongly resembled a phenomenon presently affecting thousands of other people across the country, including her father, Senator Frank Myrland. She was in a coma no doctor could explain. But without Christine there to make her case, her machinations now seemed specious, unsound, and dangerous. They certainly were criminal. Now they were in a panic; none of them knew what to do.

"People, this isn't getting us anywhere!" Garwin said, slapping a broad hand on the table, silencing the group. The little girl merely watched with furrowed eyebrows as she sucked her thumb.

Michael O'Mara, tall and spectral, looked pale enough to be ill. He swallowed. "Cecilia, we could just release her. Pin a note on her saying we're sorry. That it was all a mistake. Something like that."

Garwin trembled with rage. O'Mara had known of the plan; she hadn't. "Are you insane? Look at her! She's not an infant! She knows all our names! She even knows where we are!"

Another woman said, "Cecilia, the police aren't going to believe a five-year-old. All we have to do is send her back to L.A. Put her on a floater, like Mike says. She doesn't know who we are."

"You don't have any kids, do you Rachael," Garwin said.

"No," Rachael said defensively.

"Then you don't know how smart they are at that age!" Garwin said, trembling with her fury at the sheer stupidity of the people around her.

"They're not that smart," Rachael said arrogantly.

Little Stephie Kost took her thumb out of her mouth and started with the adult nearest to her on the left and went around the table. "Timothy, Gale, Constantine, Doug, Mike, Meryl, Hal, Ross, Erle, Carson, Rachael, Lucky Dawson and Ce-ci-li-a," she said, pronouncing Garwin's name musically.

Stephie's thumb then returned to her mouth.

"Jesus," someone said. "We're going to jail."

"Did *anybody* tell Christine that kidnapping was a federal offense?" Garwin demanded of the people sitting around the table. "Did anybody even *try* to stop her?"

She glared at Michael O'Mara, their security chief. O'Mara looked away. He was perhaps wondering what Pelican Bay prison was like this time of year.

One man, the "Timothy" sitting next to little Stephie, broke in. He said, "Now wait just a minute, Cecilia. You've backed every move Christine's made. *You're* the one who should have been watching her. Everybody in the *world* is accountable to *somebody*. Even Christine."

"Well, don't tell that to her, Tim," muttered "Gale" who sat next to him. "Not if you want to keep your job."

"It's her father," suggested "Erle." "She's used him as a big stick ever since she came here. We should have muzzled her when we had the chance."

"It's a little too late for that now," Garwin said angrily. "We've got a five-year-old here and we've got to get her back to her family without any of us going to jail."

The door to the conference room burst open just then. People turned around and nearly everyone there gasped.

The CEO of Eidolon Technologies, Virgil Swaitek, stood in the door to the conference room. His white hair was drenched with rain, his raincoat still dripping. He had just come from the parking lot and the conference room filled with his wrath.

"What's this I hear about a kidnapping?" Swaitek demanded. He then spied the little girl sitting at the far end of the conference table. "What's *she* doing here?"

Garwin lowered her head. This was too much. Christine Myrland had consigned them all to perdition. Their careers were over and everyone was going to jail.

Garwin raised her head to speak. Someone had to say something. Darkness fell suddenly. It wasn't merely that the lights went out. Darkness, like a living *thing* filled the room and it was as if everyone there had gone suddenly and thoroughly blind.

"*Hey!*" roared Virgil Swaitek. "*What's going on?*"

From somewhere at the far end of the room, a BooBaby went, "*Boo!*"

And all hell broke loose in Eidolon Technologies.

TWENTY-SEVEN

By the time Second Lieutenant Peter Mateo arrived at Eidolon Technologies, a hard rain was falling. A shuttle from the air-bus terminal had taken Koestler to Eidolon Technologies as the real Peter Mateo snoozed his way back to the Oxnard station on the reverse transit.

Upon arriving at Eidolon, Koestler found a heavy military security perimeter surrounding the sleek buildings and the vast parking lot that made up the complex. His fears lifted, however, when no cornea checks were made when he was taken through the security gate. A guard merely laser-scanned the badge Koestler had lifted from the hapless soldier on the bus. He was then waved through.

Koestler's eyes narrowed as he took the place in. To his left were Quonset huts and other temporary structures. To his right stood the three-story futuristic-looking building that housed Eidolon Technologies. All of it was enclosed by miles of rolled razor wire strung along the top of an eight-foot chain-linked fence.

A soldier made shapeless by his dark-green poncho came out of a nearby building. He had a folded umbrella in his hands. He held it out to Koestler. "Sir. You'll want this, if you're going to walk the perimeter," he said above the crashing rain.

"Thank you," Koestler said, taking the umbrella. The boy ran back to his station.

Walk the perimeter, Koestler thought. *Not a bad idea.*

Koestler proceeded to thread his way through the parking lot, his umbrella fully unfolded. He would be an obvious figure to anyone who happened to see him, so he walked with the authority and purpose of any other soldier on the perimeter.

This would disguise his true reason for walking the perimeter of Eidolon Technologies. His Night Drops. With the mini-launcher in his left hand, he shot off as many as he could, distributing the small, quarter-of-an-inch Drops every thirty feet or so. He even got a few on the roof. As he went, he kept an eye out for possible escape routes from both the building and the grounds themselves.

Koestler watched as a lone VTOL lifted from the north parking lot and disappeared to the east. It had deposited several important crates, and now a group of soldiers in rain slicks busily loaded them onto an electric flatbed that was about to be taken into the building.

Koestler armed his Clobberer and slid the goggles he would need when he activated the Night Drops into the right hand pocket of his raincoat.

He walked up to the group loading the cart. "Let me help you men!" he shouted above the rain.

One soldier looked at him, noted his rank, and smiled. "We could use all the help we can get, sir!"

Koestler set his umbrella down and began loading the crates onto the flatbed. He didn't know what was in the crates nor did he care. He was more interested in the cart itself.

Another soldier jumped into the driver's seat and switched the vehicle's power on. Three soldiers then jumped onto the rear of the flatbed.

Koestler did the same. He shouted to the driver, "Let's get out of the rain, son!"

"Yes, sir!" the driver shouted over his shoulder.

The cart moved out making no sound but a hissing from the tires on the asphalt of the parking lot.

They did not have far to go to get out of the rain. A ramp led up to a large loading dock whose corrugated metal door had already been lifted. An amber light glowed from within, welcoming them.

The cart with its mysterious cargo passed between two taciturn sentries. Once inside, the giant metal door began its descent. No one saw Koestler scattering a Night Drop or two as they went.

Koestler looked around. They had arrived at a modest transfer dock and here, Koestler saw, the going was about to get much tougher. Sentries were everywhere and all seemed very alert. In fact, Koestler wondered if the country was already at war somewhere else in the world and no one knew it but the military, and, specifically, these men.

Koestler jumped off the cart as it came to a halt. The driver got out and for the first time noticed that Koestler's boots were not army regulation. "The CO'll have you in a sling, if he sees those shoes, sir."

"That's all right, son," Koestler said, not knowing if the man was a corporal, private, or a sergeant. Calling everybody "son" seemed the logical thing to do. "I just got called in. They told me to come as is. You know how it is."

The soldier nodded.

Koestler then said, "I better check in."

The soldier turned away, letting Koestler go about his business.

Koestler marched down the hallway, moving deeper into the building.

As he went, he dropped more Night Drops onto the floor. The busy nature of both the soldiers and the civilians he saw told him that the small pellets would go unnoticed.

Koestler followed the hallway as it headed back toward the front of the building. Guards were posted at nearly every corner, but these were just sentries and they seemed to let everyone pass. Certainly they let *him* pass. He got saluted several times.

Koestler found his way to the receptionist's desk that was part of a large foyer. The receptionist, however, was a sober-looking male corporal in crisp Army attire. He also wore a standard-issue .9mm Colt.

Showtime, Koestler thought.

Koestler stood erect before the corporal. He patted his coat pocket, indicating that he was carrying something important there. "I've got a letter for Christine Myrland," he said. "Can you tell me which floor she is on?"

A Night Drop fell from his left hand onto the floor in front of the desk where the young corporal couldn't see.

The corporal's eyes narrowed suspiciously at Koestler. "No one told me that a courier was coming. I need to see your identification, sir. And, of course, the letter."

Koestler looked around at the spacious entry. Halls went to the left and the right. A bank of elevators stood just behind the receptionist's desk. These were guarded as well. From the large right-hand pocket of J. J. Moon's wonderful coat, Koestler pulled out a set of goggles, its two lenses unusually large.

"What are those?" the corporal asked. He made no move nor did he seem particularly alarmed.

Koestler removed his beret, set it on the corporal's desk. He then slipped the goggles over his head and replaced the beret. The corporal reached to his right, to the keyboard where Koestler guessed an alarm button could be found.

"Please don't do that," Koestler said.

"What the hell is this?" the corporal demanded.

The Night Drops activator was just a button on his belt. He moved his coat aside to reach it. As he did, the corporal could see that underneath Koestler's now-open raincoat was no military uniform, just a very strange vest.

The corporal reached for the alarm button, but it was too late. Koestler sent out a signal which activated the hundreds of Night Drops he'd scattered around the facility, inside and out.

Night. Domes of black null-light, each one thirty feet in diameter, rose from every individual Night Drop. The darkness was impenetrable and nothing could make it go away.

"*Whoa!*" the corporal exclaimed, pushing back in his chair. He jumped up, his arms flailing out before him like a blind man whose way had suddenly been lost.

Koestler saw all this through his goggles.

Meanwhile, in the building things crashed, alarms went off, and people started shouting, all awash in a sea of black.

Koestler jumped the desk and grabbed the corporal. He flung him to the floor, then knocked him unconscious with a savage blow to the chin.

Koestler had exactly ten minutes of darkness in which to work.

Koestler swiveled the computer screen around. Typing in Christine Myrland's name, he got a layout grid of Eidolon Technologies.

Second floor. West wing.

Koestler walked over to the elevators where the two sentries were looking around desperately in the preternatural darkness. They hadn't left their posts and were shouting above the alarms.

"Sorry, guys," Koestler said.

He pulled out his Hobble and Hobbled the man on the right first, then the man on the left. The Hobbles whirled around their legs several times, with their weighted ends falling to the ground and breaking open. Glue spilled out and the guards, now down on the marble floor, were there for the rest of the day and well into the night. As they shouted obscenities at him, Koestler kicked their guns out of reach. He removed their belts and flung those out of reach as well.

Another guard came out of nowhere, having heard the two elevator guards shouting out. Koestler pulled out a Pancake, shook it into a rigid disc, then tossed it at the new guard. The Pancake came alive just as the soldier crossed it. The soldier then crashed to the floor, knocked unconscious by the Jupiter-level-gravity tug of the Pancake. Blood oozed from the boy's broken nose.

Koestler stepped into the elevator and pressed the button for the second floor.

Night Drops only had an operative radius of thirty feet. Therefore, some areas of Eidolon Technologies would not be engulfed in the null-field. This would probably include offices and work areas that were located deep inside the Eidolon Technologies building, including the basement.

Koestler lost the beret and pushed the goggles up onto his forehead. He returned to his default face as he did. He didn't want to frighten little Stephie. *Assuming he found her. Assuming he lived.*

He then pulled out his pack of Tonya Hardings and shook out several of the discs into his hand.

The elevator doors opened to clear light. The Night Drops had not reached this far. But beyond the elevator doors were the sound of alarms and people running back and forth, many of them soldiers.

Koestler tossed out several Hardings. He flung several one way, then flung a few more the other. He then activated the gravity stays in his special shoes.

At the far end of the hallway, two soldiers came plunging out of a wall of solid black—the extent of one of the Night Drops Koestler had positioned outside the building. They saw him, saw that he was their possible intruder, and they came running after him.

Koestler pressed a button on his belt and the floor became a brilliant frozen mirror, a sudden ten-micron layer of Teflon slickness. Soldiers and civilians both found their feet flying out from under them. Their feet flew out from underneath them and they came crashing. And when they tried to stand, they couldn't, such was the fantastic slickness of the Hardings. Guns and rifles spun in wild circles out of reach.

Koestler walked past the soldiers, making for the location of Christine Myrland's office, the gravity stays in his shoes acting like cleats.

He pulled out his Clobberer and ran for the west wing. He had to work fast.

Rounding a corner, he came across a group of bewildered civilians. Only one soldier was among them, but he was unarmed. He was a high-ranking officer and it was clear that he was in command there.

"Hey, *you*! Flathead!" Koestler shouted. "Stop where you are!"

But to Koestler's right, where he had not seen, two soldiers then emerged. One of them shouted, "*There he is! Halt! Or we'll shoot!*"

Their rifles came up. So did Koestler's Clobberer. He pulled the trigger and the Clobberer sent forth a stream of brutal energy, immersing them in thunder and violent light. Within the narrow confines of the hallway they bounced back like bowling pins. They were unconscious even before they fell to the floor.

Koestler wasted no time. He turned toward the group of stunned civilians, his Clobberer aimed right at the lone military officer. Behind the group, Koestler saw that a door led to an office beyond. On the door was a name plate that said: CHRISTINE MYRLAND.

But a small woman with short brown hair leapt to one side and slapped a panel on the wall. Suddenly a security panel—actually an entire *wall*—dropped from the ceiling between them. Just as suddenly, a similar wall dropped from the ceiling behind him. Bolts threw in place with the elevator doors, locking them shut.

He was trapped.

Koestler pulled out a small cylinder. It contained several Snowballs. He popped one out and threw it as hard as he could at the security wall that had fallen between him and Christine Myrland's office. He didn't care about the wall behind him. In fact, as long as it was in place, it would keep the guards out of this part of the building.

The Snowball hit the security partition and exploded with a *crack!* sending out a burst of cold at 3 degrees Kelvin, enough to turn the metal to brittle glass. Koestler raised his boot and kicked the wall. It shattered like three-hundred-year-old glass.

Koestler ran up to the group of frightened civilians huddled at the door to Christine Myrland's office. His heart was pounding and he was sweating like an athlete having just run the four-hundred-meter hurdles.

He stuck his Clobberer into the face of the woman with the short brown hair who had engaged the security walls. She was nearest. With an anger he had never before felt, he said, "I'm Detective Rory Koestler of the Los Angeles Police Department and I *demand* that you give me Stephanie Kost *now* or I'll kill every single one of you sonsabitches!"

He shoved the snout of his Clobberer into the woman's mouth. Her security badge said: GARWIN. She stared at him wide-eyed. "Starting with *you*," he added.

TWENTY-EIGHT

KOESTLER KNEW IMMEDIATELY that these people were not made to be kidnappers. They were just civilians caught up in something over which they had no control. To a person they froze, wide-eyed, like deer in the headlights of a madman. One woman swooned. One man clutched his heart and sagged against the wall. Another looked as if he had just crapped in his pants.

Koestler pulled his Clobberer out of Garwin's mouth. At that point, a tall, white-haired man bearing some authority emerged from Myrland's large office.

"Who are you?" the tall man demanded.

Koestler rushed up to him and stuck the snout of the Clobberer on the man's forehead. He pushed the man back against the wall. "Christine Myrland has kidnapped a little girl who is a personal friend of mine," Koestler said. "Give her to me now or I'll kill you." He switched the Clobberer to its highest setting. Everyone there heard its shift in pitch.

A woman Koestler hadn't seen before emerged from the blackness that had crept into Christine Myrland's office. She had little Stephie with her.

Koestler pointed the Clobberer at the new woman. "Are you Myrland?"

"No. I'm—Christine's in the hospital," the new woman said, frightened.

Little Stephie ran to Koestler's side.

The Garwin woman had recovered her poise. She stepped forward. "Christine Myrland's in the hospital. We had no idea she had kidnapped the girl."

Koestler lifted little Stephie and propped her onto his hip, holding her. He had never held any of his own children this way. Now he wished he had. Stephie's warm little body was all that mattered to him in the world.

The tall, white-haired man cleared his throat. He said, "I'm Virgil Swaitek, the CEO of Eidolon Technologies and I can assure you, sir, that no one in my employ would authorize the kidnapping of anyone, for *any* reason, let alone this little girl."

"Then you don't know your people," Koestler said.

"I can *assure* you—" Swaitek continued.

But Koestler cut him off. "Can it, Virgil. You're going to make a phone call. Give me your phone. Your cell phone."

Swaitek pulled out his cell phone and handed it to Koestler. He let Stephie slide down to his side. She stood with her BooBaby and stared balefully at the cowering grown-ups.

Koestler kept his Clobberer aimed at Swaitek as he punched in Rux's number. He knew that Rux and a hundred other officers would be waiting for his phone call.

"*Rux,*" the captain said when the connection went through.

"It's Koestler."

"*Where are you?*"

"I'm at Eidolon Technologies in Simi Valley. I've just rescued Stephanie Kost from her kidnappers. She was taken by a woman named Christine Myrland who is apparently in—" Koestler looked at Virgil Swaitek. "Which hospital's she in?" he demanded.

"Valley Samaritan," the stout woman, Garwin, said. Several people nodded in agreement at this.

"She's in Valley Samaritan and I've got a dozen people standing here who will corroborate this. I want you to call off your dogs. That means Vincent Dunhill *and* the FBI."

He tossed Virgil Swaitek's cell phone to Cecilia Garwin. She caught it and looked absolutely terrified.

Koestler leveled his Clobberer at her. "You seem to know what's going on. Tell my captain *everything.*"

Cecilia Garwin cleared her throat and spoke into the phone. "Hello? Yes. This is Cecilia Garwin and your…friend is telling the truth. The young girl was kidnapped by one of our computer engineers, Christine Myrland. A man from the National Security Agency, Trent Andreesen, was also involved. No…I don't think the NSA's in on it. Yes. The little girl was brought to Eidolon without our knowing about it. Detective Koestler did not kidnap the little girl. Yes…that's right. Here." Garwin handed the phone back to Koestler.

"*Okay, detective,*" Rux said. "*Come in and we'll straighten this out. We'll let the FBI take over at Eidolon. But I want you to come in.*"

Koestler could hear background sounds of quick scramblings and murmured statements that did not suggest to him that anything was over yet. Certainly breaking into Eidolon Technologies—and assaulting several soldiers and civilians and causing all kinds of mayhem—wasn't something easily forgiven by anybody. Internal Affairs would be looking into this for weeks to come and he *still* could lose his job when it was all over.

All that did not bother him, however. Now that little Stephie was safe and Christine Myrland soon to be arrested, he would happily face his accusers.

But he would do it on his own terms. For now, he had to get away from Eidolon Technologies.

"What do you think *that's* all about?" Vivian Langley asked her husband as she stood at the window of their newly-erected Quonset home in the western parking lot of Eidolon Technologies. The structure was really one long room with sound-dampening section dividers creating two bedrooms and a kitchen with a modest living room area remaining.

Alex Langley walked over to where his wife had been gazing out of the rain-glazed window at the strange bubble of darkness that surrounded Eidolon Technologies. Carol Langley sat on the couch behind them with a cup of hot jasmine tea in her hands.

"Looks like Eidolon is experiencing some problems," Langley muttered. "Too bad Christine isn't here to see this."

"Why's it all dark like that?" Vivian asked.

Langley thought about this for a moment. He then said, "That looks to me like a police weapon. Some sort of crowd control device. I think the police are inside the building. I could be wrong." Though he didn't think he was.

Langley's wife, sober for two days now, looked at him. "What would the police be doing here?"

"I'll find out," Langley said. He had a good idea *precisely* what the police were doing there. He opened the front door and faced a curtain of pouring rain. He always liked the sound of falling rain.

Military helicopters, a VTOL, and half a dozen anti-gravity Eyes whipped through the air above the Eidolon building as they tried to penetrate the strange darkness that had settled about the complex. The sounds of gunfire, explosions and breaking glass could now be heard above the clatter of the rain storm.

The black fog did not appear to waver beneath the weight of the heavy rain. And to the southeast, units of army personnel stood helplessly in their ponchos, their guns ready. But clearly they did not know what to do.

Suddenly, a man wearing large goggles and carrying a little girl with a ponytail emerged from the darkness directly in front of the temporary village in the parking lot. The man in the goggles saw Langley standing in the doorway, fully illuminated. He came running over in the rain, the little girl bouncing in his arms.

"I believe it's Detective Koestler, dear," Langley said to his wife who was now standing behind him.

But when Koestler yanked off his goggles, Langley saw that he was mistaken. It was someone else. His expression changed from pleasant excitement to dour suspicion with perhaps even a bit of dread.

Apparently, the soldier saw the confusion on Langley's face and changed *his* face in response. He ran to the sheltered awning over Langley's door.

"Sorry," Koestler said, breathing hard. "I lose track of my Faces sometimes."

"You want to come in? Dry off?" Langley asked.

"Don't have time," Koestler said breathlessly.

"What happened?" Vivian Langley asked, taking the little girl.

"They *kidnapped* me!" the girl said.

Langley closed the door quickly.

Koestler was practically out of breath.

"That black fog out there," Vivian Langley asked. "Did you do that?"

Koestler nodded.

"Come here, sweetie," Carol Langley said, rising from the couch. She bore with her the blanket that was wrapped around her shoulders and surrounded little Stephie with it. Both Koestler and little Stephie had gotten soaked, even though they had only covered about fifty yards of parking lot.

Koestler turned to Langley. "I need a favor," he said. "It's a big one."

"What is it?"

"I need you to get little Stephie to the Santa Monica headquarters of the LAPD. Specifically to Captain Rux. He's my immediate superior."

Langley frowned. He had some business still to conduct with Eidolon Rex, some theories he had been puzzling through in his head. "I don't know if I can get away from here. Besides, I've got—" Langley started.

"*I'll* take her," Vivian said. She had knelt down and lifted little Stephie in her arms, rosy-cheeked and smiling.

This sudden offer surprised him. His wife had for so long been a passive creature due to her chemical pursuits that Vivian's brave offer cast her in a different light.

But Vivian was firm about this. "I can do it. I can drive right out of here and they won't even notice me or the little girl."

"My name is Stephanie!" the five-year-old said proudly.

"Stephanie," Vivian said with a smile.

"Why can't *you* take her in? Isn't that what you came here for?" Langley asked.

"It's a long story," Koestler said. "But I'm in trouble with just about every agency the federal government has, and after today, I'll be facing criminal charges for breaking into your building."

He indicated Eidolon with a jerk of his thumb over his shoulder. "Plus I made some guy crap his pants in front of about twenty people. He'll probably have *his* lawyers after me as well."

The rain rattled above them, dancing merrily on the metal of the Quonset hut. Koestler continued. "No. I've got to find a place to hide where I can mount a defense with my lawyers. But if you get Stephanie to Santa Monica, that'll be the biggest help."

"Couldn't we just turn her over to the local police?" Langley asked. "Wouldn't that be easier? It'd take most of the day to drive back into L.A."

Koestler shook his head. "There's more to this case than I can tell you about right now. It's not just about Stephie or me. It's about—" He nodded at Carol. "It's about the individuals who attacked your daughter. They're striking all over the country and we don't know who they are or why they're doing what they're doing. Hell, for all I know Christine Myrland could be behind it."

"*She is*," said Carol Langley.

Everyone looked at her.

Little Stephie was leaning her head on Vivian Langley's shoulder, sucking her thumb. Her small blue eyes were wide, watching the grown-ups speak.

"That's what they told me," Carol said.

"They who?" Koestler asked.

"I don't know," she said. "They didn't tell me who they were. They only told me what I had to do when I recovered. And that was to help my dad with the mathematics of time travel. But she *is* behind them."

Langley turned to Koestler. "It doesn't matter now, detective. Christine's in a coma herself."

Koestler blinked as if he hadn't quite heard or hadn't comprehended what he'd heard.

Langley went on. "But like I told you yesterday, I'll testify against her in court. So no matter what happens, she'll get what's coming to her."

"I appreciate that," Koestler said. "But it would look a lot better for me if either one of you could take Stephie directly to Captain Rux and tell him everything you know, everything you've seen today. I don't have many allies at this point, except Sal Briscoe. And I know he'll come and get me in his airship. I'll be safe with him. We'll hide out over the ocean until I've got my lawyers lined up in a row."

"Sal Briscoe? Are you talking about the movie star?" Vivian asked.

Koestler nodded. "Yes. But we're wasting time. I've got to get where he can pick me up. And that's got to be as far from Eidolon as possible." He looked at Vivian Langley. "I just need you to get Stephie to Santa Monica."

Koestler gave her one of his cards which had the address to the Santa Monica division on it.

Vivian glanced at her husband and he gave his consent.

Detective Koestler poked little Stephanie in the stomach with a playful finger. "Sweetie, the nice lady here is going to take you home. But the police are going to ask you a lot of questions, and when they do, tell them the truth. Don't make anything up. Okay? And I'll see you real soon."

Little Stephie made a cute "gun" out of her thumb and forefinger and said, "*Shpew! Shpew!*" she said, "shooting" him.

"Nobody will hurt you now," Koestler said. "I promise. But now it's your turn to help me. Okay?"

"'Kay," the little girl said.

Outside the rain had only gotten worse. Koestler changed his Face one more time and buttoned up his coat. He stepped back out into the rain and disappeared from sight. Something, Langley thought, he was probably very good at.

TWENTY-NINE

ONCE KOESTLER USED A PANCAKE to flatten a section of Eidolon's perimeter fence, he took every roundabout route he knew and used up every Face in his repertoire as he made his way into the San Fernando Valley. Evening had by now descended but the rain had not let up.

Koestler had chosen not to leave Simi Valley by going back along State Route 23 or the anti-gravity highway that ran above it. The FBI would have undoubtedly marshaled its forces at various stops along the way. Instead, Koestler went directly toward the San Fernando Valley, traveling east. In fact, riding a simple surface bus, he saw units of the United States Army as well as police race past, heading west, back toward Eidolon Technologies.

Before boarding the bus, however, Koestler had stumbled onto a homeless community living in an alley near the terminal. An exchange of a few dollars netted him enough diverse clothing that he could enhance his physical appearance significantly and throw everybody off, even Rux.

Looking ahead, Koestler next needed a place to hide. He needed a secure location where he could rally his forces. He'd need to contact his lawyer, he'd need to make sure all of his wives were fully informed of his situation before he went up against the FBI, the United States Army and Eidolon Technologies. Captain Rux would take care of Internal Affairs. In fact, Vincent Dunhill was the least of Koestler's worries right now.

Koestler's only real alarm for the moment was the silence from Sal Briscoe. Koestler had tried the signaling device several times, once he had gotten far enough away from Eidolon Technologies, but there had been no response. Either Sal was still out at sea in the *Fairuza Balk* or old man Moon had yet to deliver the signaling device. Koestler kept looking to the west, but the magnificent crimson airship was nowhere to be seen. He would have to hole up somewhere else.

Once in the San Fernando Valley, he changed buses again. He found a bus in Granada Hills which ran the entire length of Balboa Boulevard.

He was glad to get in out of the rain…along with everyone else on the crowded conveyance. The rain's fury seemed to hammer at everything it fell upon and Koestler had never felt so hammered in his life. His body ached from the day's exertions and his default face had begun to emerge because its subcutaneous circuitry was finally giving out. He'd be no good as a Protean for weeks now. But that didn't matter. It would take weeks to sort out the last few days.

Koestler thought about a safe house. He couldn't go back to Maria. If the FBI knew that he had already been there, they would arrest her for harboring a fugitive. She had been a saint to have taken him in in the first place. He didn't want to endanger her again. And he certainly didn't want to show up there wearing a bum's clothing. He reeked of sweat and his skin crawled with a layer of dirt and grime that would probably take an hour to scrub off with a pumice stone.

As for his other wives, they lived on the far side of L.A., a day's travel by bus, and the FBI would probably have staked out their houses anyway.

His only real hope was his sister, Rebecca, who lived in Woodland Hills. No one would expect him to go to her in a time of need. Rux knew—and would have certainly told the FBI this by now—that Koestler and his older sister didn't get along. Their quarrels were almost legendary. In fact, she had punched him once at a wedding reception—hers—when he made a smart remark.

However, Rebecca Carpenter was an MD, a pediatrician whose Oath of Hippocrates meant that she could not refuse anyone in need. Rebecca might have thought of Koestler as a slug, but she couldn't ignore her Oath. And what he needed now was her help, a meal, a shower, some rest, and enough time for Vivian Langley and little Stephie to tell the police that Koestler was not one of the "bad mans" loose in L.A.

When Koestler transferred onto another bus at Victory Boulevard in the valley, he could barely move, he was so tired. The sweat of his clothing had caked and he could feel his skin begin to itch. The other travelers on the bus looked away in revulsion.

When the bus finally came to Woodland Hills, Koestler walked the last half mile to Rebecca's home in the darkness and rain. He rang the doorbell to her large house then sank to his knees on the doormat. He could go no further.

A shrill voice of a youngster sounded out from behind the oaken door to the Carpenter residence. "*Mom! There's a dead guy on our doorstep! Want me to call the police?*"

"*Let me see,*" a woman said.

It was his sister.

At least he had the right house.

The door swung open and Rebecca Carpenter stood in the amber light of the foyer, wiping her hands with a towel. She had apparently just finished clearing the dinner table.

Rebecca Carpenter stood just an inch under six feet and had firm, capable hands. Physically she was Koestler's match and used to knock him around quite a lot when they were younger...much in the same way he had knocked around Vicki Celeste.

"I think it's your uncle," Rebecca said. She bent down to check. "It's him, all right."

The boy, an excitable nine-year-old, ran back into the house and shouted at the top of his lungs, "*Uncle Rory is here! Uncle Rory is here!*"

A herd of children—Koestler had forgotten that Rebecca had four of them—came stampeding in from the living room, yelling at the top of their lungs.

Rebecca flipped the dish towel over her shoulder and helped Koestler to his feet. A mass of children and two barky dogs piled into the hallway to witness the spectacle of their Prodigal Uncle, whom several of them had never seen before in their young lives, being delivered to them by an act of cosmic justice.

"Everybody *back*!" their mother shouted.

They stepped inside and Rebecca closed the door behind them, shutting out the rain.

"Are all these yours?" Koestler asked, water dripping everywhere.

"Mine and Andre's," she said.

Andre Carpenter, Koestler's brother-in-law, came in from another part of the house. He was even taller than his wife and wore a jaunty mustache.

Andre was an architect who designed ocean-spanning bridges.

"Great to see you, old man!" Andre Carpenter said, shaking Koestler's hand.

"Great to be seen," Koestler said.

At the end of the hallway was a vast living room presently cluttered with BooBabies and robot toys. And on the giant wallscreen was an episode of the Chacmools.

A maid came in, saw Koestler, and frowned. She put her hands on her hips. She reminded him of Erendira.

The woman pointed at Koestler. "You want me to feed this man, Misses?" She spoke as if such a task would be enormously displeasing.

"Have you eaten, old man?" Andre Carpenter asked cheerfully.

One little boy shouted excitedly, "We had *cake*! Let's have some more *cake*!" The children ran into the kitchen.

"I'd settle for bread," Koestler said to no one in particular, barely able to stand.

Koestler's sister steered him into the kitchen. The maid started unwrapping the carcass of a turkey.

"What happened to you?" Koestler's sister asked, sitting him down at the dining room table.

"Busy day," Koestler said.

Rebecca wrinkled her nose at the smell. "Tell me this is a disguise, because if you're now a homeless person, I'll break your legs."

"It hasn't come to that," he said. "At least just yet."

Koestler's brother-in-law poured some coffee for him and Koestler took it gratefully.

"I'm all right," he then said. "I was in a major undercover operation when things went wrong. Well, not exactly *wrong*. But I've got about three federal agencies after me." He looked at them. "They haven't been here, have they?"

"Yesterday," Rebecca said. "I wasn't here, but Moira chased them away."

Moira, the maid, was now putting heated bowls of chicken, string beans, and warmed mashed potatoes in front of him. Koestler started to eat. This might be his last meal as a free man.

"Where'd you get those clothes?" Rebecca asked.

"A homeless commune in Simi Valley," he said. "That's how I got away. No one looks at a bum, not even the FBI."

"How did you get here?" she then asked. "I didn't see a car outside."

"Mass transit. All the way."

"Must have cost you."

"About two thousand dollars," he said. "It was all the cash I had on me." It was all the cash he had left in the world.

The children had gathered around the table and were watching in silence, completely blown away that their uncle was there.

"Someday I'll tell you about it," he said. "Right now I've got to get to Malibu."

The food was restoring some of his energy. It was at least enough to keep him going until he reached Sal.

By the time Koestler had taken an invigorating shower and had put on a fresh change of clothing, via his brother-in-law's closet, the rain had stopped. When he emerged from his sister's bedroom, the entire Carpenter family had been waiting for him. It was as if they couldn't get enough of him—at least the kids.

Rebecca herded the flock away. "Scat! I need to talk to your uncle."

"Aw, *Mom!*" they complained. Koestler thought he could hear little Stephie's voice in there somewhere and it almost broke his heart.

"Let's go," their dad said. "Everybody!"

Rebecca moved past Koestler to the end of the hallway. There, she opened a door. "Come on in here for a minute." Koestler followed her inside. "I think you should stay the night," Rebecca said, closing the door. "You look awful and you need to rest."

"I can't," he said. "It's only a matter of time before the FBI come back here. And they *will* come back. I've got to get where I can mount a defense of some kind."

"If you live," Rebecca said.

The room was Rebecca's home office. It had all the accouterments of a physician's office, including autoclave, locked prescription cabinet and devices he did not recognize that were part of her trade.

Rebecca opened a locked door and pulled out an injection gun and several vials of fluid. She set these on the counter and began putting on a pair of latex gloves.

"No shots," said Koestler. "I'm fine."

"You are not fine," she said. "Have you looked at your skin lately?"

"I've been busy."

Rebecca stared at him soberly. Her blue eyes had the same penetrating gaze that Captain Rux's eyes had. "Be straight with me. Are you on anything? Chuckle, Bliss, JJ-180?"

This caught Koestler by surprise. "I'm a *narcotics* detective, Rebecca. I don't do drugs. My girlfriends do, but I don't."

Rebecca frowned. "The fact is you've got cysts and all kinds of debris deposits just under your skin and your lymph nodes are swollen. Stand still."

And before he knew it she had shot him in the neck with the first of three vials of innoculants. Each one stung, but only mildly. Each left a hickey the size of a dime.

Rebecca put everything into the autoclave. The gloves she tossed into a small incinerator. "I've also given you a full B-complex of vitamins, some anti-oxidants to give your immune system a boost. But I *strongly* recommend a week in detox, Rory. You also have to quit smoking, stop drinking, and you've *got* to quit whoring around. Too much sex, especially for men, throws the immune system way out of whack."

"But I don't…"

"Yes, you do," she asserted, stopping him cold. "You always have. You don't eat right, you don't exercise, and you don't have your blood cleaned regularly. I've *never* seen such bad skin in my life."

"If you knew what I've been up against, you wouldn't..."

"Cry me a river," Rebecca said. "You're on the verge of nervous collapse. And if you don't change your ways, I'm going to be giving you a liver transplant soon. The human body can take only so much. Yours has about had it."

"I'll give it some thought," Koestler said.

They walked back out into the hallway. "If you aren't any better the next time I see you, I'll take you to Betty Ford *myself.*"

"Can the kids come along?" he quipped.

"I'm serious, Rory," she said. "You're a wreck."

They passed by the living room where the kids were sitting in front of the giant wall screen watching Rene, Nyei, and Kylie carving out lines of energy. Koestler hoped that little Stephie was home by now, with her mother and Erendira, sitting before her own television screen, eating her own bowl of ice cream, safe and sound forever.

Koestler could already feel the chemicals Rebecca had injected in him going to work. Or perhaps it was just the prospect of getting to the *Fairuza Balk* where he could begin the next stage in his life. Sal was a health nut. He had a wide range of workout equipment on board his fantastic ship. Koestler could clean up there while his lawyers went to work.

"Um, listen. I could really use a car," he said to his sister.

Andre Carpenter reappeared in time to hear this. He pulled out a set of keys. "How about the Bullet?" Andre asked his wife.

They walked through the foyer to the large, five-car garage, where farthest from them was a brand new Volkswagen Bullet sports car.

"Just don't wreck it," Rebecca said. She put her arm around her husband's waist. "It's Andre's."

Koestler nodded. "Thanks. I'll have this back to you tomorrow, the next day at the latest. I only need to get to Sal Briscoe's house in Malibu."

His sister and brother-in-law looked at each other. "Sal Briscoe?" Andre Carpenter said.

Rebecca frowned. "Rory..."

"I know. I know. But he's a good friend. He'll help me out of this mess. At least I hope he will." He hefted the keys. "Thanks for all you've done."

Awkwardly, he gave his sister a peck on the cheek, something he didn't recall doing ever in his life. To hide his slight embarrassment, he quickly, and very assertively, shook Andre Carpenter's hand.

He was then in the Volkswagen Bullet and roaring out into the night.

He was about to begin the fight of his life.

THIRTY

KOESTLER WASN'T FIVE MILES FROM his sister's house heading toward Malibu Canyon when the sickness struck him.

The rain had long since stopped, but an eerie fog had moved across Interstate 101 as Koestler headed west. The fog, however, had now taken on a vile, brownish hue. It looked like a chemical residue of some kind or the aftermath of a spot fire in the Santa Monica Mountains. He couldn't understand why the Eliminator towers hadn't removed it from the air already. They were normally so efficient.

At first he thought that something was going wrong with his vision. Then he started coughing violently. He pulled the Bullet over onto the freeway's shoulder. It was the injection his sister had given him. He started to tremble uncontrollably. He started sweating. It occurred to him then that perhaps he *should* have stayed the night at his sister's house.

After the coughing and the trembling came waves of nausea. He clutched the steering wheel feeling the tremors wrack his stomach. And his skin crawled. He wrestled out of his brother-in-law's light coat and flung it onto the seat next to him.

Koestler stared out ahead at the traffic passing him by. It seemed inordinately thick for that time of night. He looked up. But overhead, where the anti-gravity lanes ran invisibly through the sky, not a single vehicle could be seen. This he found odd. There should have been hundreds, if not thousands of freight pods going both north and south with their automatic pilots.

Unless the anti-gravity lanes were being blocked far behind him and on up ahead. Perhaps the FBI and the local police had set up roadblocks and were lying in wait for him.

Koestler ventured back into traffic. He did not know if he was going to make it to Sal Briscoe's house. Despite Rebecca's medications, he knew he was close to a complete collapse. His original plan was to take a back route into Malibu, taking State Route 23 that wound through the Santa Monica Mountains. But now that seemed too extravagant, too roundabout.

He'd have to risk taking Malibu Canyon Road. If there was a roadblock somewhere along the way, he'd deal with it when he got there. He still had his Clobberer.

Koestler came to the turnoff to Malibu Canyon off Interstate 101. His headlights could barely penetrate the brown cloud that filled the sky. Yet the Eliminator tower before him was all aglow with its avoidance lights twinkling red and yellow in the night.

Normally the air around it would be swirling toward its hungry electronic cilia. That wasn't happening now. Instead, the tower was lowering into the earth, slowly disappearing.

He forgot his sweating palms, he forgot the fist of nausea in his stomach, he forgot his skin that itched with a vengeance. Incredibly, the glittering needle dotted with its constellation of warning lights sank slowly.

And off in the distance, every Eliminator tower flanking the freeway began doing the same. They simply eased down invisibly as if the very earth were soaking them up.

Koestler slowed his brother-in-law's vehicle to the barest crawl. He didn't know that Eliminator towers *did* such a thing. And no wonder the air was so brown. Someone down at city hall had turned them *off.* But why? The towers had been up for eight years now and they were the main weapons against the smog and industrial-borne toxins that had for so long polluted the Los Angeles skies. They were world wonders.

A small pesky insect started crawling on Koestler's forehead. It must have been in the car all this time. Koestler slapped it where it landed and felt its hard chitin crumple. The darkness inside the car prevented him from seeing what it was. He hoped it wasn't a spider. He was terrified of spiders.

Koestler eased down Malibu Canyon Road, relieved, nonetheless, to be out of the city.

But he wasn't.

He looked up to the canyon walls. Astonishingly, tier upon tier of homes and apartments lined the mountains that rose up to either side of the road. He was staggered by the vision. He hadn't driven this road in at least a year, but what he remembered of the picturesque road was nothing compared to *this* monstrous landscape. He couldn't even *see* the mountains for the layering of the buildings piled one upon the other. And down below, to either side of Malibu Canyon road, were restaurants and shopping malls, their garish light filling the night with ugly iridescence.

"I don't believe this," Koestler whispered.

Another insect ran up one of his pant legs. "God*damn!*" Koestler shouted as he slapped his leg as hard as he could.

But now he was sweating so badly that the moisture was actually removing debris caught up in the pores of his skin. He drove onward, following the curving Malibu Canyon road now with the windows up and the air conditioning on so no more insects would attack him. He couldn't see them, he couldn't hear them. They had to be nearly microscopic, smaller than gnats even.

But that didn't help. The car was infested with them and they were all over his skin now. They ran under his shirt, swam down his back. He squirmed in his seat, pushing back with all his strength, hoping to crush as many of them as he could.

Light from the mountainside city filled his car with a wash of color. He could have been driving through downtown Hong Kong, or Singapore, even Tokyo. The smog moved as if it had become a living organism. The city lights wavered through its brown curtain.

"Where are the damn Eliminator towers?" he shouted.

How could the city fathers allow such an abomination? Malibu Canyon was *famous*. How could it have devolved into *this* in just over a year? And in between the glittering businesses were shanties, some propped up on wobbly poles. Cooking fires drifted like ghosts in the air.

Koestler raced down the road until he finally emerged to see the Pacific Ocean. Though it was dark, he could see it by the plethora of ships and floating buildings suspended on its surface, each one agleam, riding above its shimmering reflection.

Koestler then came to Pepperdine University, a sight he saw nearly every day of the year. Koestler jerked the wheel of the Bullet over and stopped his car. He got out of the car and stood with his mouth open. He couldn't believe what was before him.

"What the hell *is* this?" he asked, astonished. "I was here this afternoon!"

When he had begun his roundabout journey to Simi Valley, he had driven up the Pacific Coast Highway, past Pepperdine. Its clean, streamlined buildings, its manicured lawns and proud statuary had become a Malibu fixture. But in one day it had become a metropolis all its own. Buildings—they were really cities in their own right—rose up over five hundred feet. They were linked by walkways and transit tubes. A monorail eased in and out of the sleek structures.

Then there was a giant neon megalith that blinked off and on.

PEPPERDINE...UNIVERSITY...PEPPERDINE...UNIVERSITY....

The school now looked like Caesar's Palace in Las Vegas. Yet, that morning Pepperdine was a pastoral vision. It had no monorail, no neon sign.

Either Koestler was going crazy or something terrible had happened to the world in the last twelve hours. *And where had the Eliminator towers gone?*

Koestler jumped in his brother-in-law's vehicle and sped down to the coast highway. He knew that Sal Briscoe would be able to explain what was happening.

The *Fairuza Balk* wasn't at its mooring station and Sal Briscoe's home was nowhere to be found. Something else had taken its place.

Koestler's vehicle snarled into the graveled parking lot of the Moon Dude Surfing Outfitter's store. Its back lot led down to Sal Briscoe's oceanside lair. Or it had twelve hours ago.

Where the *Fairuza Balk* was normally docked at her mooring station, there was now a restaurant. It was called THE HAPPY CLAM and it was all aglow in red neon, the same color as the *Fairuza Balk*, and it stretched nearly three hundred feet out onto a pier of steel pylons. It was all lit up and quite dazzling.

Koestler knew that in a hallucinatory state a person *could* perhaps mistake The Happy Clam for the *Fairuza Balk*. But what about Sal Briscoe?

Koestler heard footsteps in the parking lot behind him and he spun around, his Clobberer out. J. J. Moon, working late, had seen Koestler pull in.

The old man gave Koestler his homing device. "I thought you'd want this back. Sal Briscoe don't live there no more. *Used* to. But not no more."

"I was just *here* a few days ago," Koestler said. "I was in his *house*. And his airship was moored right there! Right there where that restaurant is! It was *huge*! You couldn't have missed it!"

The old man frowned. "Son, I think you've got one of them funny bugs in you. Lots of 'em, from the looks of it. My son was afflicted a few years back."

He pointed to Koestler's arm. In the soft glow of the amber parking lot lights, Koestler saw the skin of his forearm rippling.

"Jesus!" Koestler cried out.

Both of his forearms had it. The writhing and ripples on his skin were the tell-tale signs of Chuckle worms, thousands of them, dying from the serum that his sister had injected in him.

The old man went on. "Last nine or ten years you been coming here. You'd stand at the railing and just start talking. Sometimes you'd go down to the front of the restaurant and talk to it for a while. Then you'd go home."

"But Sal—" Koestler started. His memory was starting to return, now that the Chuckle worms inside him were dying.

"Oh, he drowned in that movie they were filming long time ago," the old surfer said. "When you mentioned him I didn't know what to tell you. I knew something wasn't right."

"All this time I've been *hallucinating*?"

There were no Eliminator towers. And there was no Sal Briscoe.

He felt sick. When the Protean Set had been dusted by Bob Thermopylae ten years ago, Koestler had somehow taken in a single, pregnant Chuckle worm. *All this time he had been the mysterious vector of Chuckle they couldn't track!*

Koestler pushed past the old man, running for his brother-in-law's vehicle, his skin crawling with the debris of dead Chuckle worms.

Koestler raced back to his house in Paradise Cove. How much of his life was real? Did he live in a condo? Did he have a five year-old neighbor that he cared for enormously? Was there an *au pair* named Erendira who frowned down upon him like mighty Zeus from the heights of Mt. Olympus?

There was no guard in the guard station at the entrance to Paradise Cove, but Koestler's pass card got him through the automatic gate. He was breathing raggedly, drops of sweat streaming down the side of his face like polluted raindrops.

He whipped around the first corner and shot down his street. The condo was still there. So was Mrs. Tenharkel sitting in her rocking chair. He jumped out of the vehicle and stumbled to his doorstep. There, on the door in plain sight, was an eviction notice.

So *some* things he hadn't imagined.

Koestler flung the note aside and palmed the lock to his door open.

Inside his home the walls came alive with their myriad advertisements. Koestler ignored them and looked around desperately.

The sliding glass door to the back patio was open. The patio door was little Stephie's normal mode of entry. She had been here already, come and gone.

"Stephanie!" Koestler shouted, trembling with sickness.

On the patio, he threw up. When he saw his vomit writhing on the cement of the patio, he threw up again.

Koestler's head reeled, his world collapsing around him. How much of the last ten years had been real? How much had been an illusion? He staggered through the side gate and began to walk up the lighted path up to the first tier of Paradise Cove. He had to see little Stephie. He had to apologize to her mother, Erendira, the gods....

Koestler fell to his knees, halfway up the darkened path, exhausted. He felt the moist earth seep through his pants.

Wearily, he glanced up.

At the head of the path he saw little Stephie. Her back was toward him and she was bent over. She seemed to be dragging something very heavy behind her. He could even hear her breathing as she struggled with whatever it was.

"Stephie," Koestler said, relieved.

His life would begin here, on this path, at this moment. He would take Stephie in his arms, take her back up the path to her mother, to Erendira, apologize for being such a shit and face whatever punishment was due him. It would be the start of a totally new life and he welcomed it.

"Stephie," he said, getting to his feet. "What are you doing? Here, honey, let me help."

The girl, he saw, was wearing a strange silver and green outfit. She also had a silver helmet on her head. But it was definitely her, because her ponytail hung behind the helmet.

"Stephie?"

The little girl turned. She was dressed as a Player. And her grip was one of the strange, incomprehensible weapons each of the Players had used.

He'd forgotten about the Players.

"Hi!" little Stephie Kost said to him. She held her weapon up at him and pulled the trigger. A wash of sudden frigid air surrounded him and he fell over.

His new life hadn't begun after all. More of the old one was still to come.

THIRTY-ONE

KOESTLER TREMBLED IN THE GRIP of a force that seemed to grip the molecules of his body, the life-force of his very being. He couldn't move. He could barely think. And he was very, very cold.

It seemed just seconds ago when little Stephie "shot" him. He expected to be lying on the cement of the pathway that led to the third tier of Paradise Cove. But when he opened his eyes, what he saw was the world rushing before his eyes. But this wasn't the world in general. It was the world specifically related to *him*. They were voices, scenes, even feelings, cascading past his visual field as if suspended on the inner walls of a whirling tornado.

His mind was being fed with his crimes, his *indiscretions*. He saw his treatment of little Vicki Celeste. He saw the years with his sister, Rebecca, and his treatment of *her*. He saw his dalliances as a cocky actor, then later as a Protean. He saw the face of every woman he'd taken to his bed, every woman he left in the lurch, including his many wives. The scenes whirled past him with such clarity that he became nauseous. But the nausea came from his disgust at the man he had been.

Was he dead…was he dying?

He didn't know.

As the images swirled around him, *information* came at him as well. A voice said, "*We had to slow you down before you could do any more damage… and that's all you ever did*."

Koestler tried to speak. He wanted to defend himself. But his tongue seemed dead and his jaw frozen. And before him, little Stephie danced in view wearing her green and silver Player's uniform.

She disappeared from view going in one direction, another figure appeared, drifting past going the opposite way. This was Clarice Kost. Though

198

Koestler had never met Stephie's mother, some dim part of his mind simply *knew* it was Clarice Kost. And she, too, wore the silver and green of the Players.

He tried again to speak, but Clarice Kost's voice intervened even as scenes whirled behind her like spangled horses on a carnival carousel ride.

"You're not a bad man. You've just never taken responsibility for anything in your life," Clarice Kost said.

Sal Briscoe had been telling him that for years.

Sal!

Koestler wanted to close his eyes. He wanted to hide from the truth, go back to sleep. But his eyelids wouldn't close, his mind wouldn't obey.

"Who...are...you?" Koestler finally managed to get out.

"Me!" little Stephie said, jumping up and down, her ponytail bobbing merrily. *"I get to say!"*

He got a glimpse of mother and daughter standing together. Clarice Kost said, *"We make adjustments in our lives in order to make our future better. The future for everybody. Little Stephie chose you. I haven't chosen mine yet."*

"Chosen?" he said, struggling to unthaw his tongue.

"Stephie chose now to stop you from doing further harm to the citizens of Los Angeles," Clarice Kost said.

"How did I—?"

But he stopped himself. He remembered the worms oozing from the pores of his skin on his drive through Malibu Canyon, the *real* Malibu Canyon.

Clarice Kost said, *"You spread Chuckle everywhere you went. Every person you touched, every sexual contact you had. You were the main vector of the spread of Chuckle, not Chloe Evers, not Jack McKimmie. Stephie had to stop you. Erendira and I were only here to supervise since she is so young."*

Chloe Evers...Chloe Evers...the name rattled around in his head, latching onto no immediate referent.

"Bob Thermopylae," Clarice Kost said, reading his confusion.

Of the blurring scenes that whipped past his eyes, Koestler saw his many girlfriends moving out through Los Angeles. Some had even gotten through the quarantine when the Chuckle worms were in their four-day passive phase and couldn't be detected. Then the worms in his girlfriends came alive and spread the disease wherever *they* went. And one of his girlfriends was still touring with *Cats*.

"So we work on our former lives to set everything straight," Clarice Kost said.

Koestler filled with confusion, but, again, Clarice Kost saw it. She said, *"We're engineers. Because of certain technical advancements in the study of time and reincarnation, we can make 'adjustments' to our past lives. But we can only choose one nexus point. Stephie chose you at this time in your life."*

Koestler swallowed. Or tried to. "Little Stephie is *me*?"

"*She'll be born one hundred years from now,*" Clarice Kost said. "*Your next life, in fact.*"

If little Stephie Kost was just four or five years-old *now*, that meant that Koestler would live a *very* long life in his current lifetime.

But as Koestler thought about it, none of what Clarice Kost said made any sense. What about all those sci-fi movies that dealt with the manipulation of time? There were always paradoxes. Alter even the *smallest* detail in the past and *all* of future history would be changed.

"I don't believe you," he said, struggling for the words. "You can't change the past. If you did...well."

"We're not travelers. We're engineers. Our time engine, Eidolon Rex, can calculate the consequences of a single 'tweaked' moment in time. If the projected results seem satisfactory to us, we go back and tweak it. That way, we make a better future for everybody, not only ourselves."

The whirling scenes, the staggering information—all were too much. None of this seemed possible.

"But how do you know *I'm* little Stephie's incarnation?" Koestler asked. As a Californian, his religious beliefs were vaguely of the New Age.

But thinking about it further, Koestler didn't know *what* he believed. Sal had often talked to him about magical passes, the foreign installation of the ego, and the necessity of recapitulating one's entire life, but he had always written them off.

Sal!

In the tumult of images, the influx of new ideas, Clarice Kost's Circean voice made his thoughts cohere. She said, "*The woman who founded our organization discovered the principles of reincarnation. She is a contemporary of yours. Her name is Christine Myrland.*"

"Christine Myrland? That woman tried to destroy me," he said, fighting to find the words, forcing them out. Little Stephie danced around him, going one way, images of his life, whirled around the other way. "*But you get a turn, too,*" Clarice Kost finally said. "*You get to choose one moment.*"

Koestler stood trembling at the very edge of his sanity. Yet, it all made sense. He had to be stopped so that he could move forward in his life...as thousands were now being stopped all over the country. This entire moment in time was the nexus for the future that humans in the late 21st century were building for themselves.

And as he thought about it, as he watched the scenes of his life flash by, Koestler knew of one moment, or at least one *gesture*, that, if he could make it, would change his life forever *if* this was truly real....

He asked for that moment. And they gave it to him.

EPILOGUE IN THREE PARTS

1

ALEX LANGLEY LISTENED TO THE RAIN as it pelted the metal roof of their Quonset hut. Instead of distracting him, however, it allowed him to relax, and it allowed his thoughts to come together finally.

A full day had passed since Detective Rory Koestler had invaded Eidolon Technologies and had rescued the little girl. Construction workers were still patching the walls and mopping up the super-Teflon lubricants left from Koestler's raid. But soon Langley would be able to get back to Eidolon Rex where he could run his latest calculations unhindered.

In the meantime, he worked at his own desk in their temporary home, finishing up his equations that would fully account for Eidolon Rex's leaps into the future. His wife, Vivian, earlier that morning had driven to Santa Monica to give a series of depositions to the LAPD detailing Detective Koestler's heroism. Meanwhile his daughter, Carol, wrapped in a blanket on the couch was working at her laptop on what would become her own Ph.D. thesis on quantum algorithmic sequencing structures.

He had never felt so happy in his life.

He knew now that time travel, *true* time travel, the kind envisioned by the popular media, was, and would always be impossible because of the enormous energies required for leaps beyond about ninety years. As it was, Eidolon Rex hadn't traveled in time, so much as he had *shrunk* it. Eidolon Rex had created a miniature time "discontinuity" in his central processing core and used that black-hole-like discontinuity in time to "pull" the future toward him in the present. Rex had become an Alcubierre "time" engine and traveled, not through space, but time.

Langley also had discovered that the energy required to "shrink" time was enormous. According to his calculations, they would only be able to move a century either way. And even that would require the power of a hydrogen bomb. The energy requirements of yet greater leaps would rise exponentially, so much so that a journey back to the time of Christ would require the explosive mass of the entire galaxy, billions of stars. That would never happen. Of this Langley was certain.

The rain had begun to lift a little and, through the window, Langley could see that the lights were back on in his wing of Eidolon Technologies.

Carol looked up from where she sat on the couch. She had a glazed look in her eyes, but it wasn't from the use of Chuckle or any other drug. She, like her father, always looked that way when lost in thought. She smiled at him.

Langley put on his raincoat and folded his laptop. All the disparate factors of his life were disparate no more, thanks to Detective Koestler. Alex Langley could now turn his attention where his attention was needed most.

It was, finally, time to go to work.

Among the traits Christine Myrland had inherited from her father, the senator, was an excellent memory. As she lay in her hospital bed in the detention unit of Valley Samaritan in Simi Valley, she made good use of it.

Though she didn't fully understand what had happened to her on the second floor landing at Eidolon Technologies, she was fully able to recall what transpired when she was *halted*. That was "their" term for it. And "they" were her distant relatives. Or something like that.

But when she had opened her eyes after the *halting* she had found herself standing in a large three-hundred-and-sixty-degree theater, a kind of near-death theater in the round where she saw images on several screens whirling around her.

At first she had thought the images were those out of her past, memories and such. But they weren't. Instead, the screens were replete with mathematical equations, the products of her *mental* past life.

And as the images whirled and her mind started making connections between the images, voices of her distant "selves" shouted at her to keep paying attention.

So she did.

And when she came out of her coma that rainy morning and found herself in a special hospital room with a locked metal door, she realized just what it was she had been shown in that strange state. She discovered that Alex Langley had not sabotaged Eidolon Rex by surreptitiously installing the computer codes he had written years ago for Telemon Ajax at Santos Aviation.

Those codes had gotten into Eidolon Rex nearly instantaneously upon Telemon Ajax's "death." Those software codes taken altogether, she had realized, were an *incarnation*, Ajax's soul. They had jumped from Ajax to Rex, over two hundred miles away. Alex Langley had written those original codes for Ajax, but when she found them at the bottom of Eidolon Rex's multi-layered programs, she had simply thought that Alex had written them in as an attempt of sabotage.

Yet, there was no reason for Alex to have done that. Telemon Ajax had imploded because of faulty design, but was sentient enough to have sent its "soul" to the next available "container." That was Eidolon Rex in nearby Simi Valley.

And she now had the mathematics to prove it.

So as Christine lay watching the rain fall outside her window, she pondered the greater implications of her discovery. Perhaps the same engrams could be found in the electrical signal configurations in the brain of a newborn child. Perhaps it was possible to determine a soul's previous life the way she could now determine Rex's previous incarnation.

It would take her years to bring all the math together. She would probably have to detail her theory in a formal paper and submit it to the most rigorous analysis for publication. Karl Moeller who ran the Artificial Intelligence unit at MIT would have to be won over with an idea as radical as this, also Keith Jenkins at Stanford. There were, in fact, half a dozen other people she knew she'd have to convince. But she did have the math. All she had to do was get it down in writing.

This would take time.

And she would have the time.

She guessed that she would spend the next several years in prison, at the very least for the kidnapping of Koestler's little neighbor. Trent Andreesen, in order to save his own hide, would probably confess to the illegal wiretaps and eavesdropping on Koestler, to say nothing of the tampering with the California Bailiff system and the computer records of several banks in the Los Angeles region.

She would happily accept any punishment now, because now she understood that you can't push people around in life without paying for it eventually. It was uncivil and *very* bad for the soul.

So, going to prison would probably be a good thing. It would certainly allow her the opportunity to concentrate so she could eventually show the world what she had discovered.

There would be no more lounging around now. No more leaning on her father or seducing men to get her dirty deeds done.

It was time to face her own demons, time for her to go to work.

ON A THURSDAY AFTERNOON, late one autumn, a long time ago, a little red-headed girl was swinging in a swing set in an empty park in Canoga Park, California. She was a little lonely because there were no other children to play with that day. But the sun was bright and a balmy wind eased through the leaves of the tall eucalyptus trees in Shadowland Park.

While she swung back and forth, singing to herself, one of the trees began to glow in a strange way. It was a time portal appearing, but she did not know this. It was not important for her to know. All that mattered was that Koestler had finally found her, found the right place, found the right time.

The little girl stopped swinging to see Koestler walk up to her. He wore his crisp new uniform and a bright new badge. He removed his silver helmet and smiled. He did not have much time.

"Are you a policeman?" Vicki Celeste asked with a sudden smile. Her voice was small, nearly birdlike and frail. It nearly broke Koestler's heart to hear it.

"Yes," he said. "I am."

"Will you play with me?"

"Sure."

The wounds he had originally inflicted on her earlier that summer had long since healed. Perhaps the memory of it had disappeared as well. Even so, it still lingered in *him*.

He set his helmet onto the sand and gently began to push little Vicki on the swing.

The air was so clean, the wind so pure. The day filled with her laughter.

Koestler was so moved by her that he had to fight an urge to run down the street and blast his ten-year-old asshole self. But he had been engineered once already in this lifetime. The process could not be done twice. He had to remain the person he was until little Stephie appeared in his life twenty-five years later.

But that really didn't matter now, seeing little Vicki this way, happy.

After she swung on the swings a while, Koestler then spun her on the iron merry-go-round. He watched as her beautiful red hair streamed outward like the cape of a hero as she passed. When the merry-go-round stopped she was breathless with laughter.

Then it was time for her to go home. A maid, or perhaps it was her mother, came out of her house across the street to the east of Shadowland Park and called her in for supper.

"'Bye!" little Vicki said, jumping up. She ran off like a happy pony.

"Goodbye, sweetie," Koestler said, holding his helmet in his hands. He waved at Vicki's mother and she waved back. He watched until they both were safe inside.

Koestler's time there was nearly through. He could already feel himself beginning to fade. He then took one last look around the world he had grown up in and prepared to return to the world he was to die in. It was time for the real work of his life to begin.

A WORD ON THE KARMA KOMMANDOS

ONE OF THE GREATEST LINES spoken by one of the truly great villains in American literature comes at the end of Flannery O'Connor's magnificent short story, "A Good Man is Hard To Find." The Misfit, an escaped criminal mastermind in Georgia, has just killed the grandmother in the story, and says: "She would of been a good woman if it had been somebody there to shoot her every minute of her life." This is Rory Koestler's story. He was a good man but he needed someone to shoot him, to bring him back around to the important things in life. In the end, he shoots himself.

This theme, however, wasn't in the original manuscript of the book.

Back in the late 1980s, Gardner Dozois had accepted the *Karma Kommandos* for publication in his Isaac Asimov Presents series when the publisher folded and the series came to a crashing end. The series had published Steven Popkes's *Caliban Landing* and Harry Turtledove's *Agent of Byzantium*. I would have been proud to be part of that line-up.

Letting the novel sit a while (plot intact), I took it out after about a decade and returned to the novel to explore some ideas that I had felt were a bit underdeveloped in the original version, ideas about personal responsibility. I'm a life-long fan of the books of Carlos Castaneda. His teacher Don Juan Matus, a Yaqui Indian sorcerer, had taught him the art of stalking the self. The Toltec lineage of sorcerers were men and women in ancient Mexico who'd managed to eradicate their egos and all the veils through which they had traditionally viewed the world. At first Don Juan used psychotropic plants to help Castaneda see that the world was only a description—a trope or a conceit, what phenomenologists would call an intentional structure or gloss. Castaneda later learned that you can also learn this path without the use of peyote. One simple way to do this is to pay attention, to be cognizant of how one's ego prevents one from seeing the "truth" by flattering oneself, by taking oneself (and one's career) too seriously. Chuckle is the main metaphor here. Chuckle allows the user to see what he or she wants to see. And the greater one's ego, the less one can see of the real world. A true sorcerer can *see* (the italics here are Castaneda's).

More than that, however, I wanted to develop the idea that there are people around us who believe that they can go through life doing (and saying) whatever they want and if anyone complains, it's that person's problem. It's the world who's at fault; it's the world that has to change. The *Karma Kommandos* is about the lessons of actual karma: how we're given opportunities daily to learn from our mistakes, to see the world as it truly is without the intercession of an interpretive ego—only most of us don't.

Originally, the *Karma Kommandos* was to be a cross between a police procedural novel and a Philip K. Dick psychedelic novel about a futuristic Los Angeles. But a simple—and quite stupid—act from my own childhood had kept cycling in the back of my mind and it ended up being the genesis of Koestler's turn-around, leading to the final scene. The concept of "work" in this novel then becomes the work we each need to do to maintain our equipoise and sobriety (a key Castaneda term) in a world with all manner of delights and distractions for the ego. Each of the three main characters in this novel get some kind of comeuppance.

I decided here to focus on facing one's demons, down to the most (seemingly) inconsequential of childhood actions. We all have them. We continue to accumulate them...until someone comes along to shoot us every minute of our lives.

Paul Cook
June 2008

PAUL COOK AT PHOENIX PICK

The Engines of Dawn

Fortress on the Sun

Karma Kommandos

The Alejandra Variations

Tintagel

Duende Meadow

Halo

On the Rim of the Mandala

www.PhoenixPick.com

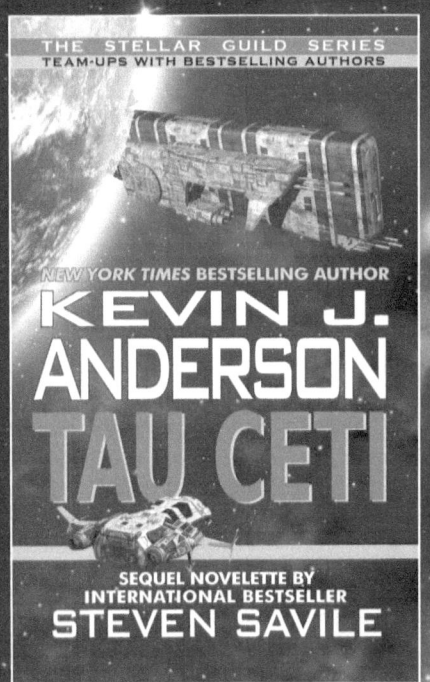